A Caster Valley Cozy Paranormal Mystery

Murder by the Bridge

By Erica St. Charles

Copyright © 2024 by Erica St. Charles

All rights reserved.

No part of this book may be reproduced in any form by any electronic or mechanical means (including photocopying, recording, or information storage or retrieval) without permission in writing from the author.

This is a work of fiction. All names, characters, places, and incidents are products of the author's imagination, or if real, used fictitiously. Any resemblance to actual persons, living or dead, events or locales, is purely coincidental

ISBN:9798335510547
Imprint: Independently published

Dedication

This goes out to my family and friends. Thank you so much for supporting me. When I was buried in worries and doubts, it was all of you who helped bring me out of it. If it wasn't for your love and support this journey would have never have been possible, and this book would have never been written.

I want to thank my dad. Thank you for always believing in me and my dreams. Special thanks to Caleb, for your amazing suggestions, editing, proofreading, and for opening yourself up to new possibilities as well as not judging my story so harshly.

I also have to thank Canva for helping me design the cover.

So, thank you all so much!

1

"Shut up!" my mom yelled.

I groaned internally at the mind-numbing pain pulsating inside my skull, and squashed my pillow over my head to block out the horrible noise. Out of all the days in the entire year, this was the one day that I did not want to hear my mother yelling.

Why, out of all the days in this month, did this have to happen on this particular day? Here I was hoping to go about my normal routine. And waking up to my mother shrieking like a maniac wasn't on my to-do list.

After stretching and putting on my glasses from the nightstand, my cleared vision. I then lifted my head, letting my eyes wandered over to the window.

Bolts of lightning zapped across the begrimed sky while in the distance, thunder rumbled. Luckily, it wasn't loud enough to cause me to jump, but did make the pain spike in my brain. Yes, I *might* be a little scared of thunderstorms. Why? Because tornadoes! But luckily this storm didn't seem to be a classic sign of a possible tornado.

I couldn't help but snicker when the thunder startled the slumbering ravens perched on the power lines. They immediately cawed and flew off over the nearby red building. If my grandma had seen that, she'd say it was a sign of terrible things to come.

I never believed her.

However, while I preferred vibrant blue, sunny sky days more, I couldn't stop myself from gazing out at the thick dark gray clouds. They blanketed the atmosphere strangely. A powerfully dread feeling sank deep in my gut. Something felt off. There was a murky heaviness that seemed to loom over this entire apartment building complex. It was as though something more than an angry thunderstorm was brewing on the horizon. I was pretty sure whatever trouble was coming had nothing to do with the storm.

Then again, maybe it did. I remembered checking the weather forecast last night on my phone. The weatherwoman had called for a cloudless and sunny day. But she had been wrong. That wasn't unusual. Weather forecasters weren't always accurate. Maybe I was just messed up in the head from the headache.

A chilly breeze drifted in through my half-opened window. Already, this was shaping up to be a not-so-normal day.

And if I thought the terrible weather was bad, I was also now experiencing the worst day of my entire existence. All I wanted to do was enjoy a pleasant morning. But as soon as my eyes drifted away from the dreary scenery outside the window, a horrid shout happened.

"I don't care!" she yelled again.

Vigorous anger sliced sharply into the depths of my brain which caused the pounding in my head to roar louder than ever, to the point, I could feel my pulse in my eardrums.

Great, I thought, bringing one of my hands up to my temples to rub the tension and pain away. A painful wince escaped past my chapped lips as soon as my fingers touched my sore head.

I wished more than anything I could stay in the safety of my warm, cozy bed and just smash my pillow constantly over my aching head to block out the horrid shouts and emotions.

Yeah, this day was *so* going the way I wanted it to. I honestly had been ecstatic about today. I didn't know why. I'm a guy, not some teenage girl excited about whatever girls get excited about. They probably got excited over something cheesy like makeup, a change of hairstyle, a first time manicure, or something that like. Okay, so, maybe I'm stereotyping a bit, but it wasn't like I knew much about what girls did or wanted.

As far as birthday presents went, I wanted one thing and one thing only: to own my first car. I didn't own one yet. Ever since two years ago, on my sixteenth birthday, all I heard was how my mom would complain about how she couldn't afford the insurance and about how paranoid she was that I would wreck a perfectly good vehicle.

Since then, I decided to get one on my own. I had a well-thought-out plan to buy one as soon as I saved up enough from my job. I guess that's what contributed to my happiness, because I was so close to having the money saved up.

Besides, today was my eighteenth birthday. This was supposed to be a momentous occasion, right? It's the time where you transition out of being a teenager to being a full-fledged adult. With that in mind, I could now think about getting a better job, moving out, or even going to college. This meant that my entire life was about to change. Honestly, that would be the least of my problems, because I wasn't even in the process of putting any of that into perspective yet. Where would I even go? What did I want to do?

It didn't matter.

Thinking about life changes was the last thing I needed on my throbbing mind. The horrid pain driving a bullet through my head was only half my problems. The other half was the yelling my mom was doing.

"I said no!"

I grunted. Might as well try and get this day over with. I got up on unsteady legs and stumbled over to my dresser. Pulling out some clean clothes, I then headed for the bathroom.

Once my ten minute shower was up and I got dressed, I walked into the kitchen to see my mom standing over by the sink. She had her black hair clipped back in a bun. She was also dressed in a black blouse with a black blazer, a black skirt down to her knee, and black dress shoes with a pearl necklace draped around her neck. If anyone in town were to drop by and see her, they would probably assume she was heading off to a funeral instead of her job at the funeral home. Well, okay, I guess they would assume correctly.

Mom was also wiping at a cup with a red washcloth. Knowing her as I do, and knowing that she didn't always pay attention to her surroundings, she'd probably been drying that cup for the last ten minutes while she shouted into the wireless landline phone squashed between her ear and shoulder.

"I don't care, Ruth!" she yelled for the umpteenth time. "No! No, this is not up for negotiation. Do not give me that hoodoo magic nonsense again! Why? You know why!"

"Mom," I said, weakly. Internally, I winced at the pain exploding in my head which made my voice crack a little. I was fighting hard to keep my voice soft. I hated interrupting anyone on the phone, especially my mom. It was impolite as my mom always told me, but I needed to know if we had any medicine.

"Stop it! Just stop it! Why aren't you listening to me?" demanded Mom as her screaming grew louder.

I shouted, "Mom!"

"Hold on!" she shouted once again before she spun around, setting the cup with the washcloth inside it on the counter. Her chocolate brown eyes landed on mine as she placed her hand over the receiver "What is it, Weston? Can't you see how busy I am? Didn't I tell you it was impolite to interrupt me while I'm on the phone?"

I flinched at the strong flow of irritation and anger surging through me. These weren't my emotions. These were the emotions pouring out of my mom.

You'd think by now I'd be used to feeling things like this and finding a way to cope and stop them from invading me. Well, usually, that was true. Usually, I had no problem separating my emotions from everyone else. Today, however, it was like my empath ability—that's the supposed term when I did an online search back when I was thirteen—was in overdrive. I wondered why...

Mom's anger seemed to grow at my silence which only made the pain already invading my cluttered mind crash like tsunami waves and only increased the discomfort.

I overheard people tell others to show more empathy and that it was the foundation needed to improve human connection and communication. If only they knew the downside to that advice. This didn't feel like a good gift at all. It was honestly a curse sometimes. Just because I had empathy didn't always help in the long run. There was this one time, back in middle school to be exact, where I had been sitting by myself reading a book in gym class, and this random guy came up, sat down beside me, and started talking about a girl he had a crush on. I remembered feeling his anxiety. I did my best to help quell it by simply listening to him. But then, once he finished talking, he got so mad at me, all because I didn't have the answer to his problem. I wasn't a therapist. I didn't always have answers.

"Weston!"

I rubbed at my aching head. "Sorry. I was just... Do you know if we have any aspirin?"

Mom grumbled and then pointed to the hallway behind me. "Medicine cabinet," she stated like it was the most obvious thing in the world when it wasn't. "For crying out loud, Weston, you know where it is! Now, stop disturbing me while I am on the phone!" She then picked up the cup again and resumed wiping the already dry cup as she angrily screamed again. "Yes, I am here, Ruth! No, it was Weston! Yes, he's fine! Yes, he is! Stop! Get back on the topic at hand!"

Not wanting to hear anymore, I staggered down the creamy white hallway. Being away from my mom seemed to soothe some of the tension. After opening the bathroom door, I flipped on the light switch. The fluorescent light bulbs flickered a few times before staying on. Mom seriously needed to change them or call an electrician for help. I would have gladly changed them for her. I knew how. I had watched her do it hundreds of times as a kid, but if I tried to grab the stool, my mom would intuitively know, yell at me, and tell me to put it back.

Okay, okay, I might have broken a bulb a time or two. Not a big deal. That was something I did when I was thirteen. I am eighteen now. Maybe I'd fix it when she wasn't home.

I opened the medicine cabinet door. Several green bottles of prescriptions were along the top shelf. They were mine. I can't believe Mom had never gotten rid of them even after I stopped taking them at twelve. There were medicines for anxiety, insomnia, and hallucinations. But because of the side effects, I decided to no longer take them, after talking to my doctor, of course. I had to convince them that I was fine. It had been harder than you know.

Shaking my head, I located the over-the-counter bottle of pain relievers. I picked up the bottle. For some reason, it felt light, too light.

Shaking it, there was no sound.

Empty.

I sighed. "Thanks for not telling me, Mom," I muttered to myself before annoyingly tossing the empty bottle into the trash can by the door. I nearly slammed the cabinet door shut in a fit of rage.

"No, Ruth, you will listen to me! I don't care about that right now!"

I wished she would stop yelling already. I gripped the sides of the porcelain sink and bowed my head so my chin rested on my heaving chest. I didn't dare glance at myself in the mirror. I would no doubt look like a mess. I could already feel a small bead of sweat underneath my black hair, and colorless dots were already dancing in my line of sight.

And to make matters even worse, my stomach was churning dangerously and I was hot.

I needed out of this apartment!

Out of this building!

I needed air!

Now!

With claustrophobia tightening in my throat and chest, I dashed out of the bathroom and down the hallway. However, I unintentionally stopped, nearly tripping over my feet on the carpet, at the entrance to the kitchen.

"For the last time, Ruth, I said that I don't care! You may not like this, but…"

Mom's rage stole my breath. One of my hands shot out impulsively. I touched the wall, supporting my shaky legs as I bent over. My other hand clutched desperately at my tightened chest. Being this close once again made me sicker. It felt like air was barely getting into my tightening lungs. The panic setting in caused my stomach to start to roll. A bout of anxiety shot through me and my heart escalated. I placed the back of my hand over my mouth and swallowed thickly.

I forced myself not to get sick by focusing on something other than Mom's anger and the sudden queasiness in my stomach. So, I let my eyes wander over to the chair. With a small smile, I tapped into my other gift of telekinesis. This gift manifested when I was a child. I discovered it accidentally after waking up from a nightmare and found several of my things floating above me. I tried telling my mom but that was when she decided to take me to a doctor. The pills had caused me to feel so numb and unfocused that I could never control it properly.

Since I wasn't on my medication anymore, and haven't been for years, I decided to use my ability whenever my mom wasn't around, or when she was busy like she was right now.

Warmth spread through me like it always did when I used my power as I kept my eyes locked onto my satchel that was hanging off the knob. The strap moved and rose by itself and then lifted before floating over to me. The second it was right in front of me, I grabbed it and threw the strap over my head so it rested on my shoulder and across my chest. I then stole a glance at my mom. Should I say goodbye? It's not like she would care or notice anyway...

"Ruth! Shut up! For once in your elderly life, shut up and listen to me!"

Without uttering a proper goodbye, I fled out of the door of our apartment and ran straight to the elevator at the end of the hall. After pressing the down arrow button, I rocked back and forth on my heels, from either the anxiety or the impatience coiling inside me. I waited for what felt like a lifetime, but in reality, it was no more than five minutes if my watch was accurate. Just when I was about to turn and take the door to the stairwell, the elevator doors dinged open

Finally!

I stepped in and hit the first-floor button and then went to the nearest corner. The tension faded all for about a second before coming back as I took in the small compacted area. I wished now that I had taken the stairs. There were four other people on. Most people would have no problem. However, I wasn't like most people and these weren't regular folks either. Well, only one was: the elderly woman.

She was dressed in a floral gown, carrying a basket of what smelled like blueberry muffins. Turning her head to me, she flashed a crooked smile. "Good morning, dearie," she said. "Would you like a blueberry muffin? You're far too skinny. Have you eaten? You know, it's unhealthy for young men such as yourself to go without breakfast for too long."

Who was this woman? And why did it feel like I knew her from somewhere?

I simply shook my head. From my empathy, I could feel nothing. There was this static buzzing inside my mind like annoying bees. I wasn't able to tell if she was upset or not. I doubted it due to the crooked smile she flashed me before grabbing my hand.

I prepared myself to be bombarded by emotions. However, there was nothing but that annoying buzzing, which grew even louder now. Touch always made my ability stronger. I wanted to pull my hand back to stop the buzzing, but she simply held it as she placed a plastic, wrapped-up muffin in my palm, and then closed her wrinkled hand around mine. An unusual coldness radiated from her hand and nearly caused me to shiver.

"This is for luck, health, and for your birthday," she said with an eerie smile.

Finally, I gathered my wits and snatched my hand out of hers, holding the muffin in my hand as I regarded her. How on earth did she know that it was my birthday? I didn't know this woman. There was no way she could have known. Unless... Was she a mind reader? Was there another person with strange abilities like me?

Doubtful, I thought.

But that meant...

"Come on, slow elevator," bellowed the nicely dressed businessman whom I presumed he was the proud parent of the little girl, who was probably about four or five, clinging to the back of his black slack pants and sucking on a lollipop. The man's anxiousness was boiling with every glance at his expensive watch that I could never afford. All the while, his daughter's curiosity had her gawking at her father.

"It won't go any faster if you yell at it," mumbled the young woman in the black strapless dress and bright red lipstick. She was busy tapping her white high heels against the side of the elevator as her annoyance and exotic emotions made my insides bubble with bile.

Those people were dead. Yes, just like that movie. However, these ghosts weren't like the ones that were portrayed in the entertainment media. These ghosts were less annoying. Some of the dead would constantly annoy me to no end until I downright drowned them out by ignoring, usually through music or by doing something on my phone. These ones right now, well, they couldn't see me. I'd tried to get them to once before, but it was like they were stuck or something.

This was why I chose the stairs over the elevator. I hated seeing these ghosts, even if they couldn't see me. It was like they were silently suffering, like they wanted to be let free. But I had no way of knowing how to do that.

And I didn't dare touch them. Also, just because ghosts were dead didn't mean that I didn't feel their emotions. I hated being like this. I hated being psychic sometimes. The telekinesis wasn't bad, but having empathy and being able to see the dead was. However, empathy was the worst of my abilities, because I was exposed to the emotions of both the living and the dead around me all the time.

It wasn't like I could do much to help anyway. Just because I had some sort of extrasensory perception didn't mean I knew how to use it properly. Like I said, my mom straight up ignored my abilities, believing they were just a fragment of my imagination, which was why she sent me to a therapist. I was told to just ignore them. That's what I've been trying to do for years. Anytime I saw them, I ignored them.

The elderly woman had been giving me weird and uncomfortable side eyed glances.

Distraction, I thought. I needed to distract myself. Just when I was about to pull out my cell phone to play a calming game I downloaded several weeks ago—some kind of Tetris-like block game I was advertised—the elevator dinged.

My eyes shot up.

The second the red needle landed on the first floor and the doors opened, I dashed out without a glance back and walked into the lobby. I was impaled so suddenly by extreme happiness that I nearly lost my balance. I managed to catch myself by grabbing the edge of the counter. Those emotions belong to the receptionist—the young woman behind the counter, who—I assumed was in her late twenties or early thirties—was waving at me.

"Good morning, Weston," she said with extreme happiness. "A little birdie told me it was your birthday."

She knew, too? Well, I could kind of understand how the receptionist knew, considering my mom and I have been living in this apartment for as long as I could remember. So, that made sense. However, that elderly woman on the elevator was just too creepy and too weird. She was no one I knew. She was no one I had ever seen, but she kind of reminded me of my grandma. But that was impossible. She didn't even live in this town.

"Would you like a blueberry muffin?" I offered the receptionist. In all the time that I've been living here, I never learned her name. I felt horrible about it, but I didn't feel it was necessary.

"Thank you, Weston. You're an absolute sweetheart," she said. And that only made her happiness brighter and galling. "But I am afraid that I can't take it. I'm allergic to blueberries. You keep it. A little sugar would do you good."

Biting back a wince, I placed the muffin in my bag. I might eat it later, maybe. I then waved politely. "Uh, yeah," I mumbled before I walked out of the translucent door.

As soon as I put my hand on the door, the receptionist said, "Oh, Weston, I hope you have an umbrella with you. The weather report said there was a storm on the way. Be careful out there."

"I figured," I said. "I always have one in my bag."

"Always prepared," she said.

And with that, I stepped outside.

The cool air caressed my face as though it was comforting me. Feeling less suffocated, I took in a deep lungful of air. The aroma of the sea salt was strong today. Guess that storm was coming up from the ocean. I leaned against the old brick building, not caring about the bizarre stares that people were shooting at me. I was just glad my stomach no longer felt like a roller-coaster. But sadly, my headache was still thundering on. It was no use. Even being out here, I could still hear my mom's booming voice from the third floor.

Gazing up, I realized why. She had the window opened. Luckily, though, her screams were muffled. However, it didn't help the anger and frustration I could still detect flooding into my head. It wasn't until I strolled to the bus stop that my head felt clear of my mom's voice and emotions and was no longer pounding as hard. This wasn't strange to me. My migraines tended to be related to my empathy. So, I took in the peace by sitting on the bench underneath the ugly green canopy. Like always, I was the only one here, which was a pleasant kindness. The tension in my shoulder blades released. I leaned back and closed my eyes unperturbed. This was the most relaxed I'd been all morning.

Suddenly, warm hands covered my eyes.

Startled, the urge to strike out with a punch or kick was strong. My reflexes had me ready to attack if necessary. I was super paranoid. I hated being touched. If you had my abilities, you would be on edge and hate sudden touch as well.

I was so close to pushing away whoever was near me, but a stream of powerfully calm emotions calmed me instantaneously and brought a bright smile to my face. I knew whose these emotions belonged to. These were the kind of emotions that I wanted to spend a lifetime drowning in. The serenity always made me feel like I belonged.

"Guess who," a familiar melodious, smooth voice said. Their heated breath on the back of my neck made me falter.

"Uh, let's see," I stammered, unconsciously licking my dry lips as I paused dramatically to cover up myself. "You wouldn't happen to be the proud owner of Ms. Hopkins' demonic cat by any chance, would you?"

With their hands still over my eyes, the person laughed. "Are you seriously comparing me, your best friend on the whole planet, to Kevin Hopkins? I am not the notorious owner of a demonic cat. So, no, I am not Kevin. That deranged kid has a crazy affinity for choking poor Stanley to his nasty demise. It's no wonder that cat turned out to be demonic."

My cheeks heated. There was no doubt that I was blushing bright red as I bit my bottom lip to keep my hilarity that was threatening to burst out of my chest, which must have been what set my best friend off into hysterical, harder laughter.

"If only you could see your face!" My best friend removed his hands from my eyes. "It's the funniest thing I've ever seen. Where's my camera?"

I straightened. "I chucked it in the ocean, keeping it far away from you."

My best friend laughed harder, his arm curling around his abdomen. The delight in his emotions made me laugh along. Why did he have to have such a stupid, yet endearing and contagious laugh?

"Can you please stop laughing?" I asked, failing to keep the laughter out of my voice. "It was quite rude of you to sneak up on me in the first place, Hayden."

This was Hayden Lakewood, the nineteen year old young man, who was still laughing like a total maniac. He was wearing his infamous amused smile on his round freckled face. He had his curly ginger hair styled differently today. Instead of his bangs being matted, he had them spiked which made his unique turquoise eyes shine brightly like when the sun hits the Caribbean Sea. He also had on a gray button up shirt with a white cardigan that had a golden trident emblem on the left pocket. He also had on black dress pants with black dress shoes. Slung over his left shoulder was his black gym bag. This was indeed my best friend in the entire world. The two of us truly had been inseparable since we were eight years old.

"Well," said Hayden, after catching his breath. "I wouldn't technically call it sneaking. I made my footsteps known. It's not my fault you look ready to fall asleep any second." His bright eyes narrowed, which caused the swirls in them to darken as he took a seat beside me. "You stayed up late again, didn't you? I told you before, Weston; those sleepless nights are eventually going to catch up with you. It seems like I'm right yet again."

I couldn't help but chuckle. He was always like this. Protective of me, worried about my health. It didn't faze me. Most people would complain, but I knew he cared about me unlike anyone had ever done before. It was nice. And I cared about him the same way. Sometimes I wondered if he only worried because I hadn't fully matured like most. He was tall, lean, and athletic from being on the swim team. But I wasn't like that. I still had baby fat cheeks and was three inches shorter than normal, and I was scrawny. Most people commented on my appearance occasionally and assumed I was younger than I really was.

"If you must know, no, I didn't stay up doing another session this time. I swear it."

Hayden's smile broadened. "That's great news. That means you took my advice for once."

"I wouldn't go that far."

"I see," he said. His bright smile faded to a gloomy frown. "What, then, is the real reason for your sleepiness, huh? Because I had assumed you would be excited about today. So, seeing you looking tired has me worried. I mean, you are the birthday boy today. Eighteen and starting all of that adult jazz. As you know, I was eighteen last year. Honestly, I never felt any different. What about you?"

I gripped the strap on my bag. I never told him about my abilities. Hell, I never told anyone. The only thing I knew was that they apparently originated from my dad's side of the family. I knew because I once talked to my grandma and she told me. My mom knew, but always chose not to acknowledge them. For me, I remember being able to feel emotions and move things from the time I was four. However, the ghost seeing ability happened after my dad's death.

I've discreetly dropped a few hints several times to Hayden. If he's caught on, he's never said anything. And anytime I tried to reveal everything, I'd lose my nerve.

I hated being able to do things and see things others can't. My empathy was like being an intruder into other people's emotions. I couldn't stop it. How would you feel if you woke up on your fourth birthday and you were able to feel your mom's discomfort just by being near her, or able to feel other people from across the hall being all passionate?

It was like a psychic hotspot emerged inside the emotional center of my brain and decided to shoot every single emotion of whoever was in proximity, without even leaving a switch or manual on how to turn it on and off. Add in telekinesis to the mix, and that was disastrous, because when my emotions were out of control, things tended to either break, crash, or shatter. And don't even get me started on the whole ghost ability, or the fact that I got glimpses of their death just by being touched, which caused me to go into fits of sorts, causing people to scrutinize me like I was a freak.

Not wanting to reveal anything out of the ordinary, I simply shrugged. "I'm fine, I suppose. Mom was having some kind of screaming fit with my grandma about something. I don't know what it was about, but she was being diabolically rude to her and I don't know why. My grandma is the sweetest person and my mom had no right to treat her like that."

"What was the argument about?"

"I think it was about some kind of event. To be honest, I wasn't paying much attention to their conversation. It doesn't matter, anyway. I was more disappointed that neither of them wished me a happy birthday."

"It's natural to feel that way." Even though Hayden wasn't outwardly expressing it, there was a jittery nervousness emitting from him. That was unusual coming from him. He was always calm.

"Why are you so nervous, Hayden?"

Hayden stared at me, startled. He then sighed. "I hate it when you do that."

I bit my bottom lip nervously. "I-I'm…"

"No, don't apologize," he said. "I know it's not your fault. You can't help it. However, you are right. You see, I was wondering… We are still meeting after you get off work, right?"

I grinned. "Of course we are."

Hayden grinned back. "Great," he said. He then checked his watch. "I have to get going. I'll drop by the magic shop at three-thirty. Don't forget."

"Have I forgotten any other time you asked me?"

"Well, no, but there's a first time for everything," he said.

"Well, I tend to never let you down."

Hayden then locked eyes with me. At that moment my heart pounded so hard. I thought it would leap right out of my chest as I held his gaze. I was lost, mesmerized by the lightest blue swirls of his eyes. My empathy, for the first time, was lost to me. I didn't know what either of us was feeling, but there was a peaceful expression on his face.

"What is it?"

"Happy Birthday, Weston," he said after a single heartbeat.

My cheeks heated again. "Thank you, Hayden. It means a lot coming from you."

Without knowing what he was going to do, Hayden wrapped his arms around my shoulders and drew me into a hug. I couldn't help but reciprocate the embrace and allowed my hands to come up and rest on my best friend's back. Our breaths hitched in sync the second I rested my head on his broad shoulder and took in the salty sea-water scent of the ocean. I never understood why he always smelled as if he'd been swimming in the ocean, and not even appearing wet. But it didn't matter. It was soothing.

He then pushed me back, much to my disappointment, but he kept his strong, nimble fingers sturdy on my shoulders. "Do me a favor."

"What favor?"

"Try and have some fun at work, okay?"

"I can't do that, Hayden. I'm way too awkward and anti-social to mingle, which is why I'm better at putting things on shelves."

"That you are," he teased. "And people should find that quality invigorating. I know it's one of the things I like about you." He smiled as his cheeks reddened. "Now, I just want you to have a good day on your birthday. It's like an unwritten law somewhere that you must have a good day on your birthday."

"It is not."

"It is in my book."

"Your book is filled with bizarre things."

He gasped. "It is not."

"If you say so," I teased, laughing.

"Just promise."

"Okay, I'll try," I promised.

"Great," he said, smiling once more before he stood up. "Well, I'll be going now. I don't want to be late. Remember, three-thirty. Don't be late."

"I won't!"

"Bye!" Hayden then took off down the sidewalk and disappeared around the corner.

"Bye," I whispered.

I couldn't stop the giant grin on my assumed reddened face, even as the bus pulled up to the curve. As soon as the door slid open and I stepped up the three steps, the once receded headache returned with a vengeance

Dizzily, I gripped the cold metal pole to keep myself grounded. I raised every shielding technique I could think of to block out the intense emotions coursing through my mind and psyche.

My eyes darted frantically around.

There weren't many people, so why was I being bombarded like this?

Sure, my empathy was strong, but this was ridiculous.

2

"Hurry up and take a seat!" yelled the grumpy bus driver.

For the first time, I observed him confusingly. This bus driver wasn't the same one as usual. Mr. Bloomingdale was the one assigned to this bus and usually was a lot nicer. Who was this new driver? This driver was different. Short and stocky with white hair balding behind his ears.

"What are you standing there for?" the driver yelled again.

"I…"

"Quit your yapping and go take a seat!"

What a jerk, I thought.

Now I wished more than ever that I had stayed at home. This man was worse because his emotions didn't seem to have a defined reason. Or if they did, it was a reason I couldn't detect. Then again, my empathy couldn't always delve deep into a person's psyche and reveal why or what made them feel that way. However, something inside me told me that I wasn't the cause of this man's rudeness.

Miserably and awkwardly, I pulled out some change from my pocket and put the money in the machine before I strode down the aisle and over to the side with fewer people. I nearly broke out into a sweat as some of them turned their gaze on me.

I took a breath, taking a seat and turning my head away to gaze out the window. I didn't know what was wrong with me today. I promised Hayden to try and have a good day, and I intended to try, but I didn't think I would be able to do it.

With an exasperated sigh, I glanced at my wristwatch—the same wristwatch that belonged to my dad. It was just a normal analog watch—and according to my watch, it was fifteen minutes past seven.

Great, I thought. If this bus didn't go any faster, I was going to be late. This stupid and crazy slow traffic jam was abnormal for a small population of ten to fifteen thousand people. Traffic like this only existed in the big cities. What could be going on?

And if that wasn't bad enough, my head felt like it had a metal rock band drummer beating away at my skull. What's worse, the girl who decided to take a seat beside me wasn't helping matters either. Her long strawberry blonde hair blew from the wind coming in through the window which she had put down and kept whacking me in the face. Every time I went to put the window back up, the girl would glare at me and insist that I leave it alone. It was pretty stupid considering there were other places where she could sit with a window down.

I wanted to yell at her because the drizzling rain was getting me wet and the coldness was causing my body to tremble. This was indeed unusual weather.

With my headache now jacked up to nearly a full-blown migraine, my concentration and thoughts were severely difficult to get together. It was hard to decipher my emotions from the emotions of everyone around me. Sure, I constructed the mental shields I'd learned from a few years ago when I did an online search, but no one had told me how to perfect them. All the advice told me was to visualize a wall between me and everyone else. And that didn't help with the emotions from the ghosts. They were cold and distant. Like the woman in front of me. She was dressed in a blue dress with a flowery hat and was busy knitting something.

"That driver is such a drag," she said, smiling. "You agree, don't you?"

I turned my head away.

Ghosts, I thought.

And if that wasn't bad enough, my shields weren't helping right now. It was like I was in the dead center of a chaotic tornado. Instead of debris, it was a whirlwind of emotions. I wasn't sure if I wanted to snicker at one of the stupidest, corniest, and dirtiest jokes that some of the athletic jocks were chuckling at on their phone. If I wanted to bite at my nails like how the anxious young female in the seat across from me was doing with her binder spread out on her lap as she mumbled things under her breath. Or if I wanted to scream out in annoyance like the girl behind me wanted to do to the older gentleman who was trying to hit on her while she was busy painting her fingernails. Who even painted their fingernails on a bus in the first place?

Let's just say that once this bus pulled up to the curve, I was one of the first people to get off. And just keeping a customary pace with the crowd of people became a struggle. I faltered quite a few times whenever someone's arm brushed against me. In those moments, I cringed as I got an overstimulating flash of their emotions and even visions of death from the ghosts I came in contact with. It felt like an atomic bomb going off in my head.

This headache is going to be the death of me for sure, I thought.

An odd sense of vertigo assaulted me, disconnecting me from reality even more. I needed to sit down and take a moment to get my heavy breathing under control and get myself together. But I couldn't yet. I first needed to make it to the magic shop without fainting like a total loser in front of strangers.

Frustrated, I willed myself to stagger and squeeze through the enormous crowd of encumbered bodies, ignoring both their protesting shouts and overwhelming emotions.

I then slowed to a complete stop when something caught my attention.

This time it wasn't emotions, sickness, or my headache. Sure, there was a deep chilling coldness rattling my bones, but it wasn't the reason I halted.

It was a sound. A weird sputtering noise caused panic to escalate my heartbeat. Cautiously, yet curiously, I turned my head.

My eyes widened.

A black pickup truck was heading straight towards me. The windows were too dark to see anyone inside.

Panicked, I darted into the nearest building.

And wished I hadn't.

The second I dashed inside was the second I collided into someone. Toppling over, my hands came in contact with said person's hand. Distasteful infuriation filled my lungs.

With a sharp gasp, I tumbled backward, crashing to the ground on my bottom. I placed my hands over my heaving chest as I forced myself to breathe deeply. When the pain faded, my cheeks heated from embarrassment. With quick, jittery hands, I seized my bag and stammered, "I-I'm so sorry. I wasn't paying attention to where I was going."

The person cleared their throat which caused my head to perk up. I was no longer purely embarrassed; I was straight up mortified. Why of all people did I have to bump into Mr. Newman? This man hated me. Okay, maybe that was a little overly dramatic. I mean, he didn't hate just me. He loathed and hated almost everyone in this town.

His salt and pepper hair was scraggly. He also never dressed like a normal museum curator. He always had on a nice brown jacket but his tan shirt today was even more wrinkled than usual, and his jeans were extra faded as though he'd worn them one too many times. And his silver blue eyes, hidden behind a small pair of glasses too small for his face, narrowed slightly and seemed even darker.

"Ah, Mr. Brooks," he said in a thick accent. "I do not appreciate you colliding with me."

"I know," I said. "I'm sorry, sir."

"Glad you know it," he sneered. "Want to tell me why you barged into my museum?"

"It was a total accident, sir."

"In that case, I suggest you hurry along to whatever place you are late to."

"Yes, sir," I said.

Mr. Newman then dusted off his clothes before he paused and gazed at me over his shoulder with those creepy eyes of his. "Word of advice, Mr. Brooks," he said. "Beware of things that lurk in the shadows." And with one pivot left turn, he was gone from sight.

Several moments after he left, I stood there gaping like a total idiot. What did he even mean by that?

Slinging my bag over my shoulder, I rubbed my face. I then turned back to the front door only to see Zelda Goodman standing in front of it. Her curly brunette hair was put up in a bun, her tanned skin seemed even tanner, and her devilish brown eyes that made every guy swoon and fall head over heels for her were even darker with the black eyeliner. I never understood why people worshiped her like she was some kind of queen. After all, she was only the mayor's daughter. The reason she hated me was partially because I didn't fall for her looks or personality.

Blocking my exit route, she crossed her arms over her large busted chest and then admired her nails. Not once did she break eye contact with me as she said, "Well, well, where do you think you are going, freak boy?"

I rolled my eyes.

Her "supposed" originality antics weren't so original. I'd heard that insult too many times. It wasn't like I was even a witch or wizard or sorcerer or whatever the hell. Sure, my abilities made me feel like a freak, and a part of me wanted to be normal, but giving it up would feel terrible. Besides, having my abilities felt like the only connection I had left between me and my dad.

Out of everyone in town, Zelda was the one I despised the most. Her murky and oily emotions of hatred fueling through her felt like a burning furnace. They were worse than the rest of the tangy emotions underneath her anger. I never understood why out of everyone she picked on me the most to bully. I did nothing to her. I never talked to her. Even back in high school, we never had a single class together. And yet, one day, as soon as I started work at the magic shop during our senior year, she singled me out. I just couldn't understand why. Sure, I was different, but it wasn't like I went around advertising it. And it wasn't like she knew, did she? Even if she did, that was no reason for her to outright target me.

All I ever did was blend in with the background. And, if at all costs: avoid the crowds. That's why I always wore dark-colored clothing.

Today, for example, I had on a black tee shirt, and that seemed to make some of the girls stare weirdly at my eyes like lovesick princesses or something. It made my skin crawl uncomfortably. My eyes couldn't stand out that much, could they? Also, I had on a pair of dark blue jeans that I bought last year for Christmas that I hadn't even worn until now. And I had on my normal white and blue striped sneakers. Oh, and I had on my favorite navy blue hoodie.

With Zelda's eyes on me, I wanted the ground to swallow me up so I could disappear. And after my unpleasant interaction with Mr. Newman, I wanted more than anything to avoid any more unnecessary confrontations.

Sometimes I wished, with all the abilities that I possessed, that I could psychically transport myself to another location. Unfortunately, I didn't have that kind of power.

I held my satchel's strap tightly and smirked as I tapped into Zelda's confidence and used it as my own. Sometimes I could use another person's emotions to help myself. I didn't do this often though.

"Zelda, this is most certainly a surprise to see you inside the museum. I thought you hated this place with a passion."

"I do hate this place," she said, smiling. "It's such a drag being here. And I didn't have much of a choice. My father made me come."

"Oh, but you brought your crew along," I said, not intimidated in the slightest. I had sensed her friends trying to sneak up on me.

Hannah Noblemen was the first to approach. She had blonde hair that she must have gotten professionally curled and put back in a ponytail. "He is such a freak."

Brianna Bloomingdale was the next person to approach. She stood beside Hannah and placed her hand on her friend's shoulder. "You are right about that, Hannah. By the way, haven't you heard the rumor?" she asked with a wicked smirk.

"No one even cares about stupid rumors," replied Hannah. "It's just stupid gossip, but you can't deny he's a total weirdo."

Zelda smiled evilly. "Indeed he is. But the rumor is no rumor, is it, Weston?" she asked, sneering.

I ducked my head, my bangs falling into my eyes. Anxiously, I grabbed tightly on my right bicep and rubbed it to comfort myself. I fought to ignore their emotions booming into my head. Why were they talking about me like I wasn't standing in front of them? Why were girls so complicated?

I swallowed the sudden lump that seemed to get lodged in the back of my throat. It took everything in my willpower to keep the sudden wave of churning nausea from rising as I took deep breaths. This proved it. They all knew.

Okay, I had to get a grip on myself. All I had to do was get past them and get to work and then pretend for the rest of the day that everything was fine like always.

"No response, freak?" asked Zelda. I could sense the disgusting hint of amusement in her emotions.

"Why don't you cool it, Zelda Goodman," I snickered. "Goodman shouldn't even be your last name. You aren't a good person. And so what if the rumor isn't just a rumor? It's not like I'm hiding who I am."

"Aren't you, though?" asked Hannah.

I couldn't help but glare at her. I wasn't hiding it. Yes, I was gay. I knew by the time I was fifteen. When guys talked about their crushes on girls, I was crushing on guys. It wasn't like you think, though. I never sexualized anything. I just knew I liked guys. I had feelings for them in a romantic sense. I didn't understand it, but when I came out to my mom that was a day she lost all respect for me. However, I kept it to myself since then. If someone asked me, I would tell them the truth even if they didn't like me anymore. I figured it was better to tell the truth and lose friends than to lie to myself.

Zelda put a hand up. "I got this, Hannah." Her brown eyes locked onto mine. "You surprise me, Weston. You've got some spark inside you." She flashed her infamous million-dollar grin. "It seems you've gotten more courageous since our last quarrel."

I crossed my arms over my chest and fought the urge to wince at the ache in my head as I fought to get my labored breathing under control. The deep belly breathing helped calm the racing of my pulse, but didn't stop the pain in my head. And again, I was close to breaking out in a sweat. This was a side effect of tapping into a person's emotions.

It also didn't help that I could feel eyes on me which made me want to flee. I hated being the center of attention.

Not wanting to say anything more, I started to hastily walk past them. Only Zelda stuck out her foot. I didn't see it fast enough to move out of the way and ended up tripping.

I fell to the ground. Hard enough that I was sure I bruised my knees. But I didn't let it get to me. I simply lifted my head and fired a heated glare in her direction causing her to flinch as I picked myself up off the floor.

The glare did nothing but cause Zelda to resume her tormenting. I should have known.

Zelda snatched my bag and ripped it open. "Ooh, what's this?" she asked as she pulled out my notebook and opened it. "Writing girlish poems?"

"No!" I shouted, fighting to grab my notebook. Hannah and Brianna, unfortunately, pinned my arms behind my back. Stupid reflexes for not making me react faster. Stupid headache for not making me respond faster.

With her devilish grin still plastered on her face, Zelda began flipping through the pages of my notebook. As her brown eyes scanned over it, I fought against the hold on me as embarrassment and anger rose in me. They were stronger than they seemed. I could have gotten out of their grasp, but being a gentleman, I didn't want to hurt them even if they were hurting me.

"Holy, guano!" yelled Zelda, laughing creepily. "I always knew you had girlish tendencies, but to write romantic poems..."

"It... It's not romantic! And they aren't poems!" I argued.

The pounding in my head worsened, and the amusement from the girls restraining me wasn't doing anything to help. Gushing water roared in my ears, and a burning sensation started behind my eye sockets as the hurricane of emotions swirled inside my head.

Something overhead clattered. I could vaguely hear it over the roaring in my ears as I continued to stare down at Zelda.

I just wanted my notebook back!

Just then, the sprinkler busted and water gushed.

Zelda shrieked and dropped my notebook.

Quickly, while Zelda's friends shrieked and released their hold on me, I tapped into my telekinesis. Feeling its warmth rush course through me, I stared at my notebook. It stopped mid-air. I then grabbed my satchel and held it open and my notebook fluttered inside.

After zipping it up, I fiercely glared at Zelda and her stupid friends. I wished so hard that they would get soaked even more. Then, like magic, the water responded. It gushed so hard and dispensed like a flood. But the strangest part, as my senses adjusted, was how the water was drenching everything except for me and the spot under my feet. I was somehow completely dry.

"What is going on over here?" inquired Mr. Newman, who walked over to us after hearing the commotion no doubt.

Zelda wrung her hands, sending water droplets everywhere as she and her friends stood there soaked. Zelda's drenched sparkly pink cocktail party dress with a white bow had water dripping heavily from the ends. The water even ruined her sparkly white heels. Her friends weren't much better. They were in the same dresses, only Hannah's was light blue and Brianna's was gold.

I fought the urge to laugh as I watched their ruined mascara run down their faces.

Zelda then pointed a long pink-painted fingernail at me. "Weston did this!"

I stepped back. "What? No, I... I didn't!"

"You did!" she shouted. "You so did! Your wicked powers rigged the sprinkler system to go off and ruin my beautiful expensive dress and shoes!"

"And don't forget about us!" shouted Hannah.

"Yeah, he ruined ours, too!" Brianna agreed.

"I didn't do this!"

"That's enough, Mr. Brooks!" demanded Mr. Newman. "The police and your mother will be hearing about this!"

3

Bent over on a bench outside of the museum, trying not to panic was the hardest thing in the world at the moment. Inside, I could hear the muffled voices of my mom, the police, and Mr. Newman yelling. And by the sound of it, they were in a heated argument, and it didn't seem to be pleasant at all.

I knew I was in a heap of trouble as I restlessly squeezed my hands. My anxiety was running a mile a minute through me as I fought to keep my leg from bouncing. This was the first time I'd ever been in this amount of trouble.

I placed my head in my hands and snaked my fingers through my black hair and tugged at it frustratingly. The guilt and anger were eating me alive. I knew I messed up. I just knew it, but the question was: what did I do exactly? I didn't rig the sprinkler system. I didn't even have that kind of know-how.

Oh no, it must have been my power. Did they get out of hand? Something, probably my conscience, told me that it had been my fault, and that was why I was in deep trouble. But I had never caused a flood or damaged anything before. I barely had the power to do much more than move objects like my bag, my pencils, a cup, and stuff like that.

"Is anyone sitting here?"

I sat up, startled.

Removing my hands from my head, I opened my eyes to see a girl standing in front of me. She had long white hair that had to be dyed, because there was no way that could ever be a natural color on someone unless they were elderly, and this girl was about my age. She had her hair pulled back with a red ribbon, but the ends of her hair were hanging past her shoulders. Her bright sky-blue eyes sparkled. I also noticed that she had on a white blouse and white denim shorts that showed off her tanned legs, with white laced-up high heeled ankle boots. There was also a silver bag hanging off her arm. This was the same girl I had seen on the bus earlier. I didn't know who she was. Though, now instead of radiating nervousness, she was way calmer.

When her question registered in my head, I shook my head, exhaled, and then scooted over some more to give her more room.

"No, please, take a seat," I said.

"Thank you," she said as she sat down. "I just needed a moment to sit down." She rubbed at her ankles. "These new heels are a killer."

"I believe you," I said, trying not to snicker. "But they do complement your outfit."

"Right?" she said as excitement radiated from her emotions like sunshine. "I thought so, too, when I saw them. I was going to walk around in them a lot more to break them in, but wouldn't you know it, the mud in our yard was so terrible that I had to carry them and change them at school. What a drag. And I might as well take them back."

"Why?" I asked. "You like them and you spent a lot of money on them."

Her sky-blue eyes gazed at me as I sensed her utter confusion. "How do you know that? Are you a mind reader?"

"Not even close," I said, shaking my head. "I just noticed that you admired them with adoration. I can tell they are expensive because I walked by that shop around the corner from here about two weeks ago and saw them in the window for like four hundred dollars."

She giggled. "Oh, yeah, I always check out that shop. Were you going to buy them for your girlfriend?"

"I'm sorry, but I don't have a girlfriend. Also, I'm just super observant. I walked past that window quite a few times and glanced in there occasionally when I noticed new items."

"Oh, I thought I heard you arguing with her in there." She pointed to the museum. "She's not your girlfriend?"

"No, goodness no," I said. "She's nowhere near my type and she's way too problematic."

The girl frowned. "I see," she said. There was now a wave of sadness coming off of her. Had I said something wrong?

Just when I was about to apologize, the girl turned to me with tears shining in her eyes. "I guess I am a bit problematic myself."

I was taken aback. "Why would you say that? You don't seem at all problematic. I can't picture you going out of your way to start unnecessary drama."

Instead of being offended, she giggled. "To be honest, I'm not, usually. I'm a good girl. I follow every rule. I always do my homework and extra credit. You see, I'm trying to get through my first year of college classes and exams with flying colors since my parents have this big plan for me. They have my whole life planned out and are paying for my tuition. But I think that's ruined now."

"What do you mean?"

"I sort of got into a fight," she said. "But it wasn't my fault. I mean, it was, but I was only defending my best friend from this guy and girl who were both verbally harassing her. They wouldn't leave her alone. She shouted at them for over five minutes, telling the girl that she wasn't hitting on her boyfriend and trying to get the guy to understand that she had a boyfriend. Anyway, I'd had enough of them tormenting her, so, I, well... I kind of punched them both in the nose." She played with the ends of her hair. "I didn't mean to hurt them. Honestly. I was just so raving mad and annoyed at their antics and the fact that they were making my friend more and more upset. I wanted to protect her, you know?"

I nodded. "You don't have to explain that to me. I get it completely." I then leaned forward and whispered, "If it had been my best friend I would have done the same thing in a heartbeat."

The girl giggled again.

I leaned back. "Though, you know, it must have been quite a sight to see."

She smiled. "I am not sure I would say that," she said. "I mean, the guy was taller than me and was probably even stronger. And the girl, well, she was about my size but way more athletic from track training."

"Even so," I said. "You are a small thing and yet you still managed to put up a fight. That's still a feat. Though, I am not promoting violence. But defending someone, friend or foe, is still admirable and never wrong."

"True," she said, swinging her left leg over her right and placed one of her elbows on her thigh, laying her chin on her palm. From her distant emotions, I could tell she was thinking about what had transpired because guilt and sorrow were beginning to seep in. "I just…" Suddenly, there was a spike of anger as her eyes narrowed. "Those stupid rules about tolerance are total bull! They help no one! My college professor was right there and watched the whole thing and when it was all over, he gave the girl and the guy a warning, lecture, and had them go on their way. While I got suspended because I hit them! I just know that now if they come back, I won't be able to protect my friend from those creeps."

"She is safe for now, right?"

"For now, I think so. But who knows for sure? I'm scared she might not be. She's not a fighter, but she isn't one to back down when she's being yelled at. She probably didn't need me to fight her battle for her, anyway. I should have just left it alone. If I had, I wouldn't be in any trouble. When I get home, my parents are going to freak out. They might even toss me out of the house. And while I'm on the streets, my best friend will be alone with those awful monsters! Why did they get away with treating her that way? It's not right!"

The guilt, the anxiety, and the panic she was experiencing were tightening in my chest. I wanted to reach over and place a hand on her shoulder to get her to calm down. But I didn't dare do that. I didn't know how she'd react to that. Thankfully, she seemed to have gotten control because the tight feeling vanished to be replaced with calmer emotions.

"This is so weird," she said. "I never talk about my problems to a stranger." She giggled. "But I've got to admit that talking to you has helped me feel better. Thank you."

"You don't have to thank me. I didn't do anything."

"Of course you did," she said with a bright smile. "You listened to me rant." She then turned her body to me. "Since I spilled my guts to you, why don't you tell me your story? I promise to listen and not interrupt once."

"You don't..."

"Please," she begged. "I'm kind of curious about you. I mean, about why you are out here. You don't seem like the type of guy to do bad things. But that argument in there must be the reason you are out here. I'm probably over stepping with this comment, but it's like you have the world's biggest guilt weighing your shoulders down."

I squeezed my hands again. "You're extremely observant."

She flicked her hair back, smiling. "I have been told that," she said with extreme confidence radiating from her. "Truth be told, I'm working on becoming a professional therapist. So, this is good practice."

"Well, you are doing a good job."

"Thank you. Now, go ahead and spill it."

I nervously rubbed my hands along my jeans to wipe the sweat beginning to wet them. "It's like you heard. I did get into an argument. She's someone who has a huge hatred for me, for reasons I don't know. But she stole something incredibly dear to me, and then the sprinklers just went off like crazy. She then started blaming me for setting it off. So, now, they called the police to investigate to see if the system was indeed rigged. No word yet. But to be honest, I don't even know how to rig something like that. Nor would I want to destroy hundreds of beautiful artifacts. So far, none of them are ruined which is a relief. I hate this because I would never do anything to get myself into trouble, but it seems I got myself into a deep predicament this time."

"Sounds awful," she said. "To blame you without any sort of proof, I mean."

"Well, the girl is persuasive. Not to mention, her family and the people in this town are superstitious and believe that anything abnormal is because of me and my family. I don't get it. Then again, she is…"

Just then the museum doors flew open and my mom stepped out. Rage was boiling through her and tearing itself into the core of my heart so hard that my nails dug into the holes in the bench.

"M…" I started to say.

"Don't even start, young man," she sneered.

I flinched.

"You are in for a world full of trouble, young man! And when we get home..." she continued but then let out an exasperated sigh. "You don't even want to know what I have planned. Now, get a move on!"

I gulped and obediently nodded. The girl, whose name I didn't even know, flashed me an empathetic smile and mouthed, "It will be okay."

I wanted to believe her, but I was too afraid to. Mom's anger was so high. So, not wanting to make it worse, I just nodded once before tottering sullenly down the sidewalk beside her. She had her arms crossed. Once at our dark blue Jeep Wrangler, she unlocked the passenger door, and then practically shoved me inside.

I fixed my eyes on the floorboard as I played with a week-old fast-food wrapper with my foot nervously. Tears stung my eyes and threatened to fall, but I fought with everything inside me not to cry. I couldn't. My mom would tell me to stop being so emotional. To her, crying was a sign of weakness. But she didn't know how hard it was for me. Being a self-proclaimed empath, my empathy made me extra sensitive. Emotions just hit me and I would feel like I was the one experiencing them. And right now, my mom's resentment and disappointment directed at me were stabbing my heart like a million knives. I didn't want this to happen. All I ever tried to do was make her proud of me. Now I was feeling horrible. And knowing that I failed her...

"How could you, Weston Walter Brooks?" my mom's sharp voice broke through my anxiety-ridden thoughts.

"Mom, listen, please, I didn't..."

"You nearly ruined one of the biggest museum exhibits!"

"But, Mom, if you'd..."

"No!" she shouted. "I don't want to hear any of your excuses! Right now, you are to remain silent until we get home. Do you understand me?"

"Perfectly," I mumbled, slumping in my seat and gazing gloomily out the window. Storm clouds were still overlaying the sky, and there were rays of violet lightning streaking across the sky now and again. But the weird part was I didn't hear any rumble of thunder.

Strange, I thought.

It was then that I realized something even stranger. The headache that had plagued me all morning was no longer there.

For the rest of the ride, I stayed silent, just gazing out the window and lost in thought. Even if there was a storm outside happening, there was also a storm raging inside me, and it seemed like the rain outside of the vehicle was listening to me, pouring all my negative emotions out.

When we got to our apartment room, Mom unlocked and opened the door. I didn't waste any time walking past her and sprinting to my room. I walked in and then slammed the door behind me before I flopped down on my bed on my stomach. I buried my head buried in my pillow and screamed out all of my frustration and pain.

I heard rattling around me as well as heavy rain splattering on my window loudly, but I paid no mind to it as I lay there, gripping my pillow like it was the last thing on earth keeping me from falling apart as silent warm tears rolled down my cheeks.

I didn't remember falling asleep, but I must have, because the next thing I knew there was a loud banging on my door.

"Weston Brooks, you wake up this instant and join me in the kitchen for dinner! It's time we discuss your punishment!"

I prolonged the torment I knew would be thrust upon me the second I stepped out that door. So, I sat on the edge of my bed for a few extra minutes and mentally prepared myself as best I could, since my thoughts were a bit jumbled. Feeling a bit more organized, I opened the door reluctantly padded into the kitchen, and sat down at the table. On the tabletop was a plate of steaming leftover spaghetti from a few days ago.

Sighing, I picked up my fork and twirled some of the noodles on the end aimlessly. I wasn't feeling hungry. Mom was sitting across from me. Her hatred was still seething, and the scrutinized glaring was making me more and more uncomfortable. I shifted in my seat for what felt like the twelfth or thirteenth time.

Mom must have noticed because her eyes narrowed deadly. "Stop fidgeting this instant, Weston! You know you are in big trouble."

"Yes, ma'am," I said, fighting to keep my ire at bay. I had the urge to shout, to scream, to yell out, to grab my stupid plate full of undercook spaghetti, and throw it at the nearest wall just to get the attention I deserved. But I pushed those thoughts and feelings down. That would only cause things to worsen. The last time I threw a dramatic tantrum like that, it ended disastrously.

"So, you want to tell me why you messed with the sprinkler system?"

"I didn't do it," I stated calmly.

"Young man, I am allowing you this one opportunity to explain yourself."

"Yes, I know, and I am explaining," I said. "I didn't do it. One minute, I am trying to get my notebook back from evil Zelda, and then the next thing I know the sprinkler just started going off."

"I will not have you lie to me!"

"I swear it, Mom!" I yelled.

"You are making this situation worse, mister!" she yelled back. "If you say you didn't do it, then can you explain why you were the only one that didn't get wet, huh?"

"I can't explain that," I said, sulking in my chair.

"Sit up straight!" she demanded.

Reluctantly, I straightened.

Ding!

My stupid phone! Did it have to go off now?

I had honestly forgotten that I even had it in my pocket. Without thinking, I pulled it out. I didn't need to know who messaged me. I had a few guesses. It could either be Hayden or even work. Or perhaps it was both. I hadn't shown up at work so my boss was no doubt angry at me, and then when Hayden had shown up and saw I wasn't there, he probably became worried and angry, and probably even felt betrayed.

Before I could press the power button and check, the scraping of my mom's chair startled me. I watched as she stood and marched her way over to me and snatched my cell phone right out of my hand forcefully. I could feel her sharp nails scratch me. "No phone at the table," she said before she shook her head. "No, you know what, no more phone, period. I don't want you talking to that crazy friend of yours ever again."

"He's not crazy, Mom!"

Mom's glare froze the blood in my veins and paralyzed me from saying the next words on the tip of my tongue. I closed my mouth as my mom sneered, "Young man, do you want to keep making this situation graver and graver?" She then slammed my phone down on the table. Judging by the booming crack, the screen was probably in pieces. That enraged me. How was I going to talk to Hayden or work or anyone else?

"I don't understand," Mom continued. "I have tried to be an exemplary mother. Where did I go wrong?"

"Mom, you…"

"This is all because of your father, isn't it? That's why there have been so many misbehaving situations. It's all because he isn't here with us, right?" she asked, but it didn't sound like she was talking to me and sounded more like she was thinking out loud.

"Mom, there is no need for you to be angry," I said without thinking.

She pointed a finger at me threateningly. "That right there! You still pretend you know what I am feeling. You still cling to this senseless notion that you have this power that allows you to magically know how I am feeling."

"It's pretty obvious," I mumbled under my breath as I moved a meatball around on my full plate of spaghetti with my fork.

"What was that?" she growled.

"Nothing," I responded.

"You know, you are so much like your father. Your sapphire blue eyes are proof of that. They blaze with that same stormy rebellion and penetrating gaze he had. I swear the only thing you inherited from me was black hair and some facial features. But you have every bit of your father's imbecilic mindset. He used to sprout nonsense all the time and did spontaneous, troublesome things until I could barely take it."

"Maybe it's good he's gone," I said, absentmindedly.

She slammed her palms down on the table. My plate and silverware rattled. "That is no way to speak of the dead!" she yelled. The venom in her voice caused the anger in her emotions to surge into an infernal rage that deprived me of proper breathing. I fought the urge to cough as my hands clenched around the edges of my chair so hard that my nails dug into the wood. I hadn't meant to provoke her like that. "Know this, Weston Walter Brooks; starting tomorrow everything is going to change. You are so lucky I sweet-talked that lovely curator into getting you out of trouble for causing that stupid prank."

I didn't like the sound of that. "What's my atonement?" I asked, panting for breath.

If my mom noticed my discomfort, she didn't pay attention. "He was too angry to decide. However, if it had been up to me, you'd be working your hands to the bone. I know you are legally an adult, but for tonight you are confined to your room."

"Why?"

She crossed her arms over her chest. "Because as long as you live in this apartment, you will obey my rules," she said. "I know I should have done this a long time ago when all of this nonsense began. But here I was, a hopeful mother, just wanting it all to be a phase that would eventually fade with time."

I couldn't take it anymore. Rather than expelling her rage, I accepted it into myself and used it to fuel my anger. "And what happened to you telling me to be myself and to love myself?" I shouted, jumping to my feet and slamming my palms down on the tabletop. The plates, glasses, and silverware clattered and shook, both from my movement and from my uncontrollable telekinesis that I could feel tingling and buzzing at my fingertips. "I can't get rid of it any more than you can! And quite frankly, I don't want it to go away! This is simply who I am!"

"It's unnatural!" she argued. "I know I told you to be yourself, but I didn't know you would turn out like this! So, you can, and you most certainly will get over this craziness! I will personally make sure of it. Therefore, you are going to march straight to your room since you don't want to eat."

"Fine," I said through gritted teeth. I pushed away from the table and clenched my fists. Sounds of creaking came from nearby, but I didn't care as I pivoted and marched away.

"Oh, and Weston," Mom said.

I stopped in the middle of the hallway. "What is it, Mom?"

"Don't talk back to me!" she shouted before she let out a frustrated groan. "You know what, never mind. Just go to your room."

I squeezed my eyes shut and wished for something, anything really, to happen and wash away her anger.

Just then, I heard what sounded like the water exploding through the pipes and then the sound of my mom's panicking shrieking.

The anger drowned.

Worried about her safety, I turned around.

My eyes widened.

Mom was standing by the sink dripping wet from the sink sprouting water like a fountain. But that wasn't the worst part. There was fright in her emotions.

She's afraid of me.

4

"What did you do?" Mom screamed.

I couldn't speak. The shock was trembling down my whole body. Had I done that?

I realized then that what happened at the museum was indeed my fault.

"Weston!"

Ignoring her heated shouts, I dashed out of the door, down the stairs, out of the apartment building's lobby door, and straight down the street. I didn't know where I was heading. I just knew I needed to get away.

Rain was pouring, and I didn't have a raincoat to keep me from getting soaked. All I had on were the same clothes that I had been wearing all day.

I found I didn't need any rain protection.

The rain wasn't even touching me which struck me as strange. But I didn't question it too much when my pounding footsteps weren't splashing water. It was like I had an invisible force field surrounding me, keeping me dry. I stored the question in the back of my mind for later. Because right this minute, I didn't care about anything. I was just focused on getting far away.

Every couple of seconds I would check behind me to see if my mom was following me. When I was far enough away, I slowed my pace and came to a stop at a lamppost. As I stood there under the light trying to catch my breath, my eyes narrowed in on the black pickup at the end of the street. Its high beam headlights blazed on me. It was like it wanted me to notice it. Wasn't this the same one that tried to run me down earlier?

The truck revved.

Panicked, I sprinted off again.

The truck followed me.

I doubted I would be faster than the truck, but I continued to sprint anyway. By the time I rounded the corner, I had lost track of it. What surprised me, even more, was the fact that I found myself in my best friend's neighborhood. Did that truck lead me here, or did I do it on my own?

Either way, I didn't care.

Seeing the familiar white brick house with the brown picket fence, tire swing hanging off the tree, and the toys scattered in the yard, I couldn't help but smile. And without hesitation, I jogged over and up the stairs to the porch. I had been here a time or two, but only when Hayden said I could. What would happen now that I was here without permission? Would he turn me away?

I hoped not.

I knocked hurriedly on the blue door with the welcome wreath full of roses hanging from it.

Bouncing up and down on the balls of my feet, I waited for the door to open.

When it finally opened, Hayden stepped out barefooted. I couldn't help the blush that heated my cheeks as I noticed that he was in a black shirt, showing off his muscles and those same dark blue jeans that always fitted him perfectly. And then there was the way his turquoise eyes widened and twinkled from the streetlight made my heart flutter with a million butterflies.

"What are you doing here?"

"I'm sorry," I said hurriedly and then glanced over my shoulder. I wanted to make sure my mom the black truck hadn't followed me. When I didn't see it, the tension in my shoulders relaxed before I hesitantly turned back and wrapped my arms around myself to try and fight off the sudden cold chill that came over me.

Hayden's eyes narrowed.

A twinge of anger and betrayal emitted from him. My heart dropped to my stomach and filled me with unadulterated pain.

"You're sorry?" he asked, growling, and then slapped my shoulder. "Weston, when I showed up at our rendezvous and you weren't there, I tried texting you and calling you. But you never responded to a single message or answered a single call. I thought we had plans."

The slap didn't hurt as much as it startled me. Hayden had never resorted to forcefulness. Or at least, he never had in my presence. Then again, I had never stood him up before either. He was right. There was a first time for everything.

Giving my shoulder a small rub, I concurred guiltily. "You're right. We did have plans. I never denied that. And I never forgot about it," I said, desperately. "I'm so sorry. You've got to believe me when I say that, Hayden. A lot happened today. I couldn't contact you back because my mom confiscated my phone and then broke the screen all because she didn't want me to have any communication with you. But, please, Hayden, believe me when I say that it wasn't intentional."

"Fine," he said. "I believe you, but what are you doing here?"

"I know you told me never to come over without your say-so first, but I... I didn't know where else to go." That wasn't completely true. I could have gone to my cousin's, but to be honest, I didn't want to get mixed up in the drama he always got himself into.

The anger that had been on Hayden's face smoothed out. "I'm sorry, too. I should have figured something happened," he said, eyes drifting over my face as though he was analyzing me to see if I was being truthful or lying. He wrapped his arm around my shoulders and pulled me into him. "You're shivering, Weston. But you aren't even wet from the rain. Did you get a ride from someone?"

I shook my head. "No," I said, taking in his confused emotions.

"It doesn't matter," he said. "You can explain when you get inside and warm up. I'll even heat some of that warm milk you love so much."

I made a disgusted face. "Please, don't," I begged. "I hate that stuff. I only drank it because my mom hardly ever let me drink any caffeinated drinks.

I'm usually stuck with milk, water, and sometimes a glass of orange juice. But you know what I would like? I would love some hazelnut coffee."

"Don't you have caffeine intolerance?"

I shrugged. "That's what my mom claims. Honestly, she's been known to lie. So, I don't think it's true. Besides, I need something to calm my nerves."

"Okay, I'll get you whatever you want," he said. "Now, come on. It's chilly out here and you are freezing."

I nodded.

Hayden led me inside. His house was gorgeous. It was warm and vibrant and smelled like apple pies. There was also the fact that it always had this serene and peaceful atmosphere that instantly made the tension in my muscles relax. I loved it. I loved that his house had this calming effect on me. It was so much better here than it was at home.

Hayden's arm slipped off from around my neck and I fought the urge to grab his arm and keep it there. It was warm and nice. I felt my cheeks heat up more. I turned my head and gazed at the brown cuckoo clock hanging on the wall. The same one with the broken wing on the bird as it chimed ten times. I couldn't believe how late it was.

A warm hand touching my shoulder made me jump a little. Startled, I turned and my wild gaze locked onto Hayden's beautiful eyes. He gave my shoulder a gentle squeeze. "It's only me," he said. "My parents aren't here."

"I remember," I said. "You told me that they were on a business trip or something."

"That's right," he said.

It was then that I noticed he was holding a towel in his hands.

"Oh, I got this for you," he said, draping the towel over my shoulders.

It took every ounce of my willpower not to blush and to keep my heart from beating out of my chest as the urge to kiss him was strong. "Thank you," I managed to say.

He smiled. "You go on ahead and take a hot shower. I laid out some clothes for you in the bathroom. Remember, Weston, you are safe here. I won't let anyone hurt you."

I didn't know what came over me. I just acted on instinct. I wrapped my arms around his neck and pulled him into my embrace as I laid my head in the crook of his neck. "Thank you so much, Hayden."

He wrapped his arms around me and patted my back. "Hey, you never have to thank me. What are best friends for?"

I chuckled. "Good point," I said, unwinding my arms from around him. "I'll, uh, go take that shower now."

Hayden nodded. "Go on ahead," he said. "You know where everything is."

I walked past him. There were two bathrooms. But since Hayden's room was downstairs, he always used the one across the hall. I know because I used to stay with him when his parents weren't home. I walked inside and pulled the chain. Light flooded the area.

After my incredibly warm shower, I dressed in some sweatpants and an old faded tee shirt that

Hayden left for me. I walked out and headed to the kitchen. Hayden was sitting on a stool with two blue mugs of steaming hazelnut coffee. It smelled wonderful.

"You're looking better," teased Hayden, smirking. "Come and sit down. While you may seem fine at the moment, I know you. You're stressing yourself out."

I sat down beside him. Our knees grazed each other slightly but neither of us moved. I curled my hands around the warm cup and smiled. The warmth was welcoming. And the sweet taste was divine. It was like drinking a piece of heaven.

"So, ready to tell me what happened?" he asked. "You only mentioned that your mother took your phone and broke it."

I nearly spurted my drink out. The vivid memory came crashing back to the forefront of my mind and I blinked rapidly. It caused the memory to crack and break away like glass and to fade into the dark recess of my mind. I turned my head as I lowered my cup. "That's true. I did."

"What happened that has you so upset?"

The lump in my throat tightened. "My mom and I got into a pretty rough heated argument."

"Again?" he asked. "What was it this time?"

"It's a long story," I said. "And it's hard to talk about because…"

"Because—" Hayden couldn't finish his sentence because bright headlights beamed in through the blinds of the window. Feeling his panic, I watched as he got out of his chair and peered out the blinds. "Oh no, it's my parents. They got back early." Before I could open my mouth, he placed his hands on my shoulders. His emotions were strange and unreadable for the first time. It was like he was scared and guilty. That made no sense to me.

"Weston," he said, keeping his voice low. "I need you to trust me and do exactly what I say. Please. I need you to take your things out of the bathroom and go hide out in my bedroom closet."

He wanted me to hide in the closet, really? I wanted to say something about that, but I held my tongue. I just gazed into his eyes before nodding as I whispered, "Okay."

I then crept as quietly as I could to the bathroom and picked up my clothes, slipped into my sneakers, and then snuck back out and darted to the bedroom across from me and closed the door just as I heard the front door open.

I leaned against the wood as I held my clothes tightly to my thudding chest.

Suddenly, the knob rattled.

My heart pounded harder. Was it Hayden's parents? Were they coming in here to tell me to go home? I didn't want to go back to that awful place. I wanted to stay here with Hayden. I wanted his warm presence, not this icy panic.

I quickly used my telekinesis, making the closet door open. I ran quiet in, closed the door, and hid against the wall just as the door to the bedroom busted open.

"See!" Hayden said. "It's like I told you. No one else is here. I was having two cups of coffee by myself. You and Mother are so paranoid."

"Well, we don't want that troublemaker friend of yours in this house," said a stern baritone voice that was too deep to be Hayden's. That must have been his father. I hadn't met the man, but the emotions I was getting from him were intimidating. I didn't want to get on the man's bad side.

Wait. Was he talking about me?

"Father, you and Mother both need to quit calling him that."

"We will when you never see him again," the man said before I heard the bedroom door open and then slam closed.

I breathed out slowly and buried my head in my knees. I tried to calm my breathing, but it was no use. I was in a dark enclosed space, and my claustrophobia was acting up. I always hated dark enclosed spaces since I was little. My therapist had tried to help me by forcing me to stay in a closet and face my fears. That only made it worse. By the time I stopped screaming and he pulled me out, I was catatonic for several days. I only know that because my doctors yelled at them for child negligence.

The hangers above my head began to rattle. Oh no. My powers were out of control again because of my lack of emotional control. I squeezed my eyes shut, rocking back and forth as I told myself to calm down over and over.

Familiar hands firmly gripped my shoulders, and all the air that left my body suddenly rushed back in as calm emotions washed over me. The panic that had been consuming me washed away. The blackness in my vision vanished as I opened them to see Hayden's concerned face.

"Breathe," he whispered calmly. "Just breathe. That's it. Take nice and slow deep breaths. They're gone and you're safe."

I took in deep breaths. My eyes never left him once. I never wanted to turn my gaze away. His turquoise eyes were so beautiful and mesmerizing. I could stare into them forever.

"Are you okay?"

And the moment was ruined when he spoke. I darted my eyes away, feeling my cheeks burning. I took in a few more deep breaths before nodding. "I'm better now," I said. "Thank you."

"No, don't thank me," he said. "I forgot about your anxiety."

"It's not your fault." I then looked over his shoulder. "Is it safe to come out of the closet now?"

A small laugh escaped from him as his hands rubbed my shoulders, causing an electric feeling to travel through my body. "Yeah," he said. A fleeting feeling came from him. "What do you say we get out of the house? The rain has stopped." He turned on the light above us before grabbing a black sweater—the same black sweater I had left for him—and then grabbing a small blanket from the top shelf.

"And where would we go?" I asked, dropping my clothes as I stood up and stepped around him.

He flashed his infamous lopsided grin. That meant trouble. "I have the perfect location. And before you even ask, I cannot tell you. It's a surprise," he said, holding up the black sweater.

I rolled my eyes. "Come on, Hayden," I said, annoyed as I put my arms through the sweater. "You know how much I hate surprises."

"Oh, I do know that," he said. "Last year's Halloween party was proof of that."

"Okay, first off, that was your fault. You were the one who dressed up as Michael Myers. What was I supposed to do when a person appeared behind me dressed in a white mask holding a knife over their head?"

"I don't know, but that girlish scream that came out of you was the most priceless thing I've ever heard. I am never in a million years letting you live it down."

"Ha, ha," I said, punching his shoulder playfully. "How about the time I placed a rubber snake in your punch?"

"Don't even go there," he said, grinning. "Though, that was a good prank. But as much as I enjoy reminiscing on old memories, what do you say we head on over to my surprise? You can think of it as a birthday surprise if it helps you."

I cracked a smile at that. "Depends on the surprise," I teased. "Besides, if it comes from you, though, I'd probably like it, especially if it gets us out of here. I don't want your family to come in and shout up a storm. But how do you plan on us getting out of here?"

"Same way I always do when I don't want my parents to know where I am," he said, smirking. "We're going out the window."

I cocked an eyebrow at him.

"You aren't afraid, are you?"

"I'm not afraid. Let's go."

We climbed out with him helping me down like I was a girl who needed help. Sure, it annoyed me. But

I wasn't fragile. I didn't care if I got hurt or scraped. I didn't care if I got my hands dirty either. But I also knew he only meant it as a way to make sure I was okay. I did the same to him from time to time.

Once safely on the ground, the two of us laughed as Hayden threw an arm over my shoulders as I held the blanket he handed me. I wondered where he was taking me. After heading down the street, he ducked behind bushes to avoid car headlights.

After walking a bit longer, Hayden led me through this little patch of woodlands until we came to this little opening. We had to crawl on our bellies to get through. Once on the other side, Hayden helped me up.

I stared in awe.

We were in a small meadow. Lilacs and lavender grew in a perfect circle. Neatly cut grass and evergreen trees surrounded and stretched as far as the eyes could see. There were even fireflies dancing. The glow of the crescent moon beaming down made specks of silver lights flake like snow falling.

"Hayden, this is…"

"Lame, right?" he asked.

I chuckled, knowing he was joking from the amusement and wonder in his emotions.

"Yeah, sure, it's super lame," I teased back.

He stuck his tongue out at me. "You were going to say incredible, weren't you?"

I couldn't help but giggle. "Actually, no," I said. "Incredible is way too mild to describe this. I don't know what adjective describes it. Perfect, beautiful, wonderful… There are so many."

With a smile, he took the blanket out of my hands and spread it out on the grass. "No one has ever found this place," he said. "I discovered it one day by accident and have used it ever since when I had bad days. I'm sorry I have never shown it to you. I didn't want you to think I was girlish or stupid. I have a reputation to uphold, you know?"

"Of course you do," I mumbled to myself before rolling my eyes skyward. I then placed a hand on his shoulder and gave it a small squeeze. "Hayden, I don't think this is stupid. It's beyond beautiful. I've seen nothing like this before."

"Aw, but you didn't deny it was girlish," he teased.

"Well, it depends on what you consider to be girlish," I said. "This would be for anyone who has an eye for beauty."

He laughed.

We then stretched out on the blanket and gazed at the starry sky with the big glowing moon beaming down on us. The storm seemed to have passed

"I'm glad you showed me this place," I said, turning on my side and gazing at him. "I wish we could have more of these kinds of moments when it's just the two of us and no one else. It's incredibly nice. I want to spend every day like this with you."

He turned his head towards me; turquoise eyes twinkling in the moonlight. "I know what you mean. But if my family catches me out here, who knows what the consequences would be."

"You don't have to explain that to me," I said. "I'm in the same boat as you are. I ran out on my mom. To be honest, she doesn't understand me. She barely has time to talk or listen to me anymore. I've disappointed her in multiple ways. And this time is the icing on the cake. So, you don't have to say anything."

He smirked. "How do you understand me so well?"

Heat radiated from my neck up to the tips of my ears. I was blushing madly. How was it possible that he could do this to me? A part of me knew I shouldn't have these thoughts and feelings for him, but I did, and I do. They've been happening since our teens, and I never dared to tell him the truth. Besides, I didn't want to ruin what friendship we had.

Shaking away my intrusive thoughts, I shrugged. "Well, I suppose you could say it's some kind of gift. Though, to be fair, I have been around you since we were kids, so, maybe I just pick up on things about you easier."

He chuckled, reaching over and placing a hand on top of mine. It was warm. Just that simple touch banished all of my worries, doubts, fears, and problems. The small touch washed them away until I forgot about every single one. With a clearer mind, I only focused on what was in front of me. There was that same calmness flooding into my body. I wasn't entirely sure if the feeling was mine or Hayden's, or maybe a combination of the both of us. It didn't matter. I was already drowning in it.

"Tell me what happened," he said almost hypnotically.

I gazed back at the starry sky as I confessed to what happened.

"The museum?" he asked. "What were you doing there instead of being at work?"

"Well, I was feeling off," I admitted. "And I just...I ran into the museum but then got blamed for the faulty sprinkler system going off." I couldn't admit the truth that it had been me since he didn't even know about me being psychic.

"Whoa," he said. "How did you manage to get blamed for that?"

"Two words," I said. "Zelda Goodman."

"That makes sense," he said. "I've met Zelda Goodman a time or two. I know how much of a bratty witch that chick can be. Did you hear what she did to her last boyfriend?"

I shook my head.

"You're in for a story then," he said. "It happened about two months ago now, I suppose. Now I only know about this because I was out on an errand for my parents. But while I out, I talked to the café owner. Apparently, Zelda had the nerve to find him and his new girlfriend."

"I hadn't heard of this. What did she do?"

"A lot," he said. "According to the owner, Zelda stormed in all high and mighty. The owner said that it was like she owned the place. Anyway, she strolled up to their table, grabbed her ex's coffee, dumped it all over his head, and even splashed his current girlfriend before she just walked away."

"Not surprising," I said. "Zelda, I swear to you, is the devil in disguise. I heard this rumor that she cheated on him with her boyfriend's best friend."

"Oh, it was no rumor. Several people, including her boyfriend, caught her in the act."

I shook my head, laughing. It didn't surprise me to hear the story. I knew how much of a troublemaker Zelda could be. And she only got away with it because both of her parents, even though they're divorced, were rich.

"But you know," he continued. "I find your situation kind of amusing because I cannot picture you getting yourself in trouble for anything. You're too good a lot of the time."

"That's not true," I said. "I just don't like getting into unnecessary trouble. Besides, if I want to get out of this town and go to good colleges than I have to keep my record clean. But with this over my head, I'm worried. What if I somehow messed up my chances? What if this does go on my record?"

"I don't think it will be," he reassured. "You barely have the nerve to kick one of those malfunctioning vending machines. I can't see you pulling off a sprinkler prank."

"That's what I tried to tell the police and my mom and Mr. Newman. They wouldn't believe me. One minute I'm raging mad at Zelda for stealing my notebook…"

"Wait," he interrupted. "The notebook we write our secret messages in?"

"The very same," I said. "You see, that's what I was doing last night. I had this new message and was going to share it with you, so I wrote it down and then was going to finish checking it over on my break at work, but I never got the chance because…" I paused. Should I mention seeing a truck? No, that would only cause him to worry more.

"Because what, Weston?" pressed Hayden.

"Because I wound up at the museum, ran into Zelda, and the rest is history."

"I'm sorry."

I leaned my head against his shoulder. "Truth be told, I don't want to do this. I don't think I can manage not talking to you every day, because once I go back home, I will have no way to talk to you. I could sneak out and see you, but you get busy, too. I can't go a day without seeing you."

"I don't want to not see you either." Something twinkled in his eyes. "Let's run away together. We are both adults. We can do whatever we want."

I laughed. "I wish we could. But we can't. We have to think financially and neither of us is there yet. My college life may be in shambles, and I have no idea how to fix that before the fall. I don't want to bring you down because of my troubles."

"Hey, you could never bring me down. Besides, you are incredibly smart and you'll figure something out. You always do," he said and then pushed himself up and crossed his legs, which made me follow and do the same. I watched in fascination as he pulled out a white box. "I had almost forgotten but I got you a birthday present."

"It's not another pen, is it? You gave me one for my fifteenth birthday."

Instead of making a joke, he frowned. "No," he said, seriously. "I promise this is something special. Do you trust me?"

"You know I do."

"Then open it."

I opened the lid. Inside were two bracelets. Both were black corded. But one had teal or turquoise beads with a circular face with the letter H in calligraphy. The other one was very similar except it had sapphire beads and a circular face with the letter W also in calligraphy.

"Hayden, they're beautiful. Did you make these?"

"I didn't," he answered. "They were handmade by a good friend of mine." He then grabbed my left hand and caressed it before taking the bracelet with his initial and sliding it on my wrist.

I bit my lip as I felt my cheeks burning.

When he was done, he held out his hand without a word.

I carefully picked up the bracelet before sliding it over his hand. What I saw in his eyes was blissful happiness.

As soon as I finished, he grabbed my hand and linked our palms together as our fingers intertwined. A pulsing sea green and bright blue light surrounded our connected hands which caused our bracelets to glow. Was this magic? Did have powers, too?

Hayden gazed at me with a giant smile. "We are bonded in a way. This bond cannot be broken by anything or anyone," he said, and then released my hand. His initial on the bracelet burnt sea green before returning to its natural white color. "When either one of us are in trouble, the bracelets will glow."

"How does that work?"

"By magic," he said, grinning.

Even though, it was meant as a joke, something about it felt like it was serious to me. Though I wanted an explanation, I found that I didn't care.

This changed nothing. I couldn't help but fling myself at him and embrace him as if the world depended on it. I buried my head in his shoulder as my arms wrapped around his shoulders. I just held him. I must have startled him a little because he tensed, but then his shoulders relaxed as his warm arms wrapped around me.

"Thank you," I said. "I can't bear to lose you. I can't. You've been with me through thick and thin."

"And you have been there for me."

We both pulled away reluctantly and gazed into each other's eyes as we kept our hands connected by our thighs. There was a magnetic pull happening between us. I could feel it. It was like we were the only two people left on the planet.

"Listen," he said softly. "I want to tell you everything. I know you are curious."

He was right. I was curious. I now knew he had to possess some kind of magic or powers.

But then, in that same moment, I knew ruin was about to happen.

And I knew everything was about to change.

5

"Hayden Lakewood!" a female voice demanded. "What is going on here?"

We broke apart and together our heads jerked up. There stood a woman who I pegged to be in her late twenties maybe even early thirties. It was hard to tell in the moonlight. She was dressed in a white flowing gown with a pair of white flats. I had to admit that she was beautiful. Her ginger hair was braided like a crown around her head.

Bewilderment shot through Hayden's emotions as he jumped to his feet. "What are you doing out here, Mother?"

This was Hayden's mom? I've never met her either. Anytime I asked about Hayden's parents, he always said they were out of town or too busy. I never bothered to ask him about it. It felt like something personal. So, I only got to see him when they weren't home. However, now that she was here, I could see the resemblance. Their turquoise eyes, their hair, and the shape of their noses. But that was all in terms of physical appearance. However, their stance, and the way their deadly intimidating gaze locked on one another as though they were in the middle of a heated battle, made me see just how much they were alike in personality.

I froze.

"You snuck out again," she sneered. It was then that her deadly gaze shifted to me.

I fought the urge not to flinch. Every instinct told me this woman meant serious business. It was a bit hard to keep eye contact.

"And now I see why," she continued, eyes once again meeting Hayden's. "Sweetheart, this fantastical dream of yours has to end. This thing, this friendship with this boy can never, ever happen. He is dooming your future forever."

"He is saving my future!"

Her voice softened. "Dear, please, come on back home, back to the place where you belong. You know you are meant to..." She reached out to grab his hand.

Hayden jerked away and crossed his arms over his chest. "I don't care!" he yelled. "I already told you and Father that I am making the future I want, my own destiny! I am not, nor will I ever follow in either of your footsteps. I.."

"You have no choice!" she squabbled. Her voice was powerful like that of a silent boom you don't always hear. "You are next in line."

"I am not!" he argued. "You and Father chose me. I had no say in it."

"Hayden, honey, you aren't thinking clearly. This craziness has to end. I am putting a stop to this, once and for all."

I had no idea what they were going on about. I turned to Hayden and the two of us seemed to gawk at each other. I wanted to reach out to him, but I couldn't move. It felt like I was either paralyzed due to the confusion and hostility in the air. Or like someone had glued my shoes to the ground itself. However, that didn't stop me from *wanting* to do something. I squeezed my eyes shut. Why could I do? I just wanted to do something to get rid of the negative emotions and to get Hayden's mother away from him.

And something did happen.

While I briefly felt a flash of warmness radiate in my chest and flow through me, it was the thud and painful grunt that had me opening my eyes.

Hayden's mom was on the ground, lying on her back. She leaned up on her elbows and stared at me with fear spreading out from her like a dark cloud.

With quickness, she pushed herself to her feet, grabbed Hayden's arm, pushed him behind her protectively, and glared at me. The hatred in her, while nowhere as sharp as my mom's, was still sizzling. Why did she feel the need to protect him from me? I wasn't going to hurt Hayden.

"Hayden," she said. The coldness in her tone paralyzed me. "Why did you not tell me that your friend had powers?"

Hayden shoved himself out of his mom's grasp. "Because it's none of your business," he sneered.

It was then his mom said something in an unknown language.

Hayden must've known what that meant because terror flooded throughout his entire body as his eyes widened and he stepped in front of his mom.

"Don't, Mother!" he shouted. "You can't hurt him! He is my friend and I will protect him. Even it means protecting him for you and Father."

Her eyes glowered. "Very well, Hayden Lakewood," she said. "You leave me with little choice." She grabbed Hayden's arm and turned his hand up. Her eyes then narrowed in on his bracelet. "Don't tell! You didn't actually bond with him? You seriously chose him over you own family?" She then said something else in an unknown language.

Whatever she said caused Hayden to wince and then let out an agonizing scream.

I gasped, hard.

Acidic bile bubbled in my stomach and erupted up my chest, but nothing came up. Instead, I lost my breath. My eyes squashed shut as tears dripped from the corners. I ignored them. I could only focus on the pain radiating in my chest and entire skull. It felt like someone was stabbing my heart and my soul.

I collapsed to my knees and placed my palms on the soft grass. My fingernails dug into the dirt as I bit back the screams lodged in my throat. If this was what dying felt like, I sympathized. Forcing my eyes open, I blurrily saw, though the tears cascading down my cheeks, Hayden fall forward. In his eyes I could see the brightness of fear in his dilated pupils.

Suddenly, an intense heat burned into my ribcage. Bringing my hands up to clutch my chest, fear shot through me as I noticed a bright red glow illuminating on my bracelet.

Panicked, I clutched my chest protectively as I crumpled to the ground. Agonizing bolts of raw pain fired through my heart, more than when I had felt it through Hayden.

With my vision fading to black, I could hear Hayden desperately crying out my name over and over.

"I'm sorry it had to be this way, Hayden," his mom said.

Blurrily, I could see them fighting against each other

And then I blacked out.

***

I came awake to the sensation of shaking and a bright light hitting my eyes.

"Weston?" a concerned voice called.

It was familiar, but I couldn't place it. My thoughts were jumbled. And through the blurriness, I could see a vague outline of a person hovering in front of me and some kind of weird light that kept flashing back and forth in my blurred vision.

"Hayden," I said, dazed. My voice sounded croaked and hoarse and felt dry. "Can you shut off that light, please?"

"Weston," the voice said again just as the light faded from my eyes and warm hands touched my face.

That wasn't Hayden. His voice sounded strange. And this touch wasn't gentle. Who was this? And why wasn't my empathy picking up on this person's emotions?"

"Who...?" I croaked out before coughing a little.

"Easy, buddy," the voice said. "It's me, Carter."

"Carter?" What was my cousin doing here?

"Yeah, it's me," he reassured.

"What are you doing here? Where's Hayden?"

"I don't know," he said, helping me to my feet and placing one of my arms around the back of his neck so my hand hung over his shoulder. "Were you out here with him?"

I nodded. "Yeah, but you didn't answer my question."

"I got a text from an unknown number telling me to come out here," he said. "I was going to ignore it, but my instinct told me to check it out. Glad I did. When I got here, I found you on the ground, out cold. Are you okay?"

Lifting my glasses and resting them on top of my head, I rubbed my eyes. "Besides having a killer headache, I'm fine. I just want to crawl into bed and sleep the pain away."

"Let me take you home then."

At the mention of home, I panicked. "No! Please! I don't! I don't want to go home!"

Carter rubbed the back of my neck and I instantly relaxed. "Okay, bud," he said. "I'll take you to my house."

I calmed. "Thanks," I said drowsily as I rested my head on his bulky shoulder.

I barely remember getting to his car, or the ride to my cousin's house, or even how he got me inside. The only thing I could feel when I was laid out on

Carter's soft bed was the pain. It was intense and still raging deep inside my chest.

I curled up, hugging my knees.

I wanted the pain to stop.

It didn't.

But somehow, I must have ignored the pain, or the pain got so intense that I ended up passing out.

6

Late! I'm so incredibly late!

Those were the thoughts running through my head as I jumped out of bed.

Melinda was no doubt going to give me one heck of a lecture the second I arrived. She was probably getting ready to plan my demise. In my head, I pictured her standing in front of the door with a steaming cup of coffee and then splashing it in my face.

I didn't mean to be late again. I had the alarm clock raring to go and went to bed early and everything. But that hadn't been good enough. Sometime during the night, during a nightmare, my clock got knocked off the nightstand.

That had been my fault.

These past two days have been hard on me. For one, I hadn't heard a word from Hayden. I had also been avoiding home like it was the plague. Since that dreadful night, I have been staying with my cousin and his nosy roommate. I borrowed his phone yesterday and sent texts and calls to Hayden, but he hadn't responded. Was he angry at me?

These two lonely days were hard, especially since the incident with Hayden's mom. I spent two horrible days missing work and having my cousin try to talk about the experience. But that was the thing. I didn't want to talk about it. And that was only half the problem. The other was that every single day I recalled the same horrific incident, and because of that, my telekinesis was out of control.

For the past two mornings, I kept waking up in a state of panic. I would find myself lying on the floor like I was still in that lovely meadow. I would remember us talking and him giving me my birthday present. And then the peaceful memory would turn into a nightmare. His mom interrupted our moment to me nearly hurting her with my telekinesis. I didn't even know my abilities could do that. I never moved anything bigger than my satchel. I never wanted to harm anyone even when I was being picked on.

And then the nightmare got worse when I began to feel the intense pain she had placed on Hayden. It felt so heavy in my chest and heart. Every time the that memory flashed in my head, I couldn't help but spring into an upright position and check myself over to see if I was okay as I heaved for breaths because my chest felt like it was burning and my insides felt hollow. It was like something was missing. And like always when I checked there was never a mark on me.

I couldn't help but wonder what it was she did to him. Why was Hayden so terrified of it? What did it all mean? Why did it have such an impact on me?

Those questions, while haunting, always went without answers. Just like how and why my telekinesis was screwing me up when I slept. This was the second time in the past two days that I had caused pictures to fall from the wall and the digital clock that was on the nightstand to be tossed across the room.

After I fixed up, I showered. I let the warm water hit me as I tried to wash away the memories of last night. I had to turn up the heat to almost scalding. I needed something to help distract me from my thoughts.

I was red from head to toe after I got out. Not that I minded. I slowly dressed before wiping the steam off the mirror. Seeing my unkempt wet hair, I picked up my cousin's comb and combed my hair, letting my bangs fall into my eyes. My cousin always insisted I needed a haircut. I would just shake my head.

Once finished with the rest of my business, I headed into the kitchen. Like always, no one was in there. So, for breakfast, I poured myself one of those branded cereals that were loaded with sugar with near full bowl of milk. I was so tired of never getting to eat anything like this. I wasn't sick, but my mom still holding a rope on me. She claimed over and over that I had a sugar and caffeine intolerance. But I had coffee at Hayden's and felt fine. Was that the reason my abilities were off? I doubted it. They'd been off even before the coffee.

Shaking my head, I turned on the faucet.

No water came out.

With a heavy sigh, I poured the remaining milk down the drain and then placed the dirty bowl and spoon in the dishwasher just as my cousin came strolling in, scathing rage bursting from him.

"Uh oh," I said, turning towards him. "Spill it, Carter, what happened this time?"

Carter jumped. "Jesus, dude, warn a guy," he said and then his eyes widened. "What are you still doing here? I thought you had left an hour ago. Aren't you late for work?"

"Work can wait. You can't," I insisted. "Now, spill. What happened?"

Carter shook his head and ran a hand through his dark brown hair with blonde highlights. "Angela happened," he said as if that made any sense.

"I thought you and Angela were best friends and roommates. What could she have done that was so bad that it's made you mad with rage?"

"What could she have done?" he echoed back as his rage rose.

I flinched; backing up until my back hit the counter. I hadn't seen him this worked up before.

"This was supposed to be a partnership. She was supposed to pay for half of the bills and I was supposed to pay for the other half. We would switch up every other week. But I just found out that she hadn't paid for the stupid water bill and now I owe two hundred dollars for all the showers and baths she takes. And not only that, but she's been acting odd around me."

"What do you mean by "odd"?"

"She's not acting as a friend should," he said. "I told her when we discussed being roommates that I held no romantic feelings for her and that she could stay with me as a roommate until she was finished with college in two years. But now, she's acting like she and I are in a relationship. She even wraps her arms around me when I'm cooking or just resting on the couch. It's starting to wig me out."

"Have you talked to her about any of this?"

"Yes," he growled. "But she never listens. She just makes the conversation about herself. The one time I told her that I was going out with my actual girlfriend, Angela got so mad at me that she picked up a vase, threw it on the floor, and then stomped out the front door. She didn't return home and I didn't hear anything from her until two weeks later after my girlfriend and I broke up. Listen, could you do that thing you do and find out what her problem is?"

"You want me to use my empathy to read her?" I asked.

"Yes. She's seriously creeping me out. I am telling you. I'm close to kicking her out. I don't want to, but this is starting to make me uncomfortable. I have tried to make this a safe environment."

"Now, hold up. I don't like using my empathy like this, but since it's bugging you so much, I will see what I can do. However, I am no mind reader. Just so you know. I also think it would be best to sit her down and get her to listen to you, or as hard as it is, tell her to leave. Help her find a place and get settled and then part ways. I know you care about her, but if she is causing you this much distress, maybe you need to think about what is best for you."

Carter nodded. "I'll think about that. Thanks, Weston. You're the best, cousin."

"I'm your only cousin," I said. "Does Mom even talk to Uncle Billy?"

"Are you kidding?" he asked, laughing. "After that huge fiasco a few years back, I was lucky he let me stay here in Caster Valley for college. I didn't want to go with him. You know how my dad's temper is." That fiasco he was referring to was from when we were eleven. Uncle Billy came to visit. While Carter and I were playing video games, Uncle Billy and Mom had gotten into a physical fight. Luckily, Carter and I got there before Uncle Billy could hurt my mom. Carter had grabbed his dad and then they left. Since then, Mom hasn't talked to him.

"Trust me, if it's anything like my mom's temper, I can imagine how terrible it must have been."

"Yeah, but seriously, Weston, you need to get going. Melinda is not going to give you any more leniencies if you continue arriving late every day."

"I'm going. I'm going," I said, putting on my sneakers, which were by the door, before grabbing my satchel. "I'm allowed to stay here, right?"

"Yes, but sooner or later you will have to stop avoiding Aunt Iris. You need to face her. But we can talk about that tonight. Get going!"

And this was where I was, after my cousin dropped me off, standing outside of the magic shop. It wasn't anything too crazy. I mean it was a two-story brick building painted black. There was a nice window to the right and a decorative door. The sign was black but Melinda's Magical Shop was in white calligraphy.

I'd been working here for the last year or two. Honestly, the whole thing had been one oddity. In fact, Hayden was the one who introduced me to this place.

So, here I was, standing like a scared cat, bouncing back and forth on my heels as I dug my chilly hands into the pockets of my jacket.

Okay, Weston, I thought. Get a grip. I have to face her wrath. All I have to do is go in and get it over with. That shouldn't be so hard.

That's what I kept telling myself. However, a larger part of me wanted to turn and run to the alleyway on the side of the building to just hide out and wait until she exited the building, so I could just sneak inside and start the day.

Just as courage swelled inside me and I placed my hand on the black brass ornate handle, a chill scurried down my spine. Goosebumps broke out on my skin just as a loud honk came from behind me.

Startled, I turned.

My eyes widened.

The black pickup truck was back and coming straight at me.

Panicked, I pushed down on the handle, and threw myself inside without a second thought.

Unfortunately, I tripped, landing face-first on the floor.

7

"Seriously?" asked my boss, who was sitting on the edge of the counter and kicking her lace-up white pointy boots. Her jet-black was unusually curly today. Like she used a curling iron and made it extra bouncy. She also had on her famous, flouncy black dress that was covered in little white stars with her bright red leggings.

She lifted her head and regarded me from underneath the rim of her pointy black hat. She moved her head to the side as if she was trying to show off her crescent moon-dangling earrings. She then giggled, a Cheshire cat-like grin curling her black-painted lips as her luminous green eyes glowered at me. She obviously wasn't impressed with my sudden and unexpected entrance.

"Don't say a word," I hissed.

"I wasn't going to say anything."

"Good."

"But if I was, I would have said that you are the world's clumsiest psychic of all time."

This was Melinda Black, my boss, and owner of this magic shop. I never bothered to understand why she always dressed up like she was going to the next Halloween party. When I met her last year, she joked that she was a witch in training, but I honestly couldn't tell if she was kidding or deceiving me. I believed, at the time, she was testing me because, somehow, she knew of my talents. How? I am still not sure. She claimed that my "aura" told her. I once, and only once, tried to question her further, but she changed the subject like it was something highly confidential.

"Ha, ha," I said, rolling my eyes and picking myself up off the rosemary wooden floor and then dusting off my jeans. "You could have, oh, I don't know, maybe, helped me instead of sitting there doing nothing, Melinda."

"And miss the chance of making fun of you?" she asked, grinning. "Never in a million years. Messing with you is so easy." She reached over and pulled out a lollipop from the jar at the end of the counter that was free of charge for anyone. After peeling off the wrapper, she started sucking on it. With a pop, her grin widened. "So, you want to tell me why you ended up kissing the floor?"

"I don't want to get into it."

"This is one of those psychic things, right?"

"Ooh, you must a mind reader," I said, sarcastically.

She scoffed like she was offended by the mere thought. "I am thankful I don't have that kind of cursed power. As you know, I am but a mere witch in basic training."

"I never see you with a magic wand or staff, nor have I heard you recite incantations or brew smell potions."

She grabbed another lollipop from the jar, and this time she chucked it at my head.

"OW!" I complained, when it bounced off my forehead. "What is wrong with you, Melinda? You could have taken my eye out!"

"Stupid boy," she said. "Magic beans! I thought you were supposed to be a powerful psychic with supernatural levels of empathy, a ghost whisperer, and telekinetic. I figured you'd be able to detect my sarcasm. I'm not magical. I do say corny spells, but they do absolutely nothing. I can't brew potions without them exploding into a black puff of smoke in my face. However, I do love dressing up as a witch, because it fits with the scenery and atmospheric vibe of my shop, and hardly anyone cares. And besides, don't you know that not all magic is the same? Not everyone needs to say silly rhyming spells."

I rubbed the sore spot on my forehead. "Haven't we already had this discussion?"

"Actually, we haven't," she said, swinging her feet back and forth with her heels banging against the counter. "You always dismiss the conversation. But, come on, Weston, you must be able to sense my intentions."

"I can't," I said. "I am not some all-powerful psychic as you put it."

Melinda rolled her eyes. "Keep telling yourself that, Psychic Know-It-All."

"I wish you would stop calling me that. If I was such a thing, wouldn't I be able to tell what you are going to do before you even do it?" I retorted. "Besides, you know, out of everyone in this town, you are the only person, so far, that I haven't been able to read. You are like a blank. I still don't know how you guessed my abilities so accurately. It's something people never figure out nor sense about me properly."

"Well, your aura..."

"I know," I said, waving her off. "You've said that before. But you never tell me what that means."

"And I never will," she said. "Besides, I am one of a kind. I'm good about how accurately reading people."

Melinda was a person I could never figure out. For one, she couldn't come up with a perfect name for this shop of hers. To be honest, I wasn't sure there was a perfect name for it, but I think she could have gone for something like Mel's Emporium, which would have probably attracted a lot more attention considering what she sells.

Off to the left side of her shop were used and new witchcraft books, either displayed on tables or organized on the bookshelves against the wall. On the right-hand side of the shop, which was where I went, the shelves consisted of several candles of various colors. Herbs, spices, and supposedly "potions" in glass vials were all aligned and alphabetized below that one. On the third self were crystals and crystal balls of different colors, shapes, and sizes. And on the last shelf were pentagram amulets and bracelets with protective stones.

Looking at the bracelets made me touch my bracelet. "Hey, Melinda, do you make those?"

Melinda glanced over at me. "Do I make what?"

"These amulets and bracelets," I said.

"Oh, no, I get those from a dear friend of mine," she said. "She makes them for me."

Under the countertop, in the glass display case, were a bunch of candies and pastries that she always advertised on the window.

While Melinda was focused on the few customers who came in, I kept myself busy by restocking the last of the candles. I sorted them by smallest to largest, round to skinny, their assorted colors. For example, I started with skinny the white candles. I put all of them off to the left safely.

I loved this place. It was calm and mellow. And somehow, I fit right in. It even strangely smelt like the ocean, mixed with that twangy coffee scent. It was the one place in town that I didn't see any ghosts or be bombarded by emotions. But there was a downside. Being here strangely reminded me of Hayden. And I hated it. I couldn't help but touch the bracelet underneath the sleeve of my hoodie.

"Who is the lucky person on the forefront of your mind that has you either wanting to snivel or throw something at the nearby wall?" asked Melinda.

She hadn't talked to me in hours, and now she decided to have a conversation. What was her deal?

"I don't want to talk about it."

"Oh, come on, you can tell me who the handsome young man is on your mind," she said with a cat-like grin.

My wide eyes gazed at her. How did she know?

"Am I that noticeable?" I asked. "Is there some kind of sign stuck somewhere on me? Or am I putting off something that makes people know? I don't stick out like a sore thumb, do I? Or is that part of your aura thing?"

Melinda stopped laughing. Her bright green eyes bored into mine like she was trying to read me or something. Honestly, it made me feel even more awkward.

"I didn't see that in your aura," she said after a full minute. "I also wouldn't say you do anything to stand out. Not all of you go around advertising your sexuality. If you must know, I have a pretty accurate gaydar that's hardly ever wrong. From the first time you stepped foot in my shop, you are the first guy who hasn't thoroughly checked me out. At first, when I noticed, I thought you were either too modest for your own good, or just a regular everyday gentleman. But then, the more I paid attention, the more I noticed that you zoned out. It was like you were thinking of someone extremely important. It wasn't until I noticed you hanging out with that boy after work that I put two and two together. And while, yes, the two of you could have honestly just been best friends, I just knew it was something deeper. I just never brought it up because it was your secret and yours alone."

I was about to respond but the jingle of the bell over the door stopped me. It was then I went rigid with tension. Not from the bell, but from the eerily familiar emotions of rage. They were diluted slightly. When I turned my head, I was unfazed to know it was her. However, I was confused. She never came here. So, what was she doing here now?

Something was different about her. At first I thought it was because she wasn't dressed in her normal black funeral work attire. She was, for the first time, in something normal. She had on black jeans, a short red blouse, and black boots. It was like she was a totally different person. And for once, her smile was genuine and not forced especially when her brown eyes locked on Melinda.

"Good morning, Melinda."

"Hello, Ms. Brooks," Melinda greeted, but even I could hear the forcefulness in her voice. "This is quite a magical surprise. What pleasures brought you to enter my little shop?"

"I'm not here to purchase anything, Melinda," she said crossly. "I am here to talk to my son." I sensed an undertone of genuine politeness underneath her bubbling anger.

"What do you want, Mom?" I asked as I finished, placing the last of the candles on the shelf.

She pushed the strap of her purse that was falling back upon her shoulder. "I am here to invite you to coffee."

8

The second Mom invited me to have coffee with her, I found myself questioning her intentions. After running away from the apartment two days ago and not showing up or calling, I figured she'd be furious with me, which wasn't far from the truth. Her emotions were seething underneath that false calm exterior that she was portraying. I knew immediately that she only wanted to be in public so that an argument wouldn't break out.

We walked to the coffee shop across the street and made our way inside. The sweet aroma of coffee hit my sinuses. However, I didn't get to enjoy the smell as I became immediately and acutely made aware of the emotions in the shop. There were several customers. However, my eyes wandered over to the three ghosts sitting at the tables in the back. While I would have preferred to just leave, I couldn't. So, I did my best to block them out as I took a few deep cleansing breaths.

Out of my peripheral vision, Mom gave me this unpleasant glance that made me shiver involuntarily.

Doing my best to ignore the emotions piercing at my head and at the ghosts staring at me, I took a seat along with my mom near the center. I would have liked it better if we got closer to the window because then I would have at least had something to distract me.

Neither of us ordered anything. Instead, Mom reached into her purse, pulled out a key, and then slid it across the table.

"What is this?" I asked.

"The key to the Jeep," she said. "It's yours."

"Why are you giving this to me?" I didn't know what was happening. She loved her Jeep. It was the last thing that she had from Dad. But she was giving it to me now. I had to wander why. I had disappointed and angered her because of my stupidity. Why would she give her most valuable vehicle to me?

"Say nothing of it, Weston Brooks," she sneered. "I already planned this for your birthday. And I would have given it to you that morning, but you fled out of the apartment before I could do it."

I wanted to dispute that she had been too busy screaming at my grandma on the phone and had blankly ignored me. But I held my tongue. We were talking and I didn't want to mess that up now.

"Thank you, Mom."

"Don't thank me," she scorned. "Besides, I have more pressing matters. I'm transferring to a new job. I packed all your belongings that I could and put them in the back of the Jeep. Everything else that I couldn't put in boxes is being sold as well as the apartment."

"You sold the apartment?" I asked, surprised. "In just two days…"

Her eyes narrowed. "After the pipes bursting, this was the best outcome."

"Does this mean that I have nowhere to go?"

"Don't be so overly dramatic," she said. "As much as I hate it, you will be staying with your grandmother right here in Kansas."

"My grandma is here?" I questioned. "I thought you told me she was in Colorado?"

"I did no such thing," she said. "I may have mentioned that she was visiting a friend of hers in Colorado. This is her hometown."

I was never told that. I thought… No, I could have sworn she told me specifically that she lived in Colorado when I was four or five. So, then, why would she lie to me?

Mom then caught my attention by checking her watch for the seventh time. It was starting to become annoying.

"Do you have somewhere to be, Mom?"

"I do," she said, pushing the strap of her purse that was falling back on her shoulder. "I booked a flight. It leaves in thirty minutes."

So, this was her plan.

"Weston…"

I swiveled my head back and forth to purge my unwanted thoughts. "You don't have to say anything, Mom," I said, trying to keep my cool. "Where are you heading?"

She gripped the strap on her purse as a wave of anger radiated from her and pierced me. "That is none of your business. Now, if you don't mind, I have a cab waiting outside. You take the absolute best care of that car, you hear me?"

"I hear you, Mom." Figured she wouldn't say anything about me.

She huffed. Without saying a single word, she got up and sprinted out of the coffee shop. She didn't hug me or even tell me she loved me. Did she even care for me?

Left alone, heaviness filled my heart. I laid my head in my arms. "Love you, too, Mom," I mumbled. Tears prickled at the edges of my eyes. I angrily wiped them away on my sleeve. I wouldn't cry because of my mom's indifference. If she wanted to act bitter, then so be it. I'd accept that. But why did it hurt so much? Why did it feel like someone was clenching my chest?

"You didn't fall asleep, did you?"

Startled and shocked, I jerked up to see my cousin standing over me. "Carter, you scared me!" I bellowed, placing a hand on my chest, feeling my pounding heartbeat.

"That's a first," he said. A grin briefly showed itself on his face before vanishing. "You are usually way more aware."

Instead of commenting, I asked, "What are you doing here?"

"As of today, I work here as the next barista," he said, pointing to the name tag on his dark green apron. "Camilla said that Cam needed extra help around here. So, I volunteered."

"Did something happen?"

"No idea," he said.

"What about your job at the gas station?"

"I quit that a while ago," he said. "Didn't I tell you about that?"

I shook my head. "Not that I remember." I wanted to know more about it, but a weird emotion creeping inside my head told me not to push the subject.

"You never answered my question."

"Huh?" I asked.

"My question," he said again. "I asked if you were okay. But I'm starting to suspect you aren't."

"Oh," I stammered before shaking my head. "No, I'm fine."

"You don't seem fine," he said, taking a seat. "Do you want to talk about it?"

"Not really," I said.

"I know it's none of my business, but it from what I saw, you and Aunt Iris were pretty close to a rough argument."

"You could say that."

"You know, talking about your problems will help you in the long run."

"So I've heard," I said.

"Do you want me to get you something? It might help calm your nerves. It could be on the house."

"Won't you get fired?"

"Nah, I would tell Camilla of the circumstances. I'm sure she'd understand."

"That's okay. I don't need anything."

"Well, just holler if you change your mind. I have an order to take." He got up and left my table.

Just then, a flash of ginger caught my attention. Turning around in my seat, I saw Hayden. He was standing next to someone I didn't know. It was a girl with blonde hair and gray eyes. She had on a white sundress. Was this one of his siblings?

It couldn't be. The emotions swirling around her were ones associated with attraction. Not to mention, the way she was gazing longingly at him made jealousy rear its ugly head and claw its way inside my chest and made my stomach feel a little nauseous.

I couldn't help but watch in horror as she leaned over and kissed him. I couldn't see Hayden's expression, but I could feel his emotions from here. Though, they weren't as bright or strong. They felt weak. All I could sense was calmness. Did that mean he liked it? Did he hate it?

The girl's eyes met mine. A smirk of pure smugness curled her brightly painted lips as she wrapped her arms around his neck. She pulled him closer to her and kissed him deeper.

I tried to turn my head away, but it was like my eyes were permanently glued to the scene in front of me.

Soon, she pulled away and whispered something in his ear. Whatever it was caused Hayden to chuckle.

My heart clenched.

I missed hearing that.

Somehow I found the strength to pull my eyes away as soon as they walked towards the exit, holding his hand as they left the shop.

Why was I feeling this hurt? I knew Hayden was straight. So, why was I—?

A loud honk then caught my attention.

I twisted my attention to the window.

The black truck was outside.

Intense fear surged inside my chest, so tight that I nearly lost my breath as I jumped to my feet. My knee banged on the edge of the table. I ignored the twinge of pain. The few customers present all raised their heads like they were marionettes, and all of their gazes landed on me like I was crazy.

"Not again," I mumbled.

Carter's anxiety and concern flashed in my mind. "What is it, cuz?" he asked, looking over at me with concern as were the other customers.

"Please tell me you see the black truck," I whispered.

"What truck?" he asked. "I don't see anything."

Of course, the truck would be spiritual and only visible to me. Why did I even ask? And what on earth did this truck want?

The truck revved.

I jerked back, startled.

Even though I was scared, my fists clenched. I had just about enough of this truck following me...

I froze as a thought occurred to me. Maybe that was it. This truck wasn't trying to scare me or run me down. Maybe, just maybe, it wanted my attention because it wanted me to follow it.

I snatched up the Jeep key that my mom left me and then dashed out of the shop.

The black truck revved again before driving down the road. It then stopped. So, I was right. It did want me to follow it. But to where?

"Weston!" yelled my cousin as he grabbed my arm and forcefully turned me around so I was facing him. "Where are you going?"

"I don't have time to explain," I said. "Can you tell Melinda I left work early? I have to do something."

"Wait…"

I yanked myself out of his grip and then unlocked the door to the Jeep and jumped inside before starting the engine.

What am I doing? I thought, ignoring my cousin's shout as I drove off.

9

I followed the black truck out of town square and down an old dirt road path that led to an old highway that was now a dead end. I watched as the truck disappeared in a puff of black smoke right by the old Caster Valley Bridge.

I slammed hard on the brake rather roughly. This was quite surprising. This was one of the town's most haunted areas. At least, according to some of the stories you read on the Caster Valley website. People came up with the dumbest ways to attract tourists.

I stepped out of the Jeep without turning off the engine. What was I thinking? What was I even doing this for? This was a whole new thing. I never saw ghost trucks or whatever this was. This could all very well be a simple hallucination. I mean, for crying out loud, I just saw a truck turn into a puff of smoke.

But somehow I felt it wasn't.

I felt this was indeed very important.

Cautiously, I walked over to the full covered bridge. It was still daylight and just a little past noon, but the sun was behind the dark clouds. I wished it wasn't because I shivered. It felt like I was freezing, but maybe that was the anxiety. I mean, this place was kind of creepy. The chills got worse and were ransacking my body. I wrapped my hoodie tighter around myself.

Taking a deep breath, I put my weight against the old iron railing. I always wondered why this place haunted. And as soon as my hands touched the cool metal, I braced myself for visions.

When nothing happened, I relaxed. Maybe this place wasn't haunted at all. Maybe whoever claimed it was only wanted publicity. If it truly were haunted, I'd be seeing dead people as well as having visions of deaths.

Just as I was going to peer over the side, a loud honk startled me. So much so that my head jerked up and my gaze turned to see a red Camaro skid to a stop. Just then, my cousin stepped out with his door wide open. "What are you doing out here? This bridge hasn't been used in years."

"You wouldn't believe me if I told you," I said. "What are you doing here? Did you follow me?"

"You bet I did," he said. "I wasn't about to let you get into a huge amount of trouble."

"Like that would ever happen."

"It does happen," he argued.

"I didn't ask you to get involved," I argued back. "In fact, I specifically told you not to follow me and to…"

"I already let Melinda know," he interrupted. "Besides, did you really expect me not to follow you? You were acting like a crazy person. Come on, cousin, what's going on? You told me about the whole empathy thing. The least you can do is explain. What's happening? Does it have to do with you empath thing?"

"You want the truth, fine. No, this doesn't have a single thing to do with my empathy. There is more to my abilities than I disclosed to you." I took a breath. "I can see the dead."

Carter blinked slowly. "Uh, excuse me? Did I hear that right?"

"You heard correctly," I said. "I see ghosts and not just that, I..." I trailed off as soon as my eyes wandered to the bottom of the hill like something was beckoning me. Near the bottom was a black truck—the same one that I had been seeing—crashed into a tree.

"Carter!" I shouted.

Carter ran over to me with concern radiating from him. "What is it?"

I pointed.

The concern faded only to be replaced with horror and terror and shock.

"We need to get help!" I suggested. "Call the police station. I am going to see if anyone needs help."

While Carter called the police, I carefully hiked down the narrow slope to the truck. I didn't know what I was thinking. I wasn't a detective or with the police department, but I knew I needed to do something. This truck led me here for a reason.

I went to open the door only a chilled hand stopped me by gripping mine. Goose bumps spread throughout my body and an electric sensation rippled through me strangely. I became acutely aware that the hand was way too cold just before a vision flashed through my mind.

I found myself behind the wheel, driving down the dark highway. I glanced occasionally at the small photograph I had a hanging. It was a picture of my wife and beautiful daughter. I missed them so much.

Sudden, a weird tickle in the back of my throat irritated me. I coughed and coughed but it wouldn't go away. It felt like I was choking. I clasped my throat with one hand and reached over for the drink to my side. My truck swerved before crashing as my head slammed into the steering wheel before total darkness invaded...

With an unintended yelp, I gasped and leaped away only to start hacking which had me falling against the side of the truck and putting my hands on my knees. My head felt like it wanted to explode and my stomach churned so much I thought I'd surely be sick. This was the downside of seeing visions of a person's death. I saw things from their point of view and got their emotions and symptoms.

Even after taking a few deep breaths, I still felt incredibly shaken up.

I reached into the pocket of my hoodie and found a pack of gum. I took a piece and chewed. After a few minutes, I managed to regain my composure and cleared the dryness from my throat. Visions tended to drain my energy and luckily my mom had allowed me to have sugar free gum.

After gaining some strength back, I peered into the cargo bed of the truck. It was covered in a bunch of fallen leaves, which gave the impression that it had been out here for a long while.

Sensing someone behind me, I turned around to see who it was.

It was Barry.

***

By the time the police got here, Carter had to help me back up to the top and over to my Jeep. I was a wreck. I could feel the emotions of Barry running through me as he died. I felt how terrified he was. Carter had a ton of questions, but luckily hadn't said a word yet.

As soon as the police cars arrived and I saw who the head detective was on the case, I knew that this meant trouble. Of course, it did. This was just great. He was the last person I needed right now.

Detective Forrester was famous. Not literally. He was just one of the only four detectives in this town. He was a great detective. He had solved dozens of cases. True, the cases he solved were small and usually involved minor fender benders or small robberies. This time was diffcrent.

But the detective wasn't the problem. It was his partner-the same partner that was called in about the museum flooding. As soon as he saw me, he immediately started ranting and raving about how I was bad luck.

I pretty much ignored him, but I couldn't stop my thoughts. I'm glad that I didn't have to see the body. Only time I saw a dead body was in a coffin.

This was officially going down in my notebook as one of the worst days of my life.

Detective Forrester was an older gentleman in his mid to late fifties I presumed from the fact his brown hair had gray and was thinning at the edges. He bore a black mustache. He was dressed in a black trench coat, holding a small notepad and taking notes with a fountain pen as he talked to someone, who I believed was the coroner.

His partner however was a bit shorter with blond hair and grayish-blue eyes. He had on a police uniform. He was just standing by the car, arms crossed, and glaring at me.

Carter was beside me, hand plastered on my shoulder. He was radiating protectiveness while the police detective was radiating hatred and suspicion.

A motorcycle pulled up behind the detective's black Mustang. A young man yanked off his helmet and hung it on the handle. He appeared to be around my age. He had short brown hair and hazel eyes, and was wearing a brown jacket and khaki jeans with neon green hiking boots. He walked over and touched the detective's shoulder.

The detective turned around. "What are you doing here? How did you hear about this?"

"I listened in again and overheard everything that you said," the young man said. "I am telling you right now that you don't know what you're talking about! He wouldn't do this! He wouldn't! He may not have been perfect, but he was turning his life around!"

Detective Forrester moved forward and went to place his hands on the young man's shoulders. "Norman, listen…"

The young man pushed the detective's hands away. "No!" he shouted. "Why aren't you listening to me? He! Wouldn't! Do! This!"

"I hear what you are saying, but the evidence…"

"Screw the evidence!" the young man retorted. "Evidence is sometimes mistaken!"

"Norman, that's enough!" yelled Detective Forrester, annoyance oozing out of his voice and emotions. "Go home this instant. We will discuss this later."

Norman growled and threw his hands in the air. As he pulled away from the detective, his gaze wandered over to me. Our eyes met briefly before I turned away and shoved my hands into my pockets.

Carter patted my shoulder before moving his hand back to his side. What was that all about?

It was then that Detective Forrester walked over to us. "Weston Brooks and Carter Morrison," he started, "you will need to come to the station with us. You both are key witnesses since you found the body."

"Is it really Barry Bloomingdale?" asked Carter.

"Unfortunately, yes."

I knew it.

Barry Bloomingdale. The same man who always drove the bus I rode on to work. The same man who always greeted everyone with a smile and talk about his family. The same man who hadn't been present in days.

Now I knew why.

He was dead, and from the sound of the conversation, they were pretty sure it was something he did intentionally.

But something about that wasn't right.

10

Here I was in a crummy interrogation room and all because I saw and followed a black truck that led me to the ghost of Barry Bloomingdale. At least, I wasn't in a ton of trouble this time.

Or, I hoped I wasn't.

I just hoped Carter was all right. I hadn't heard anything since we were brought in a few hours ago. It was one when we got here and now it's nearing six.

It wasn't long, as I sat there gathering my thoughts, that the door opened and the detectives came in and asked me the same exact questions, and I answered them the same exact way.

"Are you sure that's everything?" asked the young detective whose name I still haven't bothered to learn.

"Yes," I said. In my statement, I made sure not to reveal too much. I mean, I couldn't very well tell them about me being psychic or about how a ghostly truck led me to the crime scene, which had me fibbing a little. They wouldn't believe me. Or if they did, they would think I was loony. Besides, this town already had problems with superstitions.

"So, basically, you have no way of proving your innocence?" asked the young detective with blond hair.

Detective Forrester, who was leaning against the wall, glared at the younger officer. "Officer Wade, we heard Mr. Brooks' statement enough time now. I, for one, didn't detect anything abnormal just like his cousin which is why I let him go home already."

"But still, you have to admit this whole thing is a little unusual. No one knew Barry Bloomingdale was even missing, and then this guy and his cousin just so happened to find the truck with his body inside. And not only that, but also dead," he said. "This makes him our number one prime suspect. Not to mention that his mother, Iris Brooks, who up until recently worked at the funeral home, just skipped town. How do we know for a fact that he didn't do this in some rebellious way? He is the grandson of that crazy witch lady, isn't he?"

"Officer Wade, I am telling you to cool it on the accusations."

I anxiously rubbed my sweaty hands against my jeans. Of course, they would know about my mom's work and her abandoning me. It kind of surprised me that the younger detective knew about my grandma. But then again, they probably knew more about her than even I did considering I haven't seen her in years and then just learned she lived here.

Absently, I rubbed at the bracelet Hayden had given me out of nervousness. I wished he was here to help me.

"I can prove his innocence."

That voice...

It couldn't be...

But it was.

I knew because a wave of those calming salty emotions I admired and missed so much washed over me. I hadn't felt them since I saw him at the cafe. Feeling my heart beating faster, I turned in my seat to see Hayden. He was standing in the doorway. Though, my eyebrows furrowed. He wasn't the same. His turquoise eyes were darker, duller than they had been earlier. His clothes were wrinkled, and his red hair was less shiny and more matted.

"Hayden," I said, trying but failing to keep the surprise out of my voice. I also fought the urge to smile. Even though I was happy he was here, another part of me wanted to jump up from my seat, grab him by his shirt, and demand why he avoided me.

***

After Hayden gave his statement with me waiting outside of the room, the detectives decided to let us go. As soon as we walked out of the police station together and walked over to where my Jeep was parked, I turned to him.

"Explain," I demanded, irritated. "You haven't talked to me these past two days and then I see you with some girl, who bought you coffee, and kissed you." Yeah, I admit it, I was jealous when I had seen that.

"Weston..."

"No," I said, pain in my tone of voice. "You just showed up out of the blue and came to my rescue. I don't get it. Is it because of your mom, whatever she did, and how she feels about me? Is that why we aren't allowed to be together? What she did to us broke our friendship forever."

"You think I wanted this?" he yelled. In his emotions, I could tell he wasn't just angry. He was feeling remorseful. He didn't like this any more than I did. "I don't know what you want me to say, Weston."

My anger ebbed. "Why did you come?"

"I came because you were in trouble."

"After two days of not talking to me, of me avoiding my mom, of me staying at my cousin's, missing work, you just so happen to show up randomly and save me? I didn't think you even cared anymore."

"Of course, I still care. You don't have to pretend with me. I can tell you are hurting just as much as I am."

"How do you want me to feel? I couldn't talk to you because my mom broke my phone. But I called you on my cousin's phone multiple times and it said your number was no longer available. You could have visited me!"

"So could you!"

"How could I possibly do that?" I yelled back. "I'm not allowed to visit you when your parents are home! You don't know the amount of times I wanted to, the amount of times I thought about it. But I knew I couldn't. I bet you didn't even know that my mom basically disowned me."

"Why would she do that?"

I leaned against the Jeep as I fought not to start tearing up. This was going to be hard to admit, but I had to. "Because when I was fifteen I came out. I told her I was gay. That's part of why we were always fighting. Not to mention, she didn't want to acknowledge my abilities, which led to more fighting and why we lost our closeness."

"Why didn't you tell me?"

I blurted, "Because I have a serious crush on you, Hayden! I didn't know how you felt and if you were like me. I guess it doesn't matter now. I will be living with my grandma, who apparently lives here."

His eyes saddened. "This is all happening because of my mother."

"Well, meeting her was no walk in the park."

"I know. I never wanted you to meet her like that. I didn't know she'd come after me. She either followed us, or one of my ratty siblings did and snitched. I'm sorry, Weston. I swear I didn't know it would happen."

"What happened to you?" I asked. "What happened to me? What happened to us?"

"My mother," he said. "She placed a curse on me, but because we made a pact together, well, the curse also affects you. I don't know what this curse is, or what it entails. I never meant to keep this from you. And I guess this is a better time than not to tell you the truth. My family is full of witches."

I faltered. "I'm sorry, but did you just say that your family is full of witches?"

"Yes," he said. "My mother learned witchcraft from her ancestors. She can cast curses in Latin. I honestly never wanted to learn. But I never had a choice. She and my father have my entire life planned out. I want no part of their grand design. In fact, I pretty condemned any friendships because I knew my parents wouldn't agree. That was until I met you. You do remember that summer day, right?"

Of course, I remember it. It was a day I could never forget. It was that summer day when I just turned eight. I'd been sitting alone by the creek, watching all the small fish and naming each one of them when a voice asked me what I was doing.

I was barely startled because I had been able to tell when someone was near me due to emotions. It was also hard to scare me because of this. And when I had lifted my head I couldn't help but be marveled at the sight of a young boy, about my age, maybe a year older, with curly ginger hair. As I processed his question, I couldn't help but laugh. It was such a ridiculous thing for him to even ask me. I told him that I had been there alone naming each fish and reading a book that my mother had bought for me, back when she had devoted her time and energy to me.

We then started talking about how we didn't have friends. He then even brought up one of the strangest legends I had ever heard about supposedly seeing a magical koi fish. He had apparently said that he wanted to see it because it supposedly brought luck. He said that he had never seen one up close before. However, I had sensed that he was lying and that he was hiding something deeper. But at that age I was mature enough not to question anything out loud.

Even though his story was wildly weird, we did manage to see that legendary koi fish. And it was the most marvelous sight I'd ever seen. And now that I think about it, maybe it had been Hayden's magic that brought it to life.

"Weston?"

Snapping out of my thoughts, I found myself staring at Hayden. He had moved closer while I had taken a trip down memory lane. I wanted to be mad at him for keeping things from me, but that would make me the biggest hypocrite. Plus, those magically calm emotions of his, and the smell of sea-salt and sugar were strong that I wanted to bathe in this moment. Why must he be so different from anyone I've ever felt?

A part of me longed to comfort the hurt in his heart. But I resisted. I battled every single instinct to throw myself at him and embrace him until the hurt faded back to the same salty calmness I liked so much. He didn't deserve my coldness. But I didn't know how to feel. Questions with no answers scattered my thoughts. The answers I sought would only come from him, but I didn't want to force those same answers on him.

"Weston?"

I jumped, startled. Heat blistered my face embarrassingly and my heart fluttered uncontrollably. "Uh, yeah, I remember, Hayden, but what does that memory have anything to do with this?

"Everything," he stated. "That was the first time I ran away from home, and the first person I saw was you. You were talking to yourself, naming every single fish living in that creek. It was like those tiny creatures were the only friends you had. It was like you had a cloud of loneliness surrounding you. You looked as lonely as I felt. I knew then that I wanted to be your friend, and I needed a good excuse for you to talk to me."

"You needed a good excuse to talk to me?" I asked, fighting the urge to laugh.

He nodded twice. "Yes, I was afraid you wouldn't talk to me," he said. "That was why I told you about that legend. I was hoping it would help me call you; help me become your friend. You obviously needed one. I didn't imagine that you and I would get to see the fish since I made the whole legend thing up."

A part of me knew that. I couldn't deny it. But it didn't stop me from being his friend nor did it stop us from actually seeing his made-up legendary fish. I smiled and took one step towards him. "You needed a friend, too."

A small sincere smile lightened his face and brightened his dull eyes. "Maybe I did," he teased, smirking.

"You know my mom once told me that you were a terrible influence on me."

"Maybe she's right," he said, coyly before he frowned. "I wish you had told me about you."

"I couldn't do that," I said.

"Were you scared?"

"Yes, I was scared how you'd take it. It's like you mom said. I do have powers, but it's not as powerful as she claimed. Maybe she was mistaken.

Or maybe it only appeared that way because my telekinesis is tied to my emotions."

"She wasn't. We both saw it, Weston. You made my mother fall flat on her…" he trailed off as he started belly laughing. "To be honest, it was funny."

"Well, my telekinesis isn't usually like that. It's small things only. Is this, my abilities, going to be the reason for us to no longer be friends? Because, Hayden, I can't help who I am. And I don't' care that you have magic or something. I'm psychic. But I don't care about any of that. You're my friend. What more could there possibly be? You turn out to be a villain?"

"Yeah, right," he said. "I couldn't play the villain. Or at least, I don't want to." Like magnets, he and I took a step forward. "I don't care that you're psychic. Weston. Abilities or not, you are still my best friend of all time. Though, now that I think about it, your weird behavior makes sense now."

"What do you mean "weird behavior"?"

"You seriously didn't think I noticed how you avoid people or how you randomly stare into space occasionally?"

"Guess I couldn't hide it forever," I said. "I'm honestly surprised you are taking this incredibly well and still want to be my friend after I blurted out that I have a crush on you. I know you don't like me like that. I saw you kissing that girl. I'm sorry…"

Before I could say anything else, he interrupted by pulling me into a hug and I couldn't help but wrap my arms around his shoulders. Then we both moved until we were staring each other in the eyes.

"Weston," he whispered.

And then it happened.

He kissed me.

Exhilaration surged through me. Whether it was my emotions or Hayden's, I didn't know. Our emotions felt synced right now. Yes, the kiss was a bit awkward. But it was every bit fueled with overwhelming emotions. I couldn't help but melt into the kiss, closing my eyes as I tasted sea-salt and watermelon on my lips.

While our lips were locked, thunder boomed overhead making my eyes flutter open. Gazing up at the sky, I saw the dark storm clouds turn even blacker and then a downpour started so hard that lightning zapped, lighting up the sky like fireworks and bolted around us like a cage. In the distance, I could hear people screaming in panic. Neither of us minded. We just stood there embraced in each other's arms with our lips locked in the most sincere and loving first kiss.

It was then that Hayden's emotions zapped into me so hard that I couldn't process them.

I gasped, losing my breath, and pushed him away as I stumbled and fell against the Jeep. I fought to catch my breath. A quick gaze at Hayden made me avert my eyes. He was staring at me all crazy-like. Pain zapped through me so forceful that I gasped and placed my hands on the sodden metal and stared at the glistening grass.

"Weston…"

"Don't," I said, forcing my voice to work. I waited until the hyperactive emotions swarming through me calmed a little. They didn't. It was like a tremendous rush of water was washing over me like chaotic waves. This was something I'd never experienced before. Sure, touch strengthened my ability, but it never caused me to feel like I was in a drowning stream of emotional electricity.

"Weston, listen…"

I closed my eyes. It was now or never. Since we were being so open with each other, I guess it was time to fill him in. "There's something you don't know about me, about my powers, something that I've been afraid of admitting, Hayden."

"You don't have to say anything, Weston."

"But I do!" I screamed. Confessing this was going to be hard, I knew that. I just didn't know how hard. His salty emotions were in a pool of calmness. My emotions weren't calm, and heavy raindrops splattered on the windshield behind me and the windows of the car.

"Weston…"

I squeezed my eyes shut. "Stop, please," I begged, panting for breath. "Don't pretend anymore. Beneath that calmness in you is a heart full of hurt and betrayal. I know it. I feel it, Hayden. I can't figure out why you're angry, but I can come up with a million reasons you might be. And you have every single reason to hate me."

"I don't hate you! You are putting words into my mouth!" he shouted. "I don't understand what kind of turmoil you are experiencing, but you aren't thinking clearly, Weston. I don't know what is going on in your head, but I know how empathetic you are."

"It goes beyond that!" I yelled. "I don't just possess telekinesis, I'm also an empath. I can feel every single emotion that you and others around me feel whether I want to or not."

Hayden's eyes widened, and he took a step back. His once calm emotions were now laced with panic, skepticism, distrust, and horror. My fists clenched. This was why I was scared of admitting this. He no longer trusted me. Rain began to beat down harder as I watched in complete disbelief as the water that was pouring somehow didn't touch me or even Hayden. It was like we were encased in a force field or something.

"You..."

I couldn't take the pain anymore. I wrenched the driver's door open and plopped down in the seat. I spared one last glance at my best friend. "I'm so sorry, Hayden."

I yanked the door shut before I started the car. I remained perfectly still. I didn't dare look in the review mirror as I pulled out of the parking lot. I didn't want to see his hurtful, distrustful expression. It hurt once, and that was more than enough pain for one day.

11

Traffic wasn't too bad as I drove to my grandma's house. Then again, the last time I had seen her was years ago. I had been five. I barely remember it. And luckily my mom had enough sense to pre-install the directions into the GPS; which I followed. I drove for about two miles before I hit a dead-end street called Water Avenue. This took me down a dirt road trail through a mile extensive range of trees on either side of me until there was an opening.

In front of me was a beautiful brown log cottage with vines of flowers decorated around it. There was also a beautiful patio with a round table and comfortable brown chairs with a place to start a fire in the middle. In one of the chairs was a lone figure.

A smile broke out across my face as I turned off the engine and then got out.

My grandma came over to me. Her white gown flowed in the wind as she waddled barefooted through the grass. "It's about time you showed up, dear. I was thinking you wouldn't come. Where is that mother of yours? I thought she would be the one to drop you off."

"She took a flight somewhere."

"Oh, Weston, dear," she said sweetly and embraced me in the biggest squeeze. Her emotions were so incredibly unique. They were like an air of mysticism. "Everything will be fine. Why didn't you call me? You were supposed to be here around five."

"Mom broke my phone," I said. "I have to get a new one. And I'm sorry I'm so late. I had to talk to the police which took about five hours. Don't worry, though. I am not in trouble. They just needed a statement."

"I see," she said. "Well, you can tell me all about it tomorrow morning. For now, let's get your things into the house and up to your room. I already took the liberty to set up an old bedroom."

I thanked her.

We grabbed boxes from the back, bringing them inside. It was different from the apartment. Upon stepping through the white wooded door and walking over the threshold, it was like I stepped into a whole other realm. The first view in the interior was the living room. It was magnificent. There was a couch, an armchair, and an old rocking chair. There were several photos on the wall of relatives that I knew and didn't know. There were also crosses on every wall. I remembered Mom telling me that my grandmother was a Christian. That slightly worried me. What if I told her the truth about me? How would she react? I don't think I could handle it if she condemned me to Hell.

Looking around trying to swift my thoughts to something else, and saw how there wasn't a TV. It didn't bother me too much, though. Maybe Grandma would let me purchase one and put it in my new room.

It took us some time, but we managed to get my boxes up to the room in the second floor. I carried anything heavy. My grandma didn't deserve that kind of strain. Even though she wouldn't admit it, I could feel the waves of dull pain in her hip and back. Her arthritis was dreadful, but the way she didn't show it proved her strength. But out of the goodness of my heart and being a gentleman, I wanted to do the right thing.

After setting the last of my boxes in the corner of the large room, I laid down on the bed covered with a beautiful woven quilt of a wolf and a blue dragon. It was beautiful, peaceful, and calming. It was everything I dreamed it would be so. It had such a unique atmosphere compared to the apartment. There, it was full of chaos. Here, it was full of serenity.

I tried not to let my thoughts wander to Hayden, but it was difficult. The intense kiss we shared. The way his emotions fired through me. The way he stood there completely drowning in the rain. It all brought a sense of guilt inside me. I raised my left hand and touched my bracelet. I couldn't deny it. I missed him like no one else, and it's only been a few hours.

"Dear, can I come in?"

I jerked up. "Of course, Grandma, this is your home."

"It's your home now, too," she said. "And do you mind opening the door for me, dear? My hands are kind of full at the moment."

That took me by surprise. Why were they full? We already brought every box up, didn't we?

I opened the door.

She stood there holding a plate with a grilled cheese sandwich, something I hadn't had since I was a child and in her other hand was a steaming cup of tea. And by the sweet aroma, it was mint. Mom never let me have any.

"I brought you something to eat."

"That's kind, Grandma, but you didn't have to do that. I would have been fine."

"Nonsense," she said. "You're still a growing young man and men are always hungry. Plus, you're so scrawny already. You need more nutrition." Seeing her hands shaking, I took the plate and cup from her. Gratefulness permeated from her in waves and filled her eyes. "Thank you, dear." She smiled, showing her false teeth.

I made my way over to the bed and sat down. "You don't have to thank me, Grandma." I picked up one of the crispy pieces of toast that were oozing with cheese and took a bite. A sense of nostalgia filled me as a memory of eating a grilled cheese here once before.

She sat down beside me. "Is it okay, dear? I didn't know what to make and figured I'd make you something light since you probably shouldn't stay up too late. Especially, since you have school in the morning. I'm sure that explains your nervous energy."

I swallowed nervously. "Mom didn't tell you?"

"Tell me what?"

"That I already graduated," I said. "I have my diploma. I don't know if she packed it away in one of these boxes or just threw it out." I glanced at her. Now that I was in the light, I could see her better. Her white hair had streaks of gray and her cobalt blue eyes seemed lighter in color and brighter. So, it seemed like I got the blue eyes from my dad side of the family, even though I never got to know my dad. I wish he hadn't died when I was four.

"I see. Your mother never tells me anything. Well, dear, you're still exhausted. So, you finish eating and then head straight to bed. In the morning, we will discuss more."

After I finished my sandwich and tea, I handed the dishes to my grandma. She smiled and wished me goodnight before heading out of the room.

I changed into some sweatpants and then crawled into bed and gazed out the circular window. Seeing the moon and stars, I then closed my eyes. Hopefully, tomorrow wouldn't be so bad.

In the morning, I headed down the wooden stairs and walked straight through the living room, cutting in through the narrow hallway. Turning right, I ended up at my destination. Admiration filled me as I gawked. This was a sight to behold. It was just so clean and sparkly. It Is because of her. If I remembered correctly my grandma had an obsessive-compulsive disorder where she not only had to organize everything alphabetically but also by size and shape.

Standing over by the stove was my grandma. She was in the middle of flipping pancakes in the air and catching them in the frying pan. She was dressed in black pants and a baggy flowery shirt with white tennis shoes.

There was a pleasant aroma of her cooking. Blueberry pancakes. Excitement and appreciation bubbled in my chest. Back home, Mom never cooked pancakes. It was always instant meals and junk food. I hadn't had any homemade meals. I just hoped I wasn't getting in the way of whatever my grandma did for a living. I didn't want to keep her from her job.

"Good morning, Grandma," I greeted, planting a quick kiss on her cheek.

"Good morning, dear," she said with a bright smile. "Well, this is certainly a surprise."

"What is?"

"You," she started as if it was the most obvious thing.

"I'm not sure I understand what you mean."

"You," she said again. "I don't know. You seem different this morning. Don't get me wrong, it's better than you moping. I was just so convinced that you'd be a bit dull today or a bit gloomy. I wouldn't blame you if you were. You just moved in last night."

"I can't explain it, Grandma," I said, stopping and inhaling a lungful of fresh air breezing in through the narrow opening of the window over by the sink. "It's a beautiful day, I guess. I mean, the sky is clear. The sun is shining. The breeze is warm."

Playful mischief twinkled in the corner of her eye as she smirked. "Oh, I get it. You just want to avoid the terrible inevitable conversation, aren't you? Well, sorry, dear, but in this household that's not allowed."

"I—No... That's not..."

She laughed, grabbing her side. "Oh, relax, sweetheart. I was only teasing. I know you wouldn't do that." She grabbed a plate and stacked three fluffy, golden crispy pancakes, and smothered them in maple syrup.

I gently snatched the plate from her hands. "I wouldn't do that to you, Grandma. I don't want to do anything to get into more trouble."

She sighed. "I know that, Weston. Why don't you tell me your side of the story? Your bullheaded mother refused to tell me anything. She only said you got into trouble. Is that why you were at the police station last night?"

"Don't," I warned, frowning. Some cheerfulness lost its vibrancy as I darted my gaze to the checkered floor. "Grandma, I seriously appreciate all of this, but I'm not ready to talk about everything. I don't think you would even believe me, to begin with. I don't want to cause any problems. I don't want you to disown me, too."

"Don't say that, Weston," cautioned my grandma. "That could never happen. Nothing, and I mean nothing, could ever make me disown you. You're my grandson."

"But it could. You weren't there. You didn't see how it felt or how tough it was with Mom. She hates me. No, worse, she despises me."

"I'm sure that's not true," she said.

"It is. I know it is."

"Okay, well, that's Iris for you," she said. "She despises anything that she doesn't agree with. Besides, she never tells me how you are doing, just that you're fine. One look at you last night and I could tell you are far from fine."

"Grandma, I promise, when I feel ready, I will share with you what all happened between her and me. But I can't right now."

My grandma kissed my head. "I understand, dear. Can you tell me about last night? You told me you were at the police station."

"I did. But it was me and my cousin."

"Did Carter get you into some kind of trouble?"

"No, we found Barry Bloomingdale's truck. He's dead and we immediately phoned the police. They came out and took us to the station to give a statement. It took longer than expected because they questioned my statement. I have to call Carter and check on him, but I have to go out and buy a cell phone."

"I did hear about Barry this morning on the radio. It's such a horrible tragedy. They say he did it to himself, but I highly doubt that. I knew Barry. He was happy. You don't know this, but he and I had a book club meeting together and he was excited to discuss the next chapter of the book we were finishing."

"If you ask me, a lot of things don't make sense. Before Mom gave me the Jeep, I rode the bus and would see him. He would smile and we would talk for a few moments. From what I remember seeing, he was happy. I mean, I knew he was going through difficulties from the divorce, but he didn't seem that upset."

"He wasn't," my grandma confirmed. An eyebrow rose. "You aren't thinking what I think you are, are you, dear? Because if you are indeed thinking what I think you are, then, you better stop it right now."

"Don't worry. I won't get involved in it."

"Good." My grandma then smiled and slid over a small purple polka-dotted bag.

"What's this for?"

"Happy Birthday," she said. "I'm late on it, but I didn't forget. I told your mother to tell you, but I doubt she did."

"You didn't have to do this."

"Of course I did," she said, smiling sweetly. "Now, open it up."

Confused, I peeled back the tape. Inside was a blue smartphone.

I picked it up. "Grandma, you shouldn't have."

"I wanted to, dear," she said. "This old thing has been in my house for a while now. A neighborhood friend bought this for me last year or so. I don't know the first thing about those kinds of phones. But you young people are tech-savvy. I figured you would get more use out of it than I could. Plus, since your mother broke your old one, I figured you'd need a new one. Consider it a late birthday present from your dear old grandma."

I hugged her. "Thank you. I should get going. I don't want to be late for work. I'll set up my phone at work."

"Okay, sweetheart," she said. "Be careful. And if you find a gold cross necklace on a silver chain, please tell me. I seem to have lost it this morning."

"I will." I kissed her cheek before leaving.

12

Stuck behind a red light, a loud squeaking sound penetrated my hearing and made me turn my head to gaze out the passenger side window just in time to see a person on an old rickety bicycle wobbling up. Seeing me, he knocked on the glass and did a motion downward with his thumb.

I hit the button and the window lowered automatically. "Thank the ever-loving hell," the young man said, running a hand through his messy brown hair. "Are you, by any chance, heading towards town?"

Hearing that voice, it was the guy from the bridge. What was his name? Nick? No, that doesn't sound right. Norton? Still not right.

"Uh, hello?" he asked.

I shook my thoughts away. "Oh, uh, yeah, I am. Do you need a lift somewhere?"

"Yes. That would be nice," he said. "You wouldn't believe the morning I had. My stupid motorcycle wouldn't start this morning, so I had to use my ancient bike that got a flat about a quarter-mile back. Idiotically, I didn't see what was in front of me thanks to a squirrel. It ran out in front of me and made me divert and wound up hitting something sharp."

"I get the point," I said. "Where are you heading?"

"Mickey's Garage," he said. "Do you know where that is?"

"Nope, but you can install it into the GPS on the dashboard. Also, you can put your bike in the back. It's unlocked. There should be plenty of room. Do you need a hand?"

"That's okay. I can take care of it myself," he said as he opened the back and placed his bike in, and then shut the door. He slid into the passenger side and fixed his brown leather jacket and then ran his hands on his khaki jeans. I couldn't help a grimace when I noticed dried mud on the rim of his brown sneakers with neon green laces.

He then smiled goofily. "I appreciate this. Thanks a ton, man. I wasn't sure I was going to make it on time." He leaned over and installed the address into the GPS.

I couldn't help but notice that his down-to-earth hazel eyes were the perfect combination of green and brown. Shaking my head, I averted my gaze briefly. "By the way, I'm…"

"Weston Brooks," he said. "I know who you are. I saw you at the bridge. I'm Norman Forrester. I'm the police detective's son. But you may have already known that. What were you doing out there?"

"My cousin and I found the truck."

Norman's eyes narrowed, but there wasn't any suspicion coming off him. I could only feel a mild amount of curiosity. "How the hell did you manage that when no one else could?"

I shrugged. "Do you mind if we don't talk about it?"

"Sure. We can talk about something else like…"

I drove onward until I stopped at the next stoplight. I couldn't help it, but my gaze wandered out of the passenger window. I could distantly hear Norman's rambling voice carry on and on about something that sounded oddly like some kind of conspiracy theory, but I lacked the focus to concentrate on the words. My gaze was locked onto the graveled road leading through a long trail of evergreen trees.

"Do you know what's through there?" I asked aloud, cutting off whatever Norman was chatting about as I glanced at him.

Norman's gazed at the road. "You don't know?" he asked. "How long have you lived in this town again?"

I shrugged. "I didn't get out much.

"Well, that's the road leading up to one of the oldest houses in town. You can't see it from here because of all the overlaying trees, but there is a mansion at the top of a hill. Strangely enough, on our county's website, it is listed as one of the most haunted places to visit even though no one has dared to step foot on the property. And the sad part is that no paranormal group has ever been out here to investigate. And I have never dared to go alone. That's why…"

I tuned out more of his rambling. I wasn't interested in hearing him talk about ghosts. I mean, I saw them for a living. He didn't need to tell me about how they could manipulate things or talk to some people and stuff like that. I already knew it all.

As I continued to peer at the strange road, a weird cloud of fog began to move like a person was walking with it.

"Hey!" yelled Norman. I blinked, seeing his fingers snapping in front of me. "Dude, wake up!"

I shook myself out of my weird trance and knocked his hand away annoyingly. "Knock it off! I'm awake!"

"If that were true, you would have heard me."

"I did."

"Liar," he stated. "I've been telling you that the light has been green for about five minutes now. It's not my fault that you're the one pretending to be a zombie or brain-dead. You seriously had me spooked for a second."

"I'm sorry," I said, glancing out the window to the road again, seeing nothing. A chill ran down my spine, but I ignored it.

"I can drive if you need me to."

"I doubt you have a normal license."

"Hurtful," he said, offended. "Is it because I rode a motorcycle that you even come up with that assumption?"

"That. And it's just common knowledge that there are different licenses for different things. I do know that you need a special license for riding a motorcycle. Also, if you had a regular license you would have taken another car or rode with someone."

"First off, you may be a little right," he said. "But I wouldn't dare get a ride from my dad. He and I don't see things eye to eye. But I would have technically bought a car or a backup motorcycle."

"Why didn't you?"

"Well, for one, money is tight. And two, my dad won't let me since I still live at home."

"Strict dad?" I asked.

"Strict doesn't begin to cover it," he sneered. There was an undertone of hate in his voice, but there was barely any hateful feeling in his emotions. How was that possible? I also wondered about what he said but decided not to comment on it because Norman shook his head. "I would rather not talk about it, honestly."

"Fair enough," I said, driving, but the light changing back to red had me hitting the brake pedal so hard that the front jerked us forward.

"And this is what I call karma," he said, hands on the dashboard as he gazed at the light. "You deserved this for zoning out."

Shooting a glare at him ended our conversation. However, with the GPS, I was guided to Mickey's Garage. I lived here my whole life, but I had never been to the garage before. If there was something wrong with the car, my mom fixed it herself or called someone else. She taught me the basics of how to change the oil or how to fix a tire.

And of course, with my luck, we got there ten minutes late.

"Damn! Late on my first day of work," I heard Norman mutter under his breath, irritated.

"I'm sorry."

"This isn't on you. I would have been late no matter what. Just thanks for the ride. He's usually a pretty cool guy and understanding."

"I see. I'll apologize or do something to help if he doesn't accept. I could tell him the fault is on me that way the blame is off of you."

"You'd do that?"

I nodded.

"Thanks, but you don't have to do that. Mickey shouldn't be mad. I've known him my whole life. He's a decent guy," he said with a giant grin. But his happiness was cut short as soon as I pulled into the parking lot.

Mickey's Garage had some of the white letters peeling off the red sign. The building itself was old. Like something from the fifties. I breathed in a whiff of oil that nearly had me gagging. There was also a strange grinding sound coming from somewhere nearby. However, that wasn't what caught our attention. It was the two police cars with none flashing lights. Inside the open garage door, I could see three people inside.

Norman bellowed, "What the hell?"

"What's going on?"

"I have no idea. But I am going to find out." Norman got out of the Jeep.

I followed after him. I didn't have time to prepare my mental shields for the bombardment of emotions that drove into my head as soon as I got close enough. The deep emotional sadness coming off the man sitting hunched over in a chair was almost overwhelming me. Whatever was going on, it wasn't good.

Norman ran over to the elderly man with thinning white hair wearing oil-splattered overalls wiped his sweaty face with a rag. "Hey, Mickey, what is going on here?"

The man, Mickey, smiled. "Oh, Norman, you came. I was just about to call you after I was done talking to the police."

"What for?" he asked.

"To tell you not to come in today," Mickey replied.

Norman placed a hand on his shoulder. "Why? What happened here, Mickey?"

Detective Forrester stepped forward. "What happened here was the fact that Jerry Johnson passed away."

"What?" Norman asked. The surprise in his voice startled me, but what disturbed me the most was his emotions. I could barely feel the shock or sadness or distress. "That's... No, that is impossible. I just talked to Jerry earlier."

"Yes, I know," said Detective Forrester. "I checked your phone records."

"You went through my phone without my permission?" yelled Norman.

"You deserved it for eavesdropping last night."

With the way the detective and Norman were glaring at each other, I decided it was time to intervene.

"Hold up," I said, stepping in. This was probably the worst mistake in the century to interrupt, but I couldn't stop myself. "What exactly happened? Is it like what happened to Barry?"

Detective Forrester turned his attention to me with narrowed eyes. "Mr. Brooks, we meet again. Twice in two days. Can't be a coincidence now, can it? This is starting to get suspicious."

Mickey coughed, interrupting us. "Daryl, lay off the boys. You can tell them. They didn't have anything to do with this and you know it."

"Sir, I don't think we should," stated the detective's young partner.

"Not another word, Wade."

"Yes, sir," said the young detective. I observed the young man with suspicion. I couldn't help it. His emotions were strange. There was suspicion flickering as well as a sense of uneasiness. It was as though there was something eerily familiar about all of this. At least, that was what I was picking up from him.

"I think we are done here," said Detective Forrester. "Again, Mr. Kingston, I am sorry for your loss. And if there is anything you might think of, call us immediately."

Mickey nodded, wiping at his forehead again. "Yeah, I know the drill, Daryl. Thanks."

Once the detective and his partner were gone, Norman gazed back at Mickey. "Can you please tell me what happened here, Mickey? Jerry is a good guy. I don't understand why he died."

"I don't know either, my boy," said Mickey in a thick southern accent. "They think Jerry offed himself."

Anger and disbelief were in Norman's ever-present calm emotions which startled me slightly. "That's impossible. Jerry wouldn't do something like that. Just like Barry wouldn't either. What is going on in this town?"

Mickey shrugged. He then coughed into his handkerchief. "Your guess is as good as mine. I do agree that something unexplainable is happening. And your dad won't even do an autopsy because this is a small town. And you know how it is. They want all the evidence straightforward."

"I know," said Norman. "My dad is always shady. One time, he was called in thanks to that elderly lady who goes crazy thinking that her cats are possessed and he didn't check it out. I know I'm the crazy conspiracy nutcase around here, but he is always hiding something."

Mickey snorted. "That you are, my boy. But your father has his way of thinking. I'd think you and him would get along better. Anyway, listen; about your job and bike, I will fix it in a few days. I can't today. I'm going to close up and head home early. This stupid cold of mine has turned into a full-blown case of the flu."

Feeling like a third wheel, I nervously spoke up. "Uh, Mr. Mickey, you have my condolences."

Mickey's eyes flashed toward me. "You're Weston Brooks, right?"

"Yes, sir," I said.

"I thought so," he said. "You are the splitting image of your father."

"You knew my father?"

Mickey nodded. "I did indeed. Bryan was a great guy. You probably didn't know this, but he used to work here. He always spoke highly about you…" He trailed off as he started hacking before he hit his chest. "I hate flus."

Norman patted Mickey's shoulder. "You should get home and rest. Do you need help getting to your vehicle?"

"No, thanks," he said and then handed Norman the keys. "Here, you can lock up and leave whatever you need to?"

"Thanks, Mickey," he said. "I was going to ask if I could leave my bike with you. Not my motorcycle. Do you remember my old bike? The one you fixed like forever ago?"

Mickey bellowed out a belly laugh. "You still have that rickety piece of junk?" he asked. "I would have thought you would have sold it off or scrapped it for parts for one of those…projects of yours." He then rose to his feet.

I winced at the intense pain radiating through my knees and into my chest. He must have arthritis from that amount of pain.

Unexpectedly, a young man flashed in front of me. He was dressed in overalls, had brown shaggy hair, and amber eyes.

"Help," he whispered, eyes boring into mine before grabbing my hand.

I gasped sharply when panic invaded me just before a vision invaded my mind.

I found myself in a parked car, coughing as I struggled to breathe. I looked around, but I didn't have anything. I rolled down my window to try and help. But it didn't. I then pulled out my phone and tried to dial an ambulance but dropped it as my vision blacked out…

When the vision ended, I noticed the young man was gone. I closed my eyes, panting slightly.

"You all right there, boy?" asked Mickey.

Frightened, my eyes jerked up to see Mickey and Norman staring at me oddly.

I released a long breath. "Yeah, I'm fine," I said. "Sorry. I just... I was lost in thought."

Norman grinned. "Ignore him, Mickey. He's been zoning out for a while. He's a bit crazy."

Mickey let out another belly of laughter. "Just like his father," he said before breaking off into a hacking cough. "Gosh darn flus."

I coughed and subconsciously rubbed my chest. Something felt incredibly wrong. "Sir, I think it may be wise to go a hospital just to be sure it's nothing dangerous."

Mickey waved me off. "I'll be fine, boy. Thanks for the concern," he said. "I will head on to the wife and kids. They will help take care of me."

Norman and I watched him get into his beat-up Cadillac before I crossed my arms, turning to Norman. "I think he needs a hospital."

Norman surprised me by nodding. "You sensed it as well, huh? He's never been that bad off with illnesses." He then paused as a thoughtful expression came over his face. "You know what; I'll give his wife a call."

I gave him a strange look.

He rolled his eyes. "That sounds weird, I know. I have their numbers in case of emergencies. I've known Mickey and Valarie since I was small. They've always been like family. It's hard to explain properly."

"You don't have to explain it to me."

"Thanks," he said, pulling out his phone. "Mickey is a great guy, but he's a stubborn old mule. His wife will take care of him."

After his phone call, he and I walked to my Jeep where I helped him take out his bike and we carried it inside the garage and laid it up against the wall. As we closed up, a chill ran through me, and for a second out of the corner of my eye, I could swear I saw the young man in overalls standing in the corner, smiling. But once I blinked, he was gone.

"So, what are your plans today?" asked Norman as soon as we got in my Jeep.

"Well, I have work. I'm pretty sure Melinda is going to kill me."

"No way!" said Norman excitedly. "You work for Melinda Black?"

"Why are you excited about that?"

"Are you kidding me? That woman is capital H.O.T. Do you mind me tagging along?"

"Don't you have other plans?"

Norman shook his head. "I was supposed to work, but that isn't happening. So, I might as well hang out with you."

13

Instead of heading straight to work, Norman asked we could stop at the local cafe. I figured it would be fine considering I was late anyway since it was close to lunchtime and because the local café was also right across the street from my workplace.

Norman's stomach growled loudly when I parked the Jeep. His cheeks went tomato red as he told me he had skipped breakfast and was starving. Of all the things he could have ordered, he chose a chicken sandwich with pickles and sardines. And if that was bad enough, he dug into his backpack and pulled out a jumbo size bag of marshmallows. This only added more to Norman's weirdness. I was slowly becoming accustomed to it for only knowing him for an hour or so now.

I glanced around the shop to make sure no one was watching. Aside from the few customers and employees, everyone seemed preoccupied. Seeing that no one was paying any attention to me, I focused on the spoon and made it slide towards me.

"Dude, no way!" exclaimed Norman, taking a huge bite out of his sandwich. "Do you have magic?"

"Tone it down, will you?" I whispered, stirring my tea. I then grabbed my crispy curly fries and dipped a couple into the small ketchup cup then put them in my mouth and chewed thoroughly before swallowing. I leaned forward and lowered my voice even more. "It's not magic. I'm psychic. I don't want the entire town to know. They already call me names and think I'm a freak. How would you think they'd react if they knew the truth?"

"I think they would think it was pretty cool to have such an amazing talent. Besides, you do know this is Caster Valley, right? Secrets don't stay a secret for long," he said with his mouth stuffed which kind of disgusted me. I turned my eyes away discreetly to avoid seeing the mess.

"Don't remind me," I said. "People in town treat those who are abnormal like it's the Salem Witch Trails. Only difference is that they don't hang or drown us. Instead, they persecute by bullying either verbally, emotionally, mentally, or physically. They hate anything that is different."

"Oh, trust me, I know. And I, for one, am a little envious of you. You have this super cool talent. But being different is what makes you interesting. Do you want me to tell you how I know that?"

I glanced at him briefly. "Only when you finish your, uh, sandwich."

He ignored what I said and explained anyway. "I have a sort of talent. I'm not psychic like you, but I have this pretty weird skill or power, I don't know what to call it."

I took a slow, long sip of my tea. "What kind of talent?" I asked, genuinely intrigued. He was the first person I ever admitted my abilities to. And now he had something special as well?

"Have you lost something recently?"

"No," I said, confused.

"Do you know anyone who has?"

I thought about it. "Well, now that you mention it, my grandma lost a small golden cross. It was on a long sterling chain."

"What's your her name?"

"Ruth Hawthorn?"

Norman choked on his blueberry slushy. "You are Ruth Hawthorn's grandson?"

"Uh, yeah, is that a problem?"

"No, no, nothing like that," he said.

"Oh, I see," I said. "This is about everyone knowing that my grandma is a bit eccentric, isn't it?" Yes, my grandma was labeled as an eccentric woman all because she believed in herbal medicines that people often criticized and scoffed at and feared and labeled her as some kind of crazy witch. Only reason I knew that was because my mom told me. And when I brought up my grandma's name, they get all weird.

"I think a "bit" eccentric might be a little mild."

"Even so," I said. "She is my grandma and I love her dearly. She has been more like a mom to me than my mom. I know that sounds terrible to say, but it's the truth."

"Weston…"

"I don't want you to misunderstand. I love my mom. I do."

"Weston, you don't have to explain that to me. I get it. Your mom doesn't understand you. Let me guess. She gets angry at you all the time for things even when some of those things weren't your fault?"

"Yeah, how did you know?" I stammered.

"Because your mom is exactly how my dad acts towards me," he said. "My dad blames me for my mom's death. I was just a little kid when it happened, you know? It wasn't like I wanted to be sick or have a drunk driver hit her car. Maybe this is his way of punishing me." The pain in his voice was clear. But his emotions were strangely calm. Like I expected to feel guilt or something, but it was just a sea of calmness on the surface.

"I'm sorry about your mom," I said, sympathetically.

Norman cleared his throat and smiled, waving me off. "None of that, dude. Anyway, I was going to try and show you my talent. So, Ruth Hawthorn and a gold cross on a sterling silver chain, right?"

"Yes."

"Okay," he said and closed his eyes briefly. "I know where it is." His stern gaze peered directly into mine. "Check the right side pocket of your hoodie."

Skeptically, but curiously, I put my hand in my right pocket. What the…

Cold metal touched my fingertips.

Surprised, I pulled it out.

Sure enough, it was my grandma's necklace. How did it get there?

I was stunned. "How did you do that?"

Norman smirked; taking a large slurp from his slushy like this whole thing was no big deal. "Well, it's hard to explain. But when I was thirteen, puberty was pretty ironic for it to happen, I discovered that I had this unique ability to locate anything that someone has misplaced or lost. But the downside is it only works on items. I can't find people."

"How does it work?" I asked curiously. I couldn't help it. I found someone who had a similar talent to me. Sure, our talents were vastly different, but it was nice finding out someone else also shared a preternatural talent.

"I'm not sure," he said. "All I need is the name of the person and what they lost and it's like my mind has a built-in GPS or something like that. I get a mental image that tells me where it is. Sometimes, however, I will get a feeling towards a certain place."

"That's interesting," I said and then turned to him. "Okay, my turn. I have something to tell you too."

"Are you coming out to me? Because, dude, I already knew you were gay. Hey, no judgment from me. I just want you to know that I am a hundred percent straight."

I groaned.

"What's wrong?"

"Nothing, sorry," I said. "I'm not annoyed at you or anything. I just... I'm starting to suspect that I have this neon rainbow sign above my head that tells everyone I'm gay."

Norman laughed. "It's nothing like that. I just felt like you were checking me out." My face heated up. I was pretty sure I was embarrassingly red. "Hey, it's no big deal. I find it flattering that someone finds me attractive. I just wish a girl would look at me like that." His eyes got a dreamy glaze to them and his emotions fluttered.

I smirked. "You have someone special on your mind, don't you?"

Norman's glazed eyes returned to normal as he stared at me. "How did you know?" he asked. His eyes then widened with excitement. "Can you also read minds? Can you tell me what number I am thinking of?"

I pushed him back. "It's nothing like that," I replied. "Aside from telekinesis, I can do something else."

"What is it?"

"Don't freak out on me when I tell you this."

"I'll try not to," joked Norman.

I rolled my eyes. "I can feel people's emotions."

"No way," he said. "You're an empath? That's cool. Can you read me?"

"Excuse me?"

"Can you read my emotions?" he asked again. "I have nothing to hide. So, go ahead."

This was the first time someone wanted me to read them, and this was the first time I ever tried without subconsciously trying to block out people's emotions flooding into me. I straightened and turned in my seat. I forced myself to relax and focused all of my mind and energy on Norman.

It was strange, though.

His emotional psyche was calm. Extremely, eerily, and terrifyingly calm. Beyond the calmness, I couldn't detect what was deeper. He kind of reminded me of…

No, I wouldn't think about him right now. I wouldn't let my mind wander down that train of thought.

I reached out and gripped Norman's arm.

He gasped.

His emotions flooded me instantly. Beyond the calmness, I could now sense guilt, anger, and even fear. They all bubbled to the surface of my mind.

Wincing, I let go immediately. "I-I'm sorry."

"What happened?"

I leaned back. "I don't know. I mean, I felt how calm you were. I guess I kind of freaked. I have only met a couple of people with that level of calmness. I didn't mean to touch you so quickly. I just… Touch makes my ability stronger."

"What did you sense?"

"Nothing," I said. "I mean, at first, your emotions were strangely calm. It's like you are so well-grounded that you're completely composed of all negative feelings. Not one emotion stands out more than any other. It's almost like you are strangely balanced. If that even makes sense."

"That makes perfect sense," he said. "A ton of people commented that I have a calming nature. So, your assessment is pretty accurate. Plus, I always feel calm. I admit there was a little fear when you touched me so fast. I thought you were hurt."

"I didn't mean to scare you like that. I just freaked out," I said.

"Do you want to talk about it?"

I shook my head. "Not right now. Can I get a raincheck?"

"Sure," he said.

Just then the bell over the door rang. Usually, I would ignore such things. However, vile, oily emotion coming at me had my attention turning towards the door just in time to see Zelda and Brianna walk in. One look in my direction was all it took for Zelda to grab Brianna's hand and lead her over.

"Weston," Zelda sneered.

I gazed at them. "Hi, Zelda and Brianna," I said. "I didn't think either one of you would be out here considering your father just passed away, Brianna."

Brianna's eyes shifted away. "I could care less about that man. He was never around." I could feel that she was lying.

"You care," I said. "Deep down, you care and miss him. You're just putting up a brave face."

Brianna's eyes hardened and she slammed her palms down on the table as her deadly gaze locked with mine. "You know nothing about me or my family."

I wanted to jerk back but instead, I wasn't intimidated. Besides, I could see Barry behind her. There was a strong sense of pride and comfort came from somewhere.

"You're right, Brianna. I don't know you or your family. But I did know and talk to your dad in the mornings. He always spoke highly of you."

Brianna's eyes widened as tears welled. Without saying anything, she ran out of the shop.

Zelda glared and raised a hand. Sensing a fight about to break out, I tried to prepare myself. Before I could react, Norman, who had been quiet through the whole exchange, grabbed her arm.

"I wouldn't do that, sweetheart," he said, smirking.

"And who are you?" Zelda asked. "Are you a friend of his? Why would you want to be friends with a gay freakish weirdo?"

Norman grinned. "Because he's fascinating, unlike people like you," he said. "He has more soul and kindness. You know that putting people down only makes you out to be a bully, right?"

Zelda yanked her arm out of Norman's grip and growled. "Whatever. If you catch his curse, don't come crying to me."

14

"What was all that about?" asked Norman, sitting back down in his seat.

"Truth be told, I have no idea. Zelda has always bullied me for one reason or another. I still have no idea what those reasons might be. But she insists on always making my life a living hell."

"I can see it. Maybe it's because she has a major crush on you."

"What?" I asked. "I doubt that. Besides, she and her bratty friends know I'm gay."

"And that might be why she hates you," he deduced. "I can't say for a fact, but some people could be like that. I mean, I did see that happening on certain shows."

"Norman, this isn't a movie or a show. This is real life," I said, sipping on the last bit of my now-cold tea. "Besides, I doubt that is the case with Zelda. If anything, I get the distinct feeling it's something deeper than simply having a crush on me."

"All right, fair enough," he said. "What about Brianna then?"

"What about her?"

"Come on. Even I could tell she hates you, too. I guess I'm curious as to why you brought up her father."

I sighed. "Because she was lying," I said. "I could feel her true emotions underneath her hatred. The second I brought up her father, her true emotions were present. She's more upset over it than she is letting on." I shook my head, not bringing up the fact I saw his ghost. "I know I shouldn't have brought it up, but I can't stand it when people lie. But that isn't what's bothering me the most."

"What is bothering you?"

"Hannah wasn't with them," I said. "They are always in a group of three. I wonder where she was."

"Well, I don't know Hannah, but it might not be anything," he said.

"Maybe," I said and paid for our meal. I left a hefty tip on the table before I stood up. "Anyway, I have to get to work now. Melinda is going to give me an earful again."

Norman smirked, standing up. "This I have to see. Plus, I want to see her for myself. This should be good," he said.

***

We walked out of the cafe and went across the street to the magic shop. I opened the door and Norman went in first. Of course, Melinda was there in a red dress with a cape tied around her neck, a red witch hat, and red boots. There was a broom in her hand and she was sweeping the floor. She must have heard our footsteps because she turned. "Ah, Weston, there you are. I was sure you weren't coming in. You know, you've been late so many times now I may have to dock your pay."

"At least you aren't firing him," Norman said, chuckling.

I elbowed his ribs. "Norman," I growled quietly.

Melinda's eyed Norman with skepticism. As usual, I couldn't feel her emotions. "Oh, Weston, have you got yourself a boyfriend finally?"

I blushed. "No, he's a friend."

Norman smirked. "Besides, Wes here is not my type, but you are," he said, winking at her.

Melinda wasn't flattered. "Is that so? Well, I highly doubt that considering you barely know me, Norman Forrester."

Norman grinned. "Oh, you know me?"

"Honey, everyone in town knows who you are. You are Detective Daryl Forrester's son," she seethed. "And speaking of which, did you both hear about Barry Bloomingdale and Jerry Johnson? It's such a tragedy."

"It is. I knew both Barry and Jerry personally," said Norman. "They wouldn't have done this. I know they wouldn't have. I just have to prove it. But I can't go back to the bridge. They already cleaned it up. Man, I wish I knew where Jerry was found. He called me this morning and seemed fine."

Melinda nodded. "Well, I'm not supposed to say anything, but there was gossip earlier that Jerry was found out by that old mansion."

"Old mansion?" he asked. "You mean the one up on Chester Hill?"

"The very same," confirmed Melinda.

Norman turned to me. "That's the same place you zoned out on."

I rubbed the back of my head. "Did you have to bring that up? I said I was sorry about that."

Norman's eyes widened. "Maybe you sensed something out there," he said. "Oh, this is perfect. I have to get going. It was nice seeing you, Melinda. I hope we meet again." He winked at her and then ran out of the building.

"What do you think that was all about?" I asked.

Melinda shrugged. "How am I supposed to know? He's your friend."

"I suppose."

She huffed. "Spill it."

"Spill what?" I asked.

Her eyes narrowed. "Why your aura is acting bizarre?"

"Melinda, not today," I begged, sighing.

"O.M.G!" said Melinda with a giant grin and a strange gleam in her eyes.

"What?"

"You were kissed!"

"What... No... I mean..." I tried to ask how she knew and also didn't want to mention the truth to her.

"Ooh! That's definitely it," she said. "You totally kissed that handsome ginger-headed boy. Come on. Spill the magic beans. Did you like it?"

"I don't know. It was nice and surprising," I admitted.

"Ooh! You obviously liked it," she said.

Before I could come up with a retort, the bell dinged.

Melinda stepped past me, shoving the broom in my hands. "Hello, what can I do for you?"

With the broom in my hand, I turned to see a guy and a girl. The girl had long wavy, fiery, red hair that had to be dyed because there was no way that vivid red was real. She also had the brightest green eyes. They were brighter than Melinda's. She was dressed in a black cardigan, black shirt with vampire teeth logo saying bite me, and had black and red combat boots on. She also wore black nail polish and bright red lipstick.

The guy beside her appeared to be in his early or maybe late twenties. He had shaggy brown hair that was unruly with hazel eyes that had dark smudged under them. It was like he hadn't slept well in days. He was also dressed in faded blue jeans and a wrinkled gray shirt with a black hoodie.

The redhead removed the guy's arm that was wound around her shoulder like she was the one keeping him upright. "You sure you're okay now?" she asked strangely polite considering her standoffish emotions were filled with negativity.

The guy's face went beat red before he stuffed his hands in his pockets. "I'm fine now. I just got a bit lightheaded. I forgot about breakfast," he said, rubbing the back of his neck. I immediately sensed that he was lying.

The girl sighed. "Be glad my best friend isn't here. She'd tell you off."

I don't know why, but I stepped up beside Melinda. "Uh, hi, I'm Weston."

The girl glared at me. Even without feeling the waves of hostility from her, I could see it vividly in her eyes. I had to bite back a wince at the intensity.

"I'm Sera. That's spelled S.E.R.A," she answered.

"Oh, come on, your full name is divine," said Melinda.

"It's really not. I hate it."

"It can't be that bad," I said.

"Seraphina," she said, sighing.

Melinda smiled. "She's being modest. Her full name is Seraphina Francesca Embers."

The girl clenched her fists. "Melinda, I told you not to call me by my full name. I hate it."

Melinda chuckled. "Like I ever listen," she said. "So, what brings you here? I'm surprised you aren't with Eva."

Sera pointed to the guy. "It's his fault. I was on my way to meet Eva and the next thing I know I see him nearly faint crossing the street. I figured I'd help him out so he didn't get ran over like an idiot."

The guy's face got even redder as an air of embarrassment surrounded him. "I... That's not... I didn't faint. I was lightheaded from the lack of food and heat." Aside from embarrassment, I sensed he was also nervous. That was a given though with the ways his body was tensed up.

"So, are you here to buy something?" asked Melinda with a hint of sadness in her voice.

Sera shook her head. "Hell no," she said. "I just brought this fainting bozo in her so he wouldn't cause trouble. You guys can handle it from here. I have to go meet Eva." And with that, she abruptly left.

Melinda pinched the bridge of her nose. "That girl is such a pain sometimes."

The guy rubbed the back of his head. "I'm sorry. I can leave. I was just in a hurry. I had this job interview and I missed it. I…"

Melinda stared at the guy with a weird gleam in her green eyes. "Talk about a string of good luck. You can work here part-time."

The guy's eyes widened. "I… You're offering me a job on the spot?"

She smiled. "It's not every day I meet someone else with an equally fascinating aura as Weston here. "

I gripped the handle on the broom tighter. "Melinda," I warned.

The guy shook his head. "I…"

Melinda smiled. "No need to say anything. Just think it over. I have all day and night," she said, waving as she walked away from us.

"I'm sorry about her," I said. "She can be quite strange sometimes. Don't let it get to you. She really is a great person. Sometimes a lousy boss, though."

"I heard that, Weston. You want to see lousy. I can cut your pay again."

"Noted, Melinda," I said, smiling. I then turned my attention back to the guy. "Just decide on your own terms, uh…"

The guy's eyes widened comically. "Oh. My name is Jasper."

"Nice to meet you, Jasper," I said. "Let me get you a snack and some water. You can get better food at the cafe across the street once you feel better."

***

Close to closing time, when I finished stocking the last shelf, Melinda came over. "I'm sorry for assuming that you and Norman were a thing. It's just that handsome young man with ginger hair stopped by asking for you. Why haven't you asked him out yet?"

I blinked. I was utterly shocked. Hayden had come by and asked about me? That was strange. I thought for sure he was upset with me. Why then…

I shook my head before sighing and turning my attention to her. "It's complicated."

Just before I was about to grab my messenger bag and leave, Jasper came over to us. He shoved his hands in his pocket. "I wanted to say thank you for helping me and allowing me to stay and help out."

Melinda smiled. "Oh, such manners," she said. "You don't have to thank us. Besides, you did well stocking."

I rolled my eyes as I grabbed my bag and placed it over my head. "Flatter much, Melinda?"

She grabbed a lollipop and whacked me in the forehead with it. "Shut it. Though, he was better than you, Weston. How many things did you drop again?"

"Too many," I said, rolling my eyes. "I sadly can't stay and chat. I have to get home." Before I could walk out the door, Jasper grabbed me and pulled me away as a light above us fell and landed in the same spot I was just in.

Melinda watched us with fascination. "Are you both okay?" she asked. I couldn't feel any emotions like always, but there was something deadly in her eyes. Suspiciously, I wondered if she dropped the light on us purposefully. But why would she do that?

I dusted myself off. "I'm fine." I then turned to Jasper. "Are you…"

Jasper nodded, getting to his feet. "I'm fine as well. Sorry for the sudden move. I saw it and wanted to get you out of the way."

"No big deal. Thanks for the save." I then gave a quick wave and left before getting in my Jeep and driving off.

When I arrived home and got out of my car and walked into the house, I found my grandma in the kitchen with bags of groceries. "Grandma, I wish I had known you needed to shop. I would have done it for you."

"That's okay, dear," she said as I helped her put away the groceries. "Thanks for helping."

"It's no problem, Grandma," I said. "I need to pull my weight and help out since my mom abandoned me in your hands. It's the least I can do."

"Don't sell Iris short, Weston," she said. "She is your mother."

I sighed and placed my hands on the counter. "I know and I love her. But she did exactly what I feared she would. She disowned me. She hates me for being myself. And she hates you, too, Grandma."

Grandma walked over and pulled me into her arms. I wrapped my arms around her and cried into her white hair.

"Honey," she said. "What happened between your mother and me is not because of you. Iris hates me because I'm your father's mother."

"That doesn't make it right."

"No, it doesn't," she said.

I tried to get my pent-up emotions under control, but they were flooding out and I couldn't contain them anymore. "How could she?" I asked, desperately clinging to my grandma being mindful of her fragile body. In the back of my mind, I could hear stuff rattling from my uncontrolled telekinesis. I could also hear the sound of rain pouring on the roof. But I couldn't focus on it. I was just focused on how I was feeling for once. "Why did she leave? Why does she hate me for being who I am?"

Grandma petted the back of my head soothingly. "I don't know, dear. I don't know," she said. "Listen, you had a rough day. Maybe you should head to bed early tonight."

I aggressively wiped my eyes. "I like that idea. Thanks, Grandma." I then dug my hand into my pocket. "Oh, here," I said, placing the necklace in her hand. "I don't know how it got in my pocket, but this is the necklace you were looking for, right?"

Grandma glanced at the item and then held it to her chest as she laughed. "Oh, my, so that is where I placed it. I remember now that I placed it in your pocket for good luck. I can't believe I'm so forgetful."

I kissed her cheek. "It's not a big deal. Thank you." I then headed to my room for the night, wondering why my grandma didn't say anything about the rattling or the sudden rainstorm.

15

"Weston..." a voice whispered.

In between sleep and wakefulness, a light breeze, that felt more like someone's breath, bristled against my hair and tickled the back of my neck.

"Weston..." the voice whispered again.

"Go away," I mumbled, snuggling my head into my polyester pillow and sliding further under the covers to break off the sudden unbearable chill. I turned onto my side, finding a comfortable position.

Just when I started drifting off to sleep again, the same voice returned.

"Weston, wake up."

"Shut up and go away," I grumbled and swatted my hand.

"Don't be like that."

I kept my eyes shut and hummed. "Go away," I mumbled again this time with a large yawn as I placed my arm under my head and clapped my chapped lips together.

"That's it," the voice said. Before I could respond, the blanket was yanked off me and a hand touched my arm.

Calm emotions zapped through so fast causing my eyes to snap open. I jerked up and pushed whoever it was away.

"Who's there?" I yelled as my gaze locked onto a blurry glob.

"Take a guess."

"Norman?" I asked, reaching over to my nightstand and putting on my glasses before turning on my bedside lamp. Once light flooded the room, I glanced over. Sure enough, it was Norman. He was still in the same clothes from earlier. "What are you doing in my house? How did you get up here?"

"That's not important."

"What is important?' I asked grumpily as I checked the time on the clock. "Are you kidding me? Norman, you seriously couldn't have waited until morning? It's 11:45 at night. That means I've only been asleep for an hour! Are you insane?"

Norman put up his hands. "Hey, don't blame me for your lack of sleep. I've been awake. And this idea came to me. Do you remember what Melinda told us about Jerry?"

"You mean about finding his truck out by that creepy house you were telling me about when I picked you up?" I asked, through a powerful yawn.

"The very same," he said. "I was thinking that we should check it out. So, you get ready and I will meet you there. Tonight is the perfect opportunity. I want to find out what is happening." There was something else in his emotions that flickered too fast for me to understand before it was consumed by that ever strange calmness.

"Is there something else you are up to?" I asked.

Norman's gaze furrowed as his lips turned up into a large grin. He then walked to the window and started going out of it. "That's for me to know and for you to find out. Just meet at the place in fifteen minutes."

I got out of bed with a heavy sigh and walked over to my dresser. I rummaged for a shirt which was just a regular gray one. I quickly changed and threw my old one on the floor. I then took off my sweatpants and grabbed a pair of jeans from my closet and put them on. Only in my hastiness, I stumbled multiple times. At one time, I tumbled so much that my elbow collided into the wall, hitting my funny bone.

"Son of a…butter biscuit pie," I mumbled to myself. I made up swears that weren't exactly swears. One of my school teachers had caught a young girl cursing once in anger. Instead of punishing her like most would, she told the girl to make up swears that were silly. It's stuck with me. I don't know why.

Before getting out of the house, I eased my bedroom door halfway open and peered out. The whole house was dark and eerily quiet. Using my empathy, I sought out my grandma's unique emotions. They were there. But they were distant. I couldn't tell if she was awake or asleep.

Vigilantly, I closed the door and then sauntered over to the open window. Norman came in through here. How I didn't hear it was a mystery considering this window tended to squeak if opened too. I hadn't asked my grandma about oiling yet.

After shoving on my blue sneakers, I pushed the window open a bit more but being careful not to slam it.

A warm gush of air blasted across my face. I ignored it as I picked up my messenger bag and threw it over my shoulder. I then mounted over to the balcony. This was not going to be fun. I was glad I didn't have a height problem. I then turned my vision to the left and saw vines climbing up the side. Being as careful as I could, I scaled down safely to the ground. I used to escape out windows with Hayden, but never from two stories high, and never by myself. This felt strangely exhilarating, but I also felt guilty.

I made it around to my Jeep and got in. I turned on the ignition and then backed out of the driveway and headed to where Norman said to meet him.

16

I skidded to a stop in the gravel and turned off the engine. I then leaned over and popped open the glove compartment and pulled out the spare flashlight I had hidden in there.

The second I stepped out of my vehicle and closed the door, a bitter chill crisped over my face. I shivered. This was too cool for March. Hesitantly, I reopened the door and grabbed my hoodie from the passenger seat, and put it on before I walked. My footsteps chomping into the rocks made it sound like I was stepping on glass which made me even more uneasy.

I stopped at a creepy gate. It was huge. Though, it wasn't that odd. The old iron was so badly rusted that some of the bars were bent at weird angles and becoming so dismantled that a small child could squeeze through them if they were careful. Even the words at the top were falling apart. Only the C and M were still intact. Because of its looming appearance, it prevented me from seeing beyond the gate and tree lines. I could make out a dark pointy roof tower.

"I don't have a pleasant feeling about this," I said with a deep exhale. My breath was noticeable in the chilly environment. I involuntarily shivered. It was odd. I was in warm clothes so I shouldn't be cold.

"Did you say something?"

I jumped at Norman's sudden voice. Usually, I could detect when someone was near, but Norman's ever-calm emotions were almost undetectable. I turned and shined my flashlight at him. He was kneeling on the ground, rummaging through a black backpack he had open.

"I was talking to myself," I said. I didn't want to voice my unpleasant feeling for the second time. It wasn't like my new friend would listen to me anyway. "What are you looking for?

"This," he said, pulling out a small camcorder.

"Why?"

"Ghost hunting," he said.

I knew there was something more. He seemed like the type to go in all excitedly and then ignore everything else even if it was dangerous. I wasn't like that. I liked being cautious. And ever since Norman brought up this stupid idea, a bad feeling had been slithering around in the pit of my stomach. Sometimes being intuitive sucked.

I grabbed the walkie-talkie from Norman when he nudged me with his elbow. "What is this for?" I asked, clipping it to my belt.

"To keep in contact with each other," he said. "This place is massive and we might get separated."

"Great," I said, dispirited. "Remind me again: why do I need to be here?"

Norman rolled his bright hazel eyes. "I want answers as to why Jerry's truck was found here, and with your abilities maybe we can get them."

"Uh-huh," I said, skeptically. "There's something else."

He grinned. "Damn, you are good. I tried to hide it so well. Empathy is literally a cheat, you know?"

"Norman," I said impatiently.

"I wanted to investigate the ghost stories."

Of all things he could have said. I didn't want to get behind this idea.

"Unless there aren't any ghosts home," I said, shrugging. Deep down, I hoping there weren't any. Though, something told me that there were.

"Don't worry. I did all sorts of research. I have several camcorders, voice recorders, EMFs, the whole shebang."

"Great." I didn't bother to tell him that I could see the dead. He already liked my other two abilities; I personally didn't want him to get any more ghost-hunting business ideas.

As we pushed the gate open together, a strong gust of cold air blew past us. A sharp, uncontrollable gasp escaped my lips as I wrapped my arms around myself, trembling slightly. The coldness was deep and chilling, but it wasn't the only thing I detected. Revengeful emotions and raw pain that was both physical and mental rattled my nervous system.

Curious, I turned around. My gaze wandered. Nothing was out of the ordinary. There were no ghosts around me. So, why was I feeling like there was?

A hand touched my shoulder.

Startled, I jumped and backed away. The sudden contact had an on slaughter of concern that flooded my already sensitive nerves. The second my gaze landed on Norman, I relaxed. I took several good deep breaths, allowing my hands to fall at my side.

"I'm okay," I whispered mostly to myself.

"What happened, Wes?" he asked. "Did you feel something?"

I shook my head, ignoring his nickname for me. No one had ever called me that. I couldn't understand it. We had only just met the other day and he was treating us like we've been lifelong friends since the beginning of time. He was strange.

"I'm not sure," I said. "I thought I felt something is all. But it's gone. It must be my nerves. I'm okay. Trust me. Let's continue."

"Trusting you isn't the problem. I do trust you. I'm just concerned. I did research on empathic abilities and they can be brutal sometimes. I just wanted to be sure you okay. Don't be getting all weird on me for that. You're my friend. So, if you want…"

"No," I interrupted loudly which caused Norman's calm emotions to flicker to confusion. I flushed and then lowered my voice. "I want to be here, Norman. I'm fine. I want to continue."

Norman grinned.

We continued our stroll. I buried one of my chilled hands in the pocket of my hoodie. I didn't want Norman to notice them trembling. So, I used my other hand to point the flashlight around me. In my peripheral vision, weird shadows would dart and then disappear when my light hit them. They didn't seem like ghosts. Who knows, maybe I was going crazy.

However, my sense of uneasiness amplified the closer we got to the house. I didn't know if it was the fact that everything was way too quiet or the fact that the tall strands of wheat-like weeds were swaying calmly in the light breeze.

My heart ached at the sights. The once beautiful flowers in the once beautiful garden-like maze were all brown and withered. Even the marble angel fountain was busted. The angel's wings were missing and its sad face was cracked. And no water was gushing out of the bowl she held. It was indeed a pitiful sight.

While the plantation was so desolated, the manor was in worse condition. The old Victorian manor was just as creepy and old as Norman had described. But to me, the manor would have been lovely if it hadn't been left to rot. Overgrown vines were everywhere, crawling up the sides of the house and twirling around the columns. All of the broken shutters, hanging on by one hinge, would rattle whenever the wind caught them and would bang against the chipped painted light red panes. All of the dozen or so windows had cracks on the outside of the glass. What made it even creepier was the fact they were boarded up from the inside as though whoever lived her was keeping something from seeing them like they were super paranoid or something. What a bunch of weirdos. Though, honestly, it made me want to research this place.

The more we walked, the worse the cold got. I couldn't stop myself from wondering what happened or what I had felt. Sure, my empathy wasn't as new or raw, but things didn't always make perfect sense.

Once at the bottom of the stairs, I took in the sight. It was awful. The wood was rotted and had termites biting into it. Even the porch was a disaster waiting to happen. In the hope to relieve my frazzled nerves, I tried to envision how beautiful, lively, and new the place would have been if it had a new paint job and if all the flowers were perky and bloomed.

"Well, this is certainly creepy," I said.

"I'm more curious about what kind of people lived here," said Norman. "Boarded up windows aren't always a good sign."

"I'm not worried about that," I said, lying to myself. I was, but I didn't want Norman to go into one of his rants.

"Sure," he said, filming. "This is going to be excellent footage. My paranormal ghost-hunting business is well on its way." He then tossed me a camera. I had to use my telekinesis to bring it into my hands because Norman had a terrible aim in the dark. "Take photos for me."

"Don't get too excited," I said, snapping snapshots of the house and desolate yard. "I am one hundred percent sure nothing ghostly is going on in this house." The rotten floor boarded stairs creaked under my feet. I grimaced as a spike of fear nearly stopped me from going further. I didn't want to put any more weight on wood in case I fell though. I nearly gagged at the thought of termites and spiders climbing all over. "Ugh, this place is so grotesque. Can I go back on my word? Can we call it a day and go home?"

Norman rolled his eyes. "You can't chicken out now." I bit my tongue to keep myself from saying anything. "Besides, we both know that I am not going to back out of this. That's not who I am. I'm all in, honestly, I do want to find out the meaning as to why this house is listed as the most haunted on the town's website."

I pinched the bridge of my nose. A headache was building in my head. "Yeah, I do know that. The atmosphere in this place is already tense. Let's make this quick. The quicker we get whatever proof you are wanting, the quicker we can go home."

"Weston," he said like he was offended, but I knew better. He was just being dramatic. "I thought you were excited about this."

"You know I wasn't," I said, walking up the rest of the way carefully. I examined the white birch wood door. It didn't seem to belong with the rest of the house. It was like it was just put a few years ago which was strange. There was also the faded lion crest but the knocker ring was missing. And I couldn't help but notice how polished the golden door handle was.

Nervously, I reached out. I was a bit scared to touch the door. I didn't want to see any deaths. However as soon as my hand wrapped around the metal ornate handle, I relaxed. No images invaded me. Relieved, I turned the handle. It was locked. "Well, Norman, I don't think we will be getting inside." Good riddance, I thought. "Is that enough for you to stop this ridiculous ghost-hunting escapade and head back?"

Norman shook his head. "Not a chance," he said, grinning. "Can't you do that special trick you do?"

I glared at him. "You want me to use my telekinesis to unlock the door?" I asked. "I am not doing that. That is breaking and entering."

"How is it breaking and entering?" he asked. "You wouldn't be breaking anything."

"Okay, good point. But we would be entering a house without permission."

He gave me a pitiful look.

"Fine," I said. "You so owe me for this. If we get caught, I am so blaming this whole situation on you."

Norman smiled that goofy grin of his. "I am fine with that. And we won't get caught," he said with unusual confidence.

"What makes you so sure?" I asked. I couldn't help, but be curious. I had to know what made Norman feel this cocky and confident.

"Just a hunch," he said, shrugging.

I nearly laughed at that. I figured Norman's hunches were about as reliable as predicting the winning lottery numbers. That meant he wasn't always right. Sometimes I wished my hunches were unreliable. Maybe that would make me feel less like a freak of nature. Then again, I trusted my intuition. It saved me a couple of times.

Before I could use my telekinesis, the door squeaked open bringing me out of my deep thoughts. My gaze shot up to Norman, who was standing off to the side. "I didn't do that."

"Ooh," he said, a jittery excited feeling flooding through him and into me. "I told you. This place is haunted. Ghosts, hello, we are coming in."

I gave him a strange gaze before we peeked inside. The place was dark. When we crossed the threshold, the lanterns squeaked above us when a gust of powerful wind blew past up and slammed the door shut.

Norman grinned. "I do believe we got a ghost on our hands."

I rolled my eyes. "Don't go making any assumptions." A sudden strong musky smell hit my sinuses causing me to sneeze.

"Bless you," said Norman.

"Thanks," I said, rubbing my nose.

I scanned the foyer with my flashlight. It was huge. For the most part, it was mostly empty of all furniture. The only remains were an old rusty dead grandfather clock that had its hands stuck on midnight. Above us was a beautiful crystal chandelier. The stairs leading up were caved in and collapsed, so there was no possible way of getting to the second floor.

"I think we should split up," said Norman.

I didn't want to split up. This place was giving me absolute creeps. But I knew with Norman being excited, he would never listen to me. So, I simply nodded.

We separated. He went towards the living room while I went towards the kitchen.

As soon as I pushed open the heavy door and stepped inside the grimy kitchenette, a squeak caused my heart to leap. I hoped that wasn't what I thought it was. Moving my flashlight around, a fast-moving rat scurried over my shoe.

I screamed like a girl and jumped on the countertop behind me, hitting the back of my head on the hanging pots.

"Weston!" Norman's static voice came from the walkie-talkie that was clipped on my jeans. "Come in, Weston! Are you there?"

Hearing the concern and panic in his voice, I unclipped the walkie-talkie and pressed the button. "I'm here," I said, shakily.

"What happened? I heard your scream from the other room. Did you see a ghost?"

"No," I responded. "It was worse."

"What could be worse?"

"A rat," I said.

Norman's laughter came through the radio.

I groaned. "It's not funny."

"Oops, sorry," he said. "My finger was still on the button."

"You jerk," I mumbled, clipping the walkie-talkie back on my belt before I jumped down.

An icy coldness broke out and the air became tense. Each puff of breath made me see a white cloud in front of me. My glasses were chilled on my face. I seriously needed contacts.

Suddenly, a hand touched mine. For a split second, I thought it might be Norman. That was until my entire mind was invaded by emotions. The pain was the first one. A deep pain that felt like heartbreak and then the depression kicked in. I gasped sharply as a vision invaded my mind.

I found myself strapped to a bed. Everything was encased in a white light, but I could hear screams around me.

Panic consumed me as I heard the incoming drills. I yanked on the bands, trying to get out. But I was secured tightly.

Just then, pain in my both of my arms happened and then my head felt funny as my vision swam.

I saw a distorted face just before my eyes closed...

I jerked my hand back not wanting to stay in the vision. My chest was tight and hurting. I lifted my eyes only to be startled so much that I fell back against the stove as my eyes were locked onto a young man dressed in a nurse's outfit. There was nothing remotely familiar about him. His brown hair was wavy and his eyes were dark brown. It took me a little bit to comprehend that his lips were moving. Did he really die to some kind of experimentation?

"You must stop him."

"Stop who?" I asked.

Just then a black cat jumped in front of me and hissed at the man.

The man stepped back. "You stupid feline," he said. "You can't protect him forever. It's his destiny to help us."

The cat's hair rose like a predator ready to attack and hissed again.

The man flickered a few times until he disappeared.

I was confused. What was happening?

17

The black cat suddenly turned and sat in front of me with glowing yellow and green eyes.

"Hello, Weston," an eerily voice whispered.

"What is this? Since when do cats talk? And how do you know my name?

"Not all cats can talk, stupid. I am one of a kind. You may call me Mel. And I know you because I have been keeping a close eye on you without you noticing."

"Mel?" I asked, surprised. "Do you know who Melinda is? Are you her cat?" I didn't see a collar around her neck. But if she was indeed Melinda's cat, then that could be how she knew my name.

"You could say that," she said. "But I don't have time to get into that. You must listen to me very closely. This house isn't safe. The spirits that dwell in here have sensed your presence. It won't be long now before they come to you. You must leave now.

"What are you talking about? You mean that man who showed up a minute ago?"

Mel scratched her ear with her paw. "People who were killed in strange ways are left on earth seeking someone who can help them. That person just happens to be you. But you must be careful. Not all the spirits are nice and friendly. Some will and can hurt you."

"I don't understand," I said. "How can they hurt me?"

Mel's green vertical pupils narrowed. "I do not know exactly. You are the first psychic with telekinetic, empathic, and mediumship abilities to ever exist. There haven't been many psychics in existence to possess such gifts or talents. And empaths and mediums never last long as their abilities tend to make them go crazy."

"Crazy? Like loony bin crazy?"

"Exactly," she said. "Empaths and mediums can have a difficult time deciphering what's real and what isn't, yes. Also, we need to go. The longer we continue to talk, the more time it gives the spirits to find you. You must find your friend and escape while there is still time."

"Wait," I said.

"I promise to explain everything later, but right now your safety is my top priority. I cannot hide your aura for too much longer."

"What do you mean?" Before I could finish my sentence loud voices invaded my hearing.

"Help us…"

"Help us…"

"Help us…"

I covered my ears and turned around to see a group of different people from the elderly to adults, to teens, to young children all surrounding me, reaching out to me and begging for my help.

Frightened, I backed away.

I tried to speak, but the words got stuck in my throat. I continued to back up until I was against a wall. I didn't want these ghosts to touch me. I didn't want to see how they died.

"Please, make it stop." I placed my hands to my temples as a sharp pain erupted in my skull. It was all coming from emotions. There were so many emotions, too many to comprehend whose pain belonged to which ghost.

I slid down to the ground. Even with the ringing and gushing in my eardrums, I could distantly hear what sounded like rain and rattling. Oh no, my powers were being affected because I couldn't control my emotions.

Just then pounding footsteps approached. I glanced up to see Norman sprint forward. He phased through the spirits and didn't even shiver as he knelt in front of me. "Weston, are you okay?"

I couldn't help but watch in fascination as the spirits backed away like something was repelling them. Was it Norman?

Before I could say anything, the ceiling above rattled and then came tumbling down. Without hesitation, I threw my entire body over Norman to protect him.

Not feeling the impact, but hearing the crash and crumbling of plaster, I lifted my head to see I lifted my head to see Mr. Newman dressed differently. He was in a black trench coat and black jeans. He still had on his half-rimmed glasses with his silver blue eyes shining in the moonlight that was beaming in through the hole in the ceiling.

Did he save us from the impact?

Suddenly, his silver eyes met mine. "You have to leave!" he ordered. The determination etched into his face confused me. Why did we have to leave? And why was he here to begin with?

I opened my mouth ready to say anything, but a loud noise coming from behind me, echoing throughout the massive shambled room, prevented me from speaking a word.

Dread sank into my stomach. Terrified, my body stiffened and I slowly turned my head. I wished I hadn't though because my eyes widened and my heartbeat sped up and pounded in my chest.

A white fog drifted in as, a creepy man, dressed in a white doctor's uniform, with eyes black as night blazing at us. He loomed over us with an unpleasant satisfied grin on his face as he held what appeared to be a needle with some strange green liquid that was dripping from the end.

"Are you my new patient?" the man asked.

The urge to scream got stuck in the lump lodged in the back of my throat. Paralyzed with fear, all I could do was stare at the man in utter shuddered terror.

"No," I said.

The man's face changed into pure rage as his emotions slammed into me violently which caused me to lean back against the collapsed railing of the stairs. He then screamed as his black eyes glowering brightly and things around us started shaking violently.

I covered my ears at the sound and tried to avoid the items being tossed at us violently.

"What's going on?" asked Norman, but his voice sounded strange.

"We got to go!" yelled Mr. Newman as he grabbed my arm.

"No argument here," I said as I helped Norman to his feet, keeping my eyes on the creepy man.

The man hissed. "I never thought I would come across someone who could see me," he said in a deep menacing voice. "Come here so I can perform thorough tests on you."

I gulped, not liking the way the man's emotions changed into a gross lust as he said that.

"Weston! Come on!" Norman shouted as he yanked on my arm. "It feels like this place is going to collapse. Now is not the time to zone out, man!"

"Not much a talker I see," the man said.

I didn't comment

This either annoyed or irritated the man because he let out an angry hiss trying to lung at us. I pushed Norman to the stairs as the walls started cracking from the violent shaking.

"Leave the boys alone!" shouted Mel, the cat. She jumped in front of the three of us and hissed angrily. She lunged at the spirit. Man tried to strike her with the needle but the cat was too nimble.

The cat turned her head to me. "Get out of here!"

The man walked forward. Panicked, I scurried back. "And now, you will face your doom," the man said. However, as the man was ready to strike me, an instinct kicked into me.

I lifted my hands. "I wouldn't be so sure," I said cryptically.

The man's head tilted to the side in confusion before my telekinesis shot out of me and made the man fly backward before vanishing into thin air as the violent shaking stopped.

Breathless, a headache pierced through my brain as I lowered my hands limply as my energy suddenly felt extremely depleted. I felt clammy and could feel sweat beading across my forehead. My eyes were drooping, but I fought against it as I fought to keep my attention on Norman.

He was staring at me with wide eyes as worry poured out of him.

"Don't worry," I assured, squeezing my eyes shut. "I'm fine." I then reached into my jacket to pull out a piece of gum. Only I realized that I hadn't had any.

"Crackers," I whispered.

"What about crackers?"

"No, I… I'm out of gum."

"Is that important?"

"No," I lied.

"Liar," he said as he helped me up. I was unsteady but Norman kept his arms on me to keep me from kneeling over. I appreciated his help.

"There's no time for a round of Q&A. We have to go."

"Then we should get the hell out of here while there is still time."

I ran a hand through my damp hair and straightened myself up. "Do you think we can make it to my Jeep?"

"Maybe," he said.

I bit my bottom lip. At the moment, I was conflicted. My primal instincts wanted me to flee from this unusual scene, from the horrid estate because a psycho doctor spirit was trying to kill us. However, Norman didn't seem that afraid. He showed determination and confidence in his body language.

Just as we got to the bottom of the steps, the doctor appeared in a white fog and grabbed my arm tightly. "Got you!" he said.

I was overcome by emotions of rage, but I also got a terrible vision.

I found myself strapped to a chair, laughing manically as electricity shot through me. I wasn't afraid. I was secretly enjoying this, telling myself that if I made it out of this that I would find more victims...

I screamed out in horror, yanking out of his grasp as I gasped for breath and wrapped my arms around myself as I trembled. I could feel the electricity running through me. I could feel the man's sick emotions and thoughts. It was disturbing.

"Weston?" asked Norman.

"Watch out!" yelled the cat lunging at me. Fear shot through me, but I couldn't move only watch as the man glared at the cat which made her fly back into a wall untouched.

The cat meowed painfully as she hit the floor.

"Mel!" yelled Mr. Newman as he went to the cat's side. He then reached into his pocket and then threw what appeared to be salt at thin air.

The spirit screeched in pain before he vanished.

"Go!" Mr. Newman yelled.

Just as I was about to, a rush of white fog pushed me and Norman away from each other before I was falling back into an opened door that shut on its own.

I groaned before getting to my feet and banging on the door. "Mr. Newman, Norman, Mel, are you there?"

Not hearing a word, I sighed.

Suddenly, a weird brush of air by my ear had me turning around. I came face to face with a gorgeous woman. She was dressed in in black and purple dress with heels.

"Hello, Weston," she said, smiling kindly.

I stared at her confused. "How do you know who I am?"

She sashayed towards me and touched my cheek. Her hand was freezing but her emotions were calm, and then a vision crashed into my mind.

I found myself banging away on a door and screaming as the scent of smoke hit me. I gagged as I tried everything to break the door down to get to my family. Tears ran down my face as I collapsed exhaustedly to my knees and succumbed to the roaring flames, feeling the heat on my skin...

I pulled away with a gasp as tears rolled down my cheeks. "You... You died in a fire."

"Yes, I did," she said. "But none of that is important. My time to pass on will come in due time, Weston. You, however, need to do something to get rid of Alexander's spirit permanently."

"What do you need me to do?"

"Go to the cemetery out behind the house and find his grave. Someone there will be able to give you the next step."

I blinked slowly. "How am I to do that? I can't get out of here." I was trapped in an office room with no windows. There was a desk against that had dust on it and a bookcase near that with several missing books that were scattered all over the floor.

The woman pointed at the bookshelf. "Remove that Lovecraft book."

I walked over to the bookcase and pulled the H.P. Lovecraft book. Suddenly, I heard some kind of mechanism click before the bookshelf pushed inward, opening like a door. "What is this?"

"A secret door," the woman said. "You can get out this way."

"You didn't die in this room then?"

She shook her head. "I did not. But that isn't important. Go out to the unmarked grave and there you meet someone who can help stop Alexander.

"Who is it?"

"You will find out when you get out there," she said before disappearing.

I grabbed my flashlight out of my pocket. I was hesitant but before I could make a move, a loud bang caused the room to shake.

"Hurry," the woman's voice whispered in my ear.

I walked through the hidden door.

I hoped I could do this.

18

As soon as I walked through the tunnel, I came out through a small opening that led to outside to the backyard. I knew coming here was a big mistake.

And not knowing where Norman was, was bugging me. Was he even here with me? Was he okay? Was that ghost hurting him and the cat and Mr. Newman?

Feeling dread in my stomach, I quickened my steps as I searched the small graveyard. Violet shivers were beginning to take over me. This was why I hated being in cemeteries. It felt like I was being watched.

Flashing my light around, I hunted for the right grave marker. These all had names on them. As I approached the end of the cemetery, I tripped over something hard and fell to the ground.

While on my knees, I groaned. I moved my hands around until I found what tripped me. It was stone. Was this the unmarked grave?

I wiped away the dirt and leaves. Sure enough, there weren't any names listed. Was this the grave? Did I find it? What was I supposed to do now?

Suddenly, a little boy was standing in front of me. He had to be about five. His eyes were dark green and he was dressed in a blue sweater vest and black trousers with brown loafers.

"Hello, who are you?"

"I'm Maxwell Rivers," the young boy said. "It's a pleasure to meet you."

"Nice to meet you, too, Maxwell."

Maxwell pouted. "Mister, have you seen my toy soldier? I seem to have lost it," he said. Sadness was coming off him in waves making my heart ache.

"Do you remember where you lost it?"

Maxwell pointed to the house. "Somewhere in there. I was playing but then was told to go outside and accidentally left it behind."

"Do you remember which room?"

Maxwell shook his head. "No. If I don't find it, Papa will become angry at me for losing it. Will you help me find it, mister?"

I got to my feet. "I'll help you find it. Can you come with me?"

The little boy shook his head. "I'm not allowed to go inside until its safe. The nice lady said so. She said I was supposed to stay out here and wait. She even said a nice man would help me. Is that you, mister?"

Was it the same woman who helped me? It must have been.

"I'll help you," I promised.

The boy's emotions beamed with happiness as he grinned and then grabbed my hand. Suddenly, a vision invaded my mind.

I found myself lying in bed, clammy, and feeling sweat rolling down my face. With bleary eyesight, I gazed around my blue bedroom. Next to my bed was an I.V that was hooked up to me.

I didn't want to be sick.

Papa walked in and I smiled. He leaned over and kissed my head. I watched him confused as he injected something into my IV bag and then I was feeling sluggish and tired as my eyes closed, calling out to my papa...

I gasped, tumbling back a little, but falling on my butt as I panted for air. That poor boy, I thought as I placed a hand on my chest. His father, his own father, killed him.

"Mister, are you okay? Did I hurt you?"

Huh? Startled, I peered at the young boy, who was kneeling beside me. Worry was pouring out of him. "Are you sick, sir?"

Before I could respond, a sudden crackling static came from somewhere on me. I found the walkie-talkie on the ground...

The walkie-talkie!

I turned to my attention to Maxwell. "I have a friend who can locate your toy, but I will need you to describe it, okay? It's very important."

"Really?" he asked, tilting his head.

"Really," I said, smiling. I then grabbed the walkie-talkie and pressed the button. "Norman, come in Norman? Are you there?"

There was only static.

Please answer, I thought as I tried to contact him again.

A sudden cough came through before a voice spoke. "Weston, thank hell you are okay. Where are you?"

"I'm fine. Where are you? Are you okay?"

"Fine," he said, coughing. "I'm just hiding. Crazy stuff is still being thrown around. And Mr. Curator guy is helping the cat and…"

"Norman, listen," I interrupted. "I need you to find something with your…ability."

"You want me to do that now with poltergeist activity happening in here?" he asked and I could hear something crack. "Are you insane? I'm trying not to get killed by this pissed off spirit."

Another crashed happened.

"Norman?"

"I'm fine," he said, coughing. "So, the poltergeist might not like foul language. It just tried to hit me with a table."

I kind of wanted to snicker at that. A ghost who didn't like swearing was kind of funny. But I knew now was not the time.

"Are you safe now?"

"Yeah, do you have a name and an item detail?" he asked. "I still can't believe you want to do this now."

"Because it's important," I said. "Hold on a second." I then glanced at the boy, who had been patiently waiting for me. "Can you describe your toy now?"

Maxwell bit his lower lip. "Well, Papa got it made out it out of wood for me. It's not painted. It's one of those guards with the big hats from London who protects the Queen. Papa brought it back for me when he traveled once."

"Thank you." I talked back into the walkie-talkie. "Norman, are you still there?"

Another crash happened before he answered, "Yeah, do you have what I asked?"

"His name is Maxwell Rivers and he's missing a wooden toy soldier of a Royal Guard."

"I'm on it," he said. There was nothing but static on the other end for what felt like hours. But it couldn't have been more than a few minutes. "Okay, I got it. Coincidentally, it was nearby since I'm hiding in the kitchen. It was hidden in a cupboard. What do you need this for?"

"Tell you later. Just meet by the front door in five!"

"Weston, wait." But I ignored him. I turned my attention back to Maxwell, who had vanished.

I searched. "Maxwell?"

Thinking that the boy might have heard where his toy was, I started running to the house. "Maxwell!"

Instead of going through the tunnel that I came from earlier, I ran around to the front of the house. Once to the front door, I tried to open it. But it was like a force was holding it shut.

"Crap!" I yelled and then started banging on the door. "Doctor Alexander, let me in! I'll... I'm your new patient."

The heavy force calmed as the door came in on its own.

"About time, boy," said the doctor's creepy voice.

I took a deep breath and walked inside. The door slammed shut behind me, nipping my shoulder in the process. "That is sure to leave a bruise," I mumbled to myself.

"Glad to see you back," said Doctor Alexander's voice in my ear. I already saw his death once. I didn't want to experience it again if he touched me.

Where was Norman?

"Nothing to say before the examination begins?"

I gulped.

Suddenly, I saw something get thrown. It landed at my feet. I noticed that it was the wooden toy solider. And I wasn't the only one.

The doctor moved away as he saw the toy before kneeling. His red eyes faded to green as he picked up the toy as though it was fragile and delicate.

Overwhelming grief and guilt knocked me to my knees. My eyes clenched shut as I wrapped an arm around my stomach. I felt sick.

"Maxwell," the doctor said, his voice thick with emotion. "I never meant... I just wanted your suffering to end. And in doing so, I suffered as well. I did horrible, terrible things."

Through, the tears welling in my eyes, I could see Maxwell. He didn't feel hatred. He was feeling sympathetic. He hugged the man who was his father.

"I forgive you, Papa," Maxwell said. "It's time to go. Let's be with Mama and Auntie."

The doctor embraced his son before the two glanced at me. With a nod, I watched as they disappeared into white sparkles of light.

I released the breath I was holding and let out a small sob. A sudden hand on my shoulder caused me to jerk away from the contact. The concern I felt through the brief contact was too much. I felt like I was seriously going to be sick.

"Don't touch me," I whispered, gazing up to see Mr. Newman.

His eyes met mine as he put his hands up. "Easy, Weston," he said. "I'm not going to hurt you."

"Where's Norman?" I asked.

"Right here," a pained voice said.

I turned to see him walking, well, more like stumbling as he held his head. "Are you okay?"

Norman groaned as he stood up and straightened. "I think I'm okay," he said, pained. "A stupid chair hit my head as I was finding that damned toy you wanted."

Mr. Newman shook his head. "Come on," he said. "Let's get you boys out of here."

"Wait. Why did you come?" I asked.

Mr. Newman picked up the black cat. "A colleague of mine called me."

Norman's excitement alerted me and I turned to him as a giant grin spread across his face. "Does your colleague have the ability to know the future?"

After getting to my feet, thanks to Norman helping me up, I jabbed my elbow lightly into his ribs. Now was not the time for jokes.

Surprisingly, Mr. Newman laughed. "I do not have that kind of power. But one day you might meet someone who does."

Norman grinned. "Cryptic. I can't wait."

My gaze went back to Mr. Newman. "What about you, Mr. Newman? Are you hurt?"

Mr. Newman smiled. "I'm fine. Luckily, the salt I had left over drove the spirit away."

"Can you see them?" I asked curiously.

"Not me, no," he said. "But let's get out of here before we discuss things further. It might be calm now, but this place isn't safe."

Once outside and down the porch, I nearly stumbled as a wave of nausea swept over me, but I managed to keep my balance as I grabbed onto the railing of the stairs.

Norman, however, ran to the railing and turned an awful tint of green just before he vomited.

"I'm pretty sure I'm mildly concussed," he grumbled as he wiped his mouth.

"You definitely might be, Norman," said Mr. Newman. "It would be best to get you home."

"But I want answers," Norman said. "I didn't even find any clues about Jerry."

"Wait. What made you think Jerry came here?" asked Mr. Newman.

"Melinda told us," I said.

Mr. Newman pinched his nose. "That stupid woman," he said and then shook his head. "Jerry was never found here. He was found in the same place as Barry. I can't believe…"

A meow greeted us.

I turned to see the black cat, limping up to us and sit down beside Mr. Newman's booted feet. A rare genuine smile spread out across his face as he knelt and rubbed Mel's head. "I see you can walk. You are one cheeky cat. You and I will be having a very serious discussion, Mel."

"Yeah, later," she said. "The spirits have calmed significantly for now. And as much as I hate to break up this discussion party, Weston should not be around here any longer. The spirits could get restless again."

"Why shouldn't I be here?" I asked.

Mel meowed as she pawed at her ear. "You attract ghosts to you."

"Great." Learning all of this made my head hurt.

Mr. Newman sighed. "I know you're psychic, Weston. And none of us know the full extent of your powers. Luckily, Mel can help. She can repel spirits. But she can't be with you everywhere."

Another wave of nausea shot through me as I heard Norman gagging again.

I observed the house. There was something extra eerie about it. The house seemed to be ominously creaking. Instinctively, my empathy picked up on the sorrow, the anger, and the terror. It was nearly overwhelming.

"You want more answers; meet me tomorrow afternoon at the museum. I will explain everything," said Mr. Newman. "For now, take Norman and go home."

I wanted to protest, but he held up his hand stopping me.

"I mean it, Weston. You need to get going." And with that, he scooped Mel up into his arms before walking inside the house, leaving me and Norman alone.

I knew this trip had been a bad idea from the start.

19

Norman turned his head to me as I held him up. "You don't mind giving me a ride home, do you? I had to hitch a cab. My motorcycle wouldn't start. I tried everything. Hopefully, once Mickey is better, he can do an inspection and fix it for me."

"Norman," I said interrupting him.

"Yes?"

"I don't mind giving you a ride."

After helping him into my Jeep's passenger side, I then went around and hopped into the driver's seat.

"By the way, do you have my camera?" he asked.

"It's in my bag," I answered.

Norman grabbed my bag and opened it and rummaged around before he grabbed the muffin that I forgot was in there. "What is this?"

"A muffin," I said.

"Okay, genius, I already knew that. I meant what is it doing in your bag?"

"Oh, I forgot I still had it on me. A woman on an elevator gave it to me weeks ago."

Norman inspected it. "Well, can I have it? I am hungry."

"Didn't you hear me? It's been in there for weeks."

"Yes, but there doesn't seem to be anything wrong with it. Why didn't you eat it?"

"I'm not big on muffins."

Norman gaped at me. "A person who doesn't like muffins can't be human," he said, peeling off the plastic and taking a large bite. "Blueberry," he said with his mouth already full before he took another bite. "It's quite good." Just as he said that his eyes closed and his head collided against the window with a clonk.

"Norman," I said a bit panicked. He didn't answer. I reached over and shook his shoulder. He still didn't respond.

Just then a knock on my window made me jump. I turned in my seat to see a beautiful young woman with brown straightened hair and bright green eyes. "Do you need any help?"

I rolled down the window. "I'm sorry?"

The woman smiled. "I live just down the street. I was on a late-night walk and saw your vehicle as I walked past. I thought maybe something was wrong." Her eyes then traveled over to Norman who was still out cold. "Is he okay?"

I didn't know why, but this woman gave off a frightening vibe even though she was being friendly. But maybe that was just me being paranoid and on edge from a bit ago.

"Mister, are you okay?"

I blinked out of my stupor. "Uh, yeah," I said. "And my friend just had a terrible breakup and asked me to find him since he didn't have money for a cab."

"That was mighty kind of you," she said. "You must be a good friend to help him out."

"Well, I couldn't let him be alone."

The woman smiled. "You have a good heart. I'll let you get him home now," she said.

I backed up when she moved back and then drove away.

***

The second I got home and tried to sneak in through the front door, carrying Norman on my back, who was out like a light and snoring, the lights came on and Grandma was sitting in the rocking chair.

I swallowed thickly. "Grandma, what are you doing up late?"

"Funny," she said. "I was just about to ask you that, sweetheart. Who is that?"

I wanted to lie, but instead, I told the truth. "This is Norman. He is a friend. He, uh, ate something that didn't agree with him and I decided to bring him inside."

"Lying isn't good, sweetheart."

"I'm not lying. I just… Okay, I had to check out something with him. He couldn't do it alone. He did eat something and the next thing I know he's passed out. I could have driven him home, but I didn't know where he lived."

Grandma leaned forward. "This isn't going to get you into trouble, is it?"

I shrugged. "I hope not, Grandma. But it might. I keep ignoring things, but maybe I need to just embrace them. I can't keep hiding."

She got out of her chair and came over to me. She placed a hand on my shoulder and smiled. "You are so much like your father. My son, too, couldn't let things go. He would be so proud of you. Let's get your friend comfortable. And then in the morning, we are all going to have a serious, and I do mean serious, talk."

I nodded.

Grandma then checked up on Norman. She first checked his forehead and then checked his pupils. I knew she used to be a nurse years ago, but had long since retired. I watched as she hummed. "Interesting," she said. "Dear, did your friend happen to take any sleeping pills?"

"No, I don't think so," I said. "He just ate a muffin when he passed out."

"May I see this muffin?" she asked.

I handed her the muffin from my bag that I discarded on the armchair.

"Thanks." While she went to the kitchen, I got Norman settled on the couch. I found a blanket in the closet downstairs and draped it over him. Norman snored like a bear as he sprawled out on his stomach. He was seriously knocked out and from a muffin. Did it really have sleeping pills like my grandma said in it?

In the morning, after deliberately delaying the inevitable talk by taking a fifteen-minute shower, I slowly got ready to face the inevitable. Once I walked downstairs and stepped into the kitchen where Norman was cradling a cup of what smelled like chamomile tea while my grandma sat there with sternness on her face. There was nothing in her emotions that I could detect and that worried me even more.

Her eyes glared at me. "Weston, dear, there you are."

As I sat down, none of us spoke a word and the intense awkwardness was causing me to shift in my seat until I couldn't take it anymore.

"Grandma, you said we needed to talk. Can you do it now? This atmosphere is making me uneasy."

Norman glanced between us. "You know what; I think I am going to leave. This seems like a family matter. I want to thank you, Ms. Ruth, for letting me stay. It meant a lot. I'm much better."

"But, Norman, what about…"

"Don't worry. Thanks for the help last night, Weston." He then stood up and ran out the front door before we could stop him.

"I think you scared my new friend away, Grandma."

She glared at me sternly. "I did no such thing. I will say you are lucky to have brought your friend here. What I found in that muffin was no sleeping pill. It was belladonna."

"What's belladonna?"

"A very powerful plant from the nightshade family," she explained. "Usually, in small doses, it is harmless and only causes sleep. However, it's more potent and dangerous in large doses."

"Meaning…"

"Meaning if your friend had eaten anymore, he might not have woken up ever again."

"He would be…dead?"

She nodded. "If he had eaten another bite or two, he might have just wound up in a coma. But if he had eaten the whole thing, well, he would be dead."

I rubbed my hands. "I see."

"Why don't you tell me about what happened and where you went last night?"

I told her everything. I told her about the ghosts, about Norman wanting to ghost hunt, about nearly getting killed…

When I was done, I nervously stared at her.

She sighed. "I'm going to help you understand something."

"Understand what?" Something about this upcoming conversation was making me feel extremely uneasy.

Instead of answering, she signed the cross and then clasping her and praying. "Lord, please, give my grandson strength," she said before sashaying over to the fridge and then placed a stool on. Standing on it, she grabbed an old brown box. I had noticed the box many times since moving in but never questioned the contents inside. I figured it was best to not ask. After she stepped down and came over, she placed the box on the tabletop and then opened the lid.

There was a large brown jacket.

"What is this, Grandma?"

"Touch it."

"Okay," I said, confused. Why was she showing me this and why did she want me to do this?

Hesitantly, I reached in. The second my fingertips touched the rough fabric, emotions of protectiveness, fright, and then terror zapped through me before pain exploded in my head before a vision flashed in my eyes.

I found myself on the ground, a dark figure stood over me. I couldn't see who it was as the person was shrouded in the darkness of the room. But I could feel soft hands on my throat; breathing near my face. I was doing this to save my son.

Just then, something stabbed into my neck and I felt incredibly sluggish and tired. However, before my eyes closed, I felt my mouth being open before feeling my life being sucked out...

As fast as I could, I jerked my hand back and the vision broke instantly. I found myself on my knees; hand on my chest as I coughed. It was like I had been the one who was dying. I could still taste something weird in the back of my throat as tears fell.

"Dad," I managed to croak out before sobbing. "I saw Dad."

Grandma slid a cup of tea over to me. "I want you to sip on that. It will help bring your strength back."

I shakily got to my feet and sat down on the stool before I took the drink. I wanted to gulp it down but Grandma told me to sip on it and I trusted her. I didn't want to anger her right now anyway.

After taking a sip, I said, "I saw Dad's death. He was being pinned down by someone, I couldn't see who. I still feel Dad's terror and can still taste something weird on my breath."

Grandma's eyebrows furrowed before she went over to the cabinet. She opened it and pulled out a small jar. She come over and shook a tiny bit of it in my tea. "Taste that."

"What is it?"

"Taste it first."

I did as she said. I picked up my tea and took a small taste before coughing.

"Is that what you taste?"

"Yeah," I said, feeling a little woozy all of a sudden.

Grandma steadied me by grabbing my arm. "Easy, dear," she said. "It will fade in a second. I didn't give you a lot. Just enough to make you a little dizzy."

"What was that?"

"That, my grandson, was belladonna."

"Like the stuff that was…"

"In the muffin," she said, finishing my thought before she put the lid back on the box. "I was hoping I was wrong. I just needed confirmation about what happened to my son."

My eyes widened in surprise before my brows furrowed. "Is that why you don't want me involved? The same thing that…killed Dad, and what is happening now, it's all connected?"

"Yes, honey," she said. "You see, it all started on your fourth birthday. We all got along a bit better, but Iris still didn't like me all that much. She was only nice because she married my son and because you seemed to adore me to pieces."

I smiled at that.

"Your father came to me the day before because you told him that your imaginary friend was trying to hurt you."

"I had an imaginary friend?"

"Yes, imaginary friends are usually ghosts," she explained. "Young children are susceptible to seeing them. It's not all that uncommon. However, your imaginary friend wasn't always nice to you. Sometimes we caught you talking to yourself and laughing, but sometimes you'd have bruises as well. Your dad was worried. Iris was also worried that instead of letting me help, she went to a child psychologist."

"I don't remember any of that."

"I imagine not. You were only four when it happened."

"What happened?"

"It all started at the lake. We fed the fish and then skipped rocks. But then you wandered off on your own. We didn't notice it at first until we heard you screaming. You had fallen into the deep side of the water. You hadn't even learned how to swim just yet. Your father dove in after you. You weren't breathing for a good seven minutes before your father resuscitated you. After that, we went our separate ways…"

"But…"

"I'm getting there," she said. "That night, your father called me, telling me that he had a talk with you. Apparently, your imaginary friend pushed you into the lake. Of course, this after he found out the truth about what your mother did. Iris had CPS called on him about child abuse. Your father never hurt you.

She didn't want to believe that your imaginary friend hurt you. And you, being as you were just coming into your empath powers, sensed their anger and took off. We searched for you. Iris and I managed to find you by the lake. You were unconscious, but we couldn't find your father anywhere. He was missing for several days before we got a call from the police, saying they found his body."

"So, it was my fault that Dad died."

She gripped my arms. "Never think that, Weston."

"But if I hadn't run away then he'd still be here," I said, tears falling once again.

"Hey, your father saved your life. He would give up everything in the whole world to protect and save you. I should know. I would have done the same thing."

"What happened after that?"

"After that, we had the funeral. However, as soon as you crossed into the cemetery, you went hysterical. You were shouting at thin air, saying that people were touching you, and that you could see their deaths. You were so out of control that your telekinesis was acting up causing tree limbs to crack and fall and even caused people who were trying to help you to fly away from you. No one was hurt, but your mother got angry. And because of your empathy, you sensed hers and everyone's fear and passed out. Iris was so angry and annoyed that she took you away. I tried to reassure her and tell her that what you had was a gift, a hard gift, an unpredictable gift, but a gift nonetheless."

"Is that why Mom hates me because Dad died on the night of my fourth birthday?"

Grandma took my hand and held it. "Sweetheart, your mother doesn't hate you."

"I wish I could believe that," I said, pulling out of her grasp. "She does, though," I said. "I know she does. I felt every time she talked to you on the phone or brought you up."

"I think she blames me for not saving your father. But it's not like I can locate anyone. I'm not a magician. However, Iris would like to believe that. In fact, when you started causing thing to break in your room, saying that you could feel everyone's emotions so clearly, and mention ghosts talking to you and wanting your help, that your mother demanded I find a way to get rid of it. She didn't understand that it's a part of you. I can't take that away."

I stared at her in shock. "So, is that when I stopped being able to see you?"

She ran a hand through my hair. "Iris got a restraining order against me. She said that I was the reason behind your delusional behavior, and as a result, I wasn't allowed to be near you."

"Mom told me you lived in Colorado."

"I did, but only for a year or two. After that, I came back home. Though, I avoided being around, I did call occasionally to check up on you both."

"Why are you telling me this now, Grandma?"

"Because I feel you will need this information if you keep getting wound up in dangerous situations, situations that I can't help you with. Ghosts are going to be coming to you for help, you know? Iris is lucky

I managed to put salt packets around your apartment to keep them at bay."

"Why salt?"

"Salt is pure and keeps spirits at bay and even hurts them," she said as she reached over and placed a small vial in my hand. "Use this in times of need."

"This is all way too much." Without much else to say, I stormed out of the kitchen and ran to my Jeep. As soon as I got inside, I placed my hands on the steering wheel. My head was pounding so much that I was a bit nervous to drive. But I needed to get away before my grandma could come and get me.

So, I put the Jeep in drive and skidded out of the driveway.

20

I headed towards town. I should have headed to work, but I was too caught up in my thoughts and needed some time to calm down. So, after parking, decided to take a short walk. As I started walking down the sidewalk to clear my head, a chill radiated down my spine as the ghost of a woman started towards me.

Not wanting to draw attention, I turned and nearly tripped. Out of instinct, I grabbed a hold of someone's arm. A deep sense of frustration anger and concern all flowed into me.

"Weston, hey, you okay?" That was Carter's voice.

I pulled my hand away. The pounding in my head was worse than ever. I placed my hands on my temples, but it didn't alleviate the pain. It was stupid to think it would.

"Weston, cousin, talk to me."

Once the buzzing in my head quieted, I lifted my head to stare into my cousin's brown eyes. "I'm...better."

"What happened?"

"It's a long story."

"Come on," he said. "You can tell me over a cup of coffee or in your case a cup of tea. You obviously need a pick me up."

We walked into the coffee shop. To be honest, I wanted to be outside more. Once inside, the place felt heavier than normal which was odd considering it wasn't even crowded.

"Let's just get our drinks to go," I suggested.

"Is your empathy acting up again?"

"You could say that," I muttered as I kept my hands in my jacket pockets. Ever since my grandma and I talked and since I touched Carter, I now wanted to avoid touching others as my head felt like it was going to explode. At least I didn't get visions from the living only from objects that were on the dead when they died or from the dead themselves or the place where they died and only when touch was involved.

"You can go outside and wait for me. I don't want you overwhelmed," he said.

"Thanks." I pulled out some dollar bills and handed them to him. "Here. Buy me a hazelnut coffee."

"I thought you couldn't drink coffee?"

"Must have been mistaken," I said, shrugging. "Actually, that was a lie Mom told me."

"Not surprising," he said.

I left the building only to get stopped by a girl, who strolled up to me. This wasn't someone I had met. She had long strawberry blonde hair braided like pigtails and blue ribbons at the ends. She was also dressed in a black skirt with a red blouse and silver high heels. I thought maybe I had recognized her.

The closer she drew closer, the more I wanted to get away. There was darkness in her emotions.

The second she was right in my face, I found myself staring into her bright greenish-blue eyes. "Stay the hell away from Hayden."

So that was why she seemed familiar. This was the girl I had seen with Hayden, whom he kissed.

Wait.

What right did she have to come strolling up to me when I hadn't seen him in days? I mean, I did miss him and wondered where he was considering our shared kiss...

I shook my head and then glared at her. "I haven't been near him. He's been spending all his time with you."

She smiled. "That's right. He is. But he hasn't been lately. He's told me all about you. Like how you are his best friend and would do anything. Why can't you just leave him alone?"

"I'm sorry, but I don't know who you are. I told you I haven't been with him. If anything, he has been leaving me alone."

Just then, the door behind me opened and Carter came out. The second his eyes landed on the girl, his emotions strangely flared to anger. "What are you doing here, Angela? I thought you had morning classes."

Angela smirked. "I did. But they got canceled. The professor got sick."

So this was the infamous Angela. I had never met her face-to-face before. She was more intimating than what Carter explained.

"So, you just decided to come and talk to my cousin?" he asked.

"Yes, exactly," she said with an innocent smile that made me want to roll my eyes. It was then I got a hint of flirtation in her emotions. "I can't believe you never introduced us. Your cousin is a real cutie."

This was making me ill.

Her eyes then stared fondly at the coffee cups in his hands and she grabbed one. "Oh, did you get this for me? You shouldn't have."

"That's not…"

"I see!" she squealed. "You bought this as a way to apologize, right?"

"Apologize? For what?" he asked.

"For our recent argument, silly," she said. "I know I made you mad, but you made me upset too. So, I take it you thought about it and this is your way of apologizing." She then took a sip of the coffee and spat it out nearly on me. Luckily, I had taken a step back.

"Uh, this is hazelnut," she said, disgusted. "I hate hazelnut." She then shoved the cup into my hand. When she did, her fingers grazed mine.

Just then, strong emotions invaded me. I could feel satisfaction, an odd swirling darkness, suspicion, and even glee.

Before I could wonder, the connection was lost the second as her hand left mine. Unintentionally, I let go of the cup. It hit the ground and hot contents pilled over her open-toed shoes.

"You bastard!" she scorned, clenching her fist. "What is your problem?"

Carter protectively stood in front of me when she tried to advance. "Stay away from my cousin. He has nothing to do with anything. You are the one who stole his coffee. You owe him an apology."

"Hell no," she huffed. "I'm going to go home to soak my feet in cold water." She turned and walked away.

"Well, that was intense."

"You have no idea," said Carter. He then started apologizing for what happened, but it wasn't his fault. I never met Angela. Now that I had, I wish I didn't. I knew my cousin mentioned her attitude, but I didn't realize how much she reminded me of Zelda.

Afterward our brief conversation, I headed to work even though I was late again. I walked inside with anticipation. I expected Melinda to start yelling, but instead, I found her talking to the receptionist from the apartment building I used to live in.

Melinda's eyes immediately locked onto mine. "Ah, there he is, Rosemary."

Ah, so, her name was Rosemary. I could not believe I never knew that.

Jo then turned to me and smiled. Her emotions were as bright and cheerful as ever as she stepped forward. "Thank goodness. I've been searching everywhere for you."

"Oh, sorry about that," I said. "I was... helping a friend. How did you know to come here and find me?"

"That's quite all right. Your mom spoke about your job once."

"She did? I had no idea."

"That's okay. I'm sorry for stopping by like this in the first place. I just needed you to come to the apartment building later. The person living in your old apartment found a box with your belongings. I know this is sudden, but if you can come by after work and pick up the box, it will be much appreciated."

"I can do that. It's not like I have anything to do after work."

Rosemary smiled. "Great. See you later then." She then left.

Melinda returned the smile. "So..."

"Don't, Melinda," I said.

"Ah, you're mad at me, aren't you?" she asked.

"As a matter of fact, I am," I said. "You sent Norman and me on a wild goose chase, didn't you?"

Melinda smirked. "Not a complete wild goose chase," she said. "I bet you got a clue or something."

"Yeah, sure," I said.

"Come on, Weston, what's wrong?"

Anger swelled inside me as I clenched the counter. "We could have been killed, Melinda!" I yelled. "You know more than you are letting on. The same way Mr. Newman isn't telling everything. Something is going on and you lead me right into a dangerous situation. Not only me, but Norman, too. Now, you might not have known that, but it's true."

Just as I let out my anger, a jar behind me exploded.

21

Work was awkward at best. Melinda and I avoided each other after I cleaned up the glass from my telekinesis disaster. This wasn't our first argument, but it was the first time that I ever caused something to explode in her store, and I felt horrible for it. I figured she'd scream at me or fire me, but instead she just sashayed off to who knows where.

As soon as it was closing time and I was about to head out for the day, Melinda grabbed my arm.

"Wait," she said.

I turned to her confused.

"I wanted to apologize. I didn't know that place was dangerous and I didn't know that you and Norman nearly got hurt. I swear."

"It was never gossip you overheard, was it?"

"No," she said. "But I would never send you or Norman into anywhere dangerous."

"I believe you, Melinda," I said. "And I'm sorry, too, for the jar."

"That," she said, waving her hand. "Don't worry. Accidents happen. Now, you best get going."

Before I turned and left, I looked at her. "Do you own a cat?"

"A cat?"

"A black cat."

Melinda shook her head. "Nope. I don't own one. But there is one that appears every now and then. I fed it once and gave it the name."

"Was it Mel?"

"How did you know that?"

"Just a hunch. By the way, that isn't a very kitty name."

Melinda stuck her tongue out at me. "Sue me then at giving cats terrible names. I'm not a cat kind of woman. I was just helping out the poor thing. I thought naming her after me was helpful. Though, I guess I could have chosen a much better name."

I laughed and then headed out, driving to the apartment building. When I got there, a sense of nostalgia washed over me. I did miss this place a bit. I think I even missed my mom. I wish she would call or something that way I knew she was okay. But it was hopeless. I was, after all, a disappointment. As I walked in, a black-and-white photo from the seventies caught my attention. I was shocked to see that it was the same people I had seen on the elevator on my birthday. The young man with the little girl and the woman, and like I predicted there was no elderly woman. Sometimes it was hard to tell the dead from the living.

"Ah, I see you're fascinated with that photo," a voice said. It looked like the elderly woman from the elevator.

I turned my attention to her. Surprised, I couldn't help but stare. "It's you... You gave me that muffin?"

The woman blinked. There was an air of confusion around her as she leaned on her cane. "I'm sorry, dear, but I have never met you a day in my life."

"But..." I then shook my head, chuckling nervously. "I'm sorry. This is going to sound crazy, but you just look like someone I saw before."

The woman smiled. "No problem."

I then turned back to the photo. "Who exactly are they?"

The elderly woman shakily pointed to the guy. "Well, that man used to be a big-time businessman." She then pointed to the little girl. "And that little four-year-old cutie pie is his beautiful daughter." And finally she pointed to the woman who had her arms crossed. "And that woman, well, she was super popular. You might not know this, but she was a big-time movie star."

"I see."

"Weston?" a voice called from behind me.

I turned to find Rosemary holding a box. "Sorry. How long have you been there?"

"Just got here," she replied. "Who were you chatting with?"

My eyes widened before I turned my attention to the elderly woman, who waved at me before vanishing.

I blinked. "Uh," I stammered before running the back of my neck nervously. "You know, just myself. Is that mine?"

Rosemary giggled. "Another person who talks to themselves," she said. "Welcome to the club. I'm the same way." She then handed me the box. "And yes. You know, Weston, we miss you around here. You always made it lively."

"I... I don't know about that. But I do kind of miss it a little. But it is what it is."

"True. I do hope you decide to drop by from time to time."

"I'll try." After walking back out to my Jeep, I placed the box in the passenger after I got in on the driver's side. Instead of going through the box, I leaned back in my seat and closed my eyes. I couldn't stop my mind from returning to that elderly woman. I could have sworn she was the same one who gave me that muffin... But that couldn't be because she was a spirt. The event couldn't have been a hallucination, could it? I mean, Norman did find the muffin in my bag, so it had to be real. So, then, was it just that the woman looked like her? Did she have a twin?

Not wanting to think about it anymore, I decided to check out what was inside the box. Pulling back the cardboard tabs, I peered in. Inside there was one of my mom's favorite Dean Koontz novels.

Ignoring that, I found a strange ring. It was silver and black and the inside was electric blue. It couldn't be my mom's. She rarely wore any rings. Was it Dad's?

There was also a weird sterling silver pocket watch with a yin-yang on the front. I also found a pouch. But I didn't know what was in it. I didn't open it. I then moved stuff around and found a strange wooden box with a pentagram on the front of it. What's inside?

Before I could do anything, my phone started vibrating in my pocket.

I took it out and slide the green call button, and then answered, "Hello?"

"Where are you?" demanded Norman.

Not wanting to damage my eardrums, I moved the phone away a little. "What do you mean?"

"You were supposed to be at the museum," he said. "Don't you remember?"

Oh, shoot. I had forgotten about that.

"Weston?"

"Uh, yeah, I'm on my way now," I said. "Be there in a couple of minutes."

I made it to the museum within ten minutes. I hopped out after turning off my Jeep and then ran inside.

"There you are," said Norman, holding up a folder. "We've been waiting for you. What were you doing?"

I rubbed the back of my neck. "Uh, well, I kind of forgot. Things haven't been going great today. But it's not important. Where is Mr. Newman?"

"He got a call from his office. Anyway, come check this out."

"What it is?" I asked, walking over to the table where a lot of Manila folders were spread out.

Norman smiled. "Well, I just started on the information in this folder."

"What's in it?"

"Police files," he stated. "Yes, before you ask, I stole my dad's files and copied them for myself. He never suspects anything because I do it late at night. I keep the copied files for myself. Anyway, check it out and see if anything stands out."

I leaned over and glanced over the files. Not much stood out except for the fact that all of them were males. They all had different names, different races, different ethnicities, different interest, different jobs, etc. They didn't seem to have any connection until I focused on the names again.

"This is weird," I said.

Norman's emotions flared with a strange sense of pride. Before I could question him, Mr. Newman was walking over to us. He was dressed in a suit and had on a jacket. His silver blue eyes locked onto me.

"Ah, Weston, we were wondering when you would show up."

"Yeah, sorry," I said. There was something in Mr. Newman's emotions that had me worried. "Is there something wrong?"

"I just received a call. A colleague of mine just passed away. So, I sadly can't stay and chat."

"Who was it?" asked Norman, perking his head up.

"Henry Hunter," he said before he started out the door.

The amusement from Norman made me stare at him. He stood there with his arms crossed and a giant grin on his face. "You noticed a pattern, too, haven't you?"

"Whoever it is behind everything is going after males, possibly with names that rhyme, and seem to have the same first and last initials."

"Correct. And I suggest we follow after Curator Newman. He might be the only person who can answer important questions."

"Did you just figure that out?"

Norman glared at me. "Hey, I hit my head and then got knocked out by belladonna in a muffin. Yes, I know about it. Your grandmother told me. There is no telling what damage that did to me. I was pretty much out of it."

"You said a chair hit you?"

Norman shrugged. "When you asked me to find the toy soldier, a stupid chair flew across the room and hit me upside the head pretty hard because I could see stars. You still have a lot of explaining to do. Who the hell was that Maxwell kid you were talking about? I was out of it for a lot of what happened. Also, was there a talking cat, by chance?"

"Uh, kind of," I said, rubbing the back of my head. "I promise you will get the truth once we figure things out. You have my word," I said as we walked out of the museum.

Norman opened the passenger door. "What do you say we follow him?"

"No way," I said. "He will know for sure."

"Come on. I doubt he will suspect anything."

"And what if he does? Besides, didn't you bike here?"

"I grabbed a cab. My bike is still at the mechanic shop and I can't get my motorcycle fixed until Mikey orders a part, but he is severely out of commission."

"What do you mean "out of commission"?"

"Oh, yeah, I didn't tell you. His wife took him to the hospital. Your hunch was spot on."

"He's not…"

"No, he's not dead," Norman said. "Luckily, he is very much alive and kicking. But his wife told me that he is in the hospital and that the doctors are doing several tests. She also promised that she'd keep me updated on his condition when she can."

A terrible sadness overcame me. I assumed it was from Norman as I had hardly known Mikey. The man was incredibly nice when I met him and I knew I didn't want anything to happen to the man.

Norman eyed the box still in the seat. "What do you want me to do with this box?"

"Put it in the back seat." I climbed into the driver's side as Norman placed the box in the back seat.

As soon as I started following behind Mr. Newman's blue Sudan, Norman started droning on about the strange bizarre deaths. And I was only paying half attention as I drove.

"What's in that box anyway?" asked Norman as he turned to the box in the backseat.

"I don't know exactly. Rosemary, or rather, Jo, the receptionist at the apartment I used to live at with my mom, said the people who moved into our old apartment found the box. She asked me to pick it up which I did. I didn't have time to go through it before you called me."

"Oh, so, that is why you didn't show up?"

"Well, partially. I honestly did forget about it. My head hasn't been too focused today."

"Oh. Was it because of your grandmother? Is she mad at you?"

"Not exactly," I said, sighing. "I don't want to talk about it right now if that's okay."

"Of course, Wes," he said with a smile before he reached into the back and grabbed the box. "What's in here anyway?"

"Don't go through it. I haven't had the chance to do it."

"But there might be something interesting in here," he said as he picked up the ring. "This seems interesting."

As soon as we were at a stop sign, I reached over. "Come on, Norman. Hand it over." As soon as I touched the ring and Norman's hand, two things happened instantaneously. The first was I became bombarded with all sorts of feelings from extreme happiness that almost made me tear up to peaceful emotions that were all too quickly replaced with frustration, giddiness, and concern

The second thing that happened was the vision of my dad. I was back in that dark room struggling against that dark figure again. I could feel his terror all over again.

I yanked back and my head collided into the window. "Holy starlight," I muttered as I rubbed the back of my head. I already had a headache rearing its ugly head and now I clonked my head into the window. Not only that, but my energy felt drained.

"Weston!" a voice said and panic was seeping into my head.

I placed a hand to my head before I felt something made of paper pressed into my hand. I fought the urge to scream out at whatever or whoever not to touch me, but soon the voice returned. As the confusion faded, I realized it was only Norman.

"Eat that, Weston."

I eyeballed what was in my hand. It was a chocolate bar that was half-opened. I took a bite out of the bar, tasting milk and nuts.

I closed my eyes as the pounding in my head slowly faded and rested my aching head on the steering wheel.

"What was that?"

"What?" I asked groggily.

"That," he said. "You zoned out on me for a good five minutes and then acted like you were having some kind of fit. I know the symptoms of low blood sugar. And I don't think that was it. What happened?"

"I can't tell." Just then, I realized what we were doing. It was then that I also realized that we were at. "Where is Mr. Newman? Did we lose him?"

"I don't know," he said as he got out of the vehicle. "I saw him come this way. After that, I lost track because you nearly fainted at the wheel. If you were unwell you could have told me."

Even with him out of the Jeep, I could feel his irritation behind the thick layer of calmness he was trying to keep contained.

I got out and leaned on the side of my vehicle. "I'm sorry, Norman." What else could I say? I was such an idiot.

"Tell me what happened then," he demanded.

I was left staring at him. I couldn't tell him what was going on, could I?

Just before I could open my mouth and say something, a gentle yet freezing breath breezed across my neck and caused me to shiver.

"Weston," a voice whispered in my ear.

I turned around to see an older gentleman in a gray and blue plaid sweater vest and jeans with brown dress shoes. His eyes were hazel and his short hair was curly with gray streaks.

"Who are you?"

The man didn't respond with words. Instead, he grabbed my hand and a vision invaded me.

I found myself behind the wheel of a vehicle as I pulled out my phone, punching in a number, hoping that he'd pick up before I started coughing, dropping the phone, and began clawing at my throat. I was struggling to breathe before my car swerved and crashed into a tree...

The vision ended and I coughed. Emotions of anxiousness and terror raged through me as I touched my throat before I hacked one last time. "Henry," I said, struggling to catch my breath. "You're Henry Hunter, aren't you?"

"You must put a stop to her."

"Who is she?" I asked hoarsely. This was Henry's ghost, and he was the second one to ask me to stop some woman. But without any specific information, I couldn't stop anyone.

The man flickered a few times before he vanished.

Just when I thought it was over, several other ghosts appeared before me in a flicker and surrounded me. I saw Barry and Jerry in the crowd, but some of them I didn't recognize.

As if my head wasn't already pounding insanely, the emotions these ghosts were feeling were intense and I had no mental block to block them out.

Putting my hands on my head, I collapsed to my knees on the asphalt.

"Go away," I whispered. "Don't touch me."

A familiar voice called out to me as my vision darkened.

"Hayden," I called out just as blackness took over my sight, and succumbed to it.

22

I was dreaming. I knew because I was back in the meadow, lying on the blanket with Hayden beside me and we were holding hands as we watched the stars together.

He then turned towards me and caressed my cheek. "You must wake up, Weston. You still have work to do," he whispered.

And then he was gone as soon as my eyelids fluttered open. My vision was blurry, but as some awareness slowly began to seep in, I noticed that the bed under me felt off and the room around me seemed different even if I couldn't see properly.

I leaned over to get my glasses only for my hand to slide through the air and cause me to tumble out of bed. Instead of hitting a hardwood floor, I landed on a flurry carpet. What was going on?

Something told me I wasn't at home. I was somewhere else. But where was I?

I tried to wrap my head around what happened. I remembered being with Norman and following Mr. Newman and then something to do with ghosts.

Suddenly, I heard loud voices. It sounded like yelling. I got up and used the wall since without my glasses I was nearly blind. Feeling a cold knob, I leaned what I assumed was the bedroom door.

I didn't mean to eavesdrop on a conversation. But I was confused. And those voices...they were Norman and his father's. Did that mean I was at Norman's place?

"Why did you bring him here?"

"I didn't have a choice. He collapsed on the road."

"Then you should have taken him to the hospital."

"I couldn't do that."

"Why not, Norman?" his father asked.

"Because his mother disowned him," Norman said with defiance in his tone. "Everyone in town knows it. Also, what if he has no insurance? He can barely afford the bills."

"So what?" his father asked. "He's a fully functioning adult just like you. It isn't your responsibility to look after him. You know he's a prime suspect in these strange suicide cases."

"How so?" asked Norman. "If it truly is suicides like you say, then, why do you suspect Weston in all of this? Are you going to say that he was there and making them hurt themselves?"

"Norman, I don't have time to get into the details. But know this. Everywhere that boy goes trouble follows him."

"You are the only one to believe that."

Sudden footsteps started approaching.

I quickly moved back to the bed, hitting my knee on something sharp as I did.

The door opened. "You're awake."

I could see Norman's blurry outline. "Do you know where my glasses are?"

"Yeah," he said. I watched his blurry outline move before I heard what sounded like a drawer being slid open and then his blurred figure walked towards me. "Here you go." He placed them in my hand. "When you passed out, I took them off you and placed them in a safe place."

"Thanks." I put them on. When the blurriness cleared, I examined his room. There were posters all over the walls. Most of them were alien-related. He had a UFO one. There was one with a flying saucer over the pyramid. The ones that weren't related to aliens were punk rock bands. I knew Norman was a little weird, but that was completely strange. He also had a desk with a laptop on it with a black piece of tape over the camera and folders stacked off to the side.

Norman sat on the bed. "How are you doing?"

"I'm fine."

"Uh-huh," he said. "And I am the gingerbread man which means I don't believe you."

"I know what that means, Norman. I do know sarcasm when I hear it. I am fine."

"Sure. You were the one who passed out in the middle of the road after talking to yourself or rather talking to a ghost. Why didn't you tell me?"

"I'm sorry," I said. "I'm not used to talking about these things. Ghosts are complicated. I was told to ignore them my whole life."

"You could have told me. I wouldn't have treated you any differently."

"I know," I said, guilty.

"So, have you always been able to see ghosts? What do ghosts even look like? Do you feel them before they show up?"

I snickered at his questions. "According to my grandma, I had an imaginary friend. She said that imagery friends are ghosts. Usually, they are harmless. And as kids get older they outgrow it. However, in my case, because I could see them and then had a near-death experience, it woke it up inside me."

Norman hummed. "How did you nearly die?"

"I nearly drowned when I was four. According to my grandma, I was dead for proximately three minutes. It was a little while after that event that I began to see ghosts permanently and even saw how they died."

"That's terrible for a four year old."

"Yeah, as for you other questions: ghosts look like you and I. They don't seem different. They sometimes can be a little transparent, but not by much. I sometimes wouldn't even know if they were dead or not if not for small things. When I was little I got ghosts and real people mixed up. And while my empathy does work on the dead and living, but it doesn't' help me differentiate. Since I got older, I can see and feel subtle differences. Did you feel anything when you pass through them?

"I passed through them?"

"Twice," I said. "Once on the road and once back at the mansion."

"Huh," said Norman with interest in his tone. "I didn't feel anything. Then again, I wasn't paying attention to my surroundings at the time. I will have to take note of it more often."

"You do that."

There was momentary silence before Norman spoke up again. "Was Henry's spirit the reason you passed out?"

I looked at him confused.

"I heard you say Henry's name."

"Oh," I said. "No, he wasn't the problem. It was the multiple that showed up."

"I see, so what did Henry want."

"He didn't say much."

"What did he say?"

"He wants me to stop her."

"Stop who exactly?" he asked.

"I wish I knew. Henry didn't stick around long enough to tell me anything more before the other ghosts showed."

"I see," he said. "Do you know who the other ghosts were?"

I shook my head. "I don't get out much. So, I don't socialize like I should."

Norman chuckled. "Well, I can't blame you there. We do live in a town with a population of 3,503. I don't know if I would want to socialize with that many people either."

"So, the multiple ghosts caused you to pass out like that?" he asked. "I mean, were they in your

Jeep? You were on the verge of collapsing long before that."

"It's complicated."

"I think I at least earn an explanation for you almost passing out at the wheel."

"You're right." I leaned back on the bed. "Aside from seeing the dead, I also see how they died. It's usually through contact with a ghost or something the ghost had on them when they died. I touched the ring you were holding and saw how my dad died again."

"Again?" he asked. "You mean you experienced it once before?"

"Yeah," I said, rubbing my arm. "First time was from my dad's jacket. I didn't know he also had on his ring. Then again, I wasn't paying much attention. The visions are so fast that I don't always process everything I see."

"So, you can see the same death multiple times?"

"It happened a lot when I was a kid. The same ghost would touch me once or twice and I would see it over and over. But that's not everything. My empathy is another part. Contact makes it worse. Whether from people or ghosts, I can feel their emotions."

"Has it always been like that?"

"Sometimes," I said. "There were times as a kid where I'd be overwhelmed which would cause my mom to shelter me away from others and school and try and tell me not to be delusional. Just recently, it feels stronger. I'm not sure why."

"That's interesting. Is that what happened when we were tailing after Curator Newman?"

"I guess I overloaded because I was touching you and the ring you were holding at the same time."

"That's never happened before?"

"Not like that. Sure, someone may touch me when I am in a vision. But I never touched something of the dead and a living person at the same time. It was like an explosion went off in me."

"What did you sense from me?"

"It's all mixed together now. But I briefly felt your giddiness and your concern before it was drowned out by my dad's terror."

"What happened to him?"

"Someone killed him in a dark room. I don't exactly know how. Usually, death visions are like a ghost's last memory."

It was then that Norman and I sat in silence for a while before Norman spoke up again.

"Can I ask you a question?"

"Sure."

"Who is Hayden?"

"Where did you hear that name?"

"From you," he said. "Right before you fainted like a total girl, you said Hayden. Is he your boyfriend?"

"I wish," I mumbled as I fell back on Norman's bed. "But sadly he's not. He is engaged to a woman. We aren't allowed to be with each other."

"Why? You like him, right?"

"Of course I do. I always have. I had thought he liked me back considering..."

"Considering what?"

"Promise you won't laugh or be weirded out?"

"You two didn't...do the deed, did you?"

230

I scrunched my nose in disgust. "No. We simply kissed. Why would you even think that?"

Norman rubbed the back of his neck. "Sorry. I didn't mean to ask that. I just read some things online."

"Not all of us are like that. I'm not. The internet is a weird place and you can't believe half of it."

"I see." He then smiled. "So, you guys kissed. Was it your first?

"My first true kiss, yes."

"True kiss?" he asked.

"Well, I never told anyone, but Zelda Goodman kissed me when we were twelve. I pushed her away."

"Is that when she started bullying you?"

"Almost," I said. "It was a year later when she started the bullying nonsense."

Norman hummed but didn't say anything else about instead he asked, "So, how do you know Hayden doesn't like you back?"

I thought back to our kiss. "I honestly don't know. I do know that his mom doesn't approve."

"How do you know?"

"Because she caught us," I said, sighing.

"In the middle of the kissing action?" he asked.

"What?" I asked, horrified. "No. No. No."

Norman threw his hands up. "Sorry. I just had to ask."

I rolled my eyes. "She caught us when Hayden and I were in this meadow. We were just chatting and talking about the stars and then…then she just showed up and took him away."

"That sucks."

23

After spending time with Norman, I headed to work. As usual, Melinda wasn't pleased by my lateness. However, like always, she joked about docking my pay. Jasper, still being new, hadn't been around the shop too much due to Melinda sending him on errands. That kind of surprised me. Melinda never allowed me to run errands. Was there a reason for that?

While on my break, I pulled the file that Norman loaned me out of my messenger bag and placed it on the counter. Studying it didn't help anything. The men were all different. Their ages were different, too. Their race was also different. They all had different jobs. So, then, what was it this woman wanted with them?

"What are you gazing at so intently?" asked Melinda.

"Just some research," I said.

"Does it have to do with the mysterious deaths?"

"Should have known you would guess that," I said, annoyed. "I know I shouldn't be involved in this, but there is something off about this whole mess. I know I am missing something. My gut tells me that. And whoever the woman is behind all of this seems to be going after men only."

Melinda jumped up and sat on the counter beside me. "Hmm, if you ask me, sounds like a succubus."

"What's a succubus?" I asked.

"You know, a female demon that preys on lonely men and drains them, well, sexually," she said. "It's in mythology."

"Tell me more about them?"

Melinda crossed her legs. "Well, not much to tell. A Succubus goes after men who are lonely and feeds on their live energy."

"Melinda, you are a genius!" I shouted.

"Well, that's…" she started. "Wait. Why am I genius?"

"Barry Bloomingdale. He just got divorced."

"Well, yes, but…"

"And Jerry Johnson, he just got over being dumped, right?"

"And again, yes, but…"

"And Henry Hunter, he was a widower because he lost his wife."

"Okay, but…"

"But there has to be more. Barry wasn't sad. I know. I felt his emotions every day. He was happy. And according to Norman, neither was Jerry. And I doubt Henry was either. I just didn't sense any loneliness in either of them. So…"

"Weston!" The anger in Melinda's tone startled me.

"Huh?" I asked.

"You do realize that a succubus is a myth, right?"

"And I'm apparently psychic."

"Weston, psychics aren't a myth. A succubus is. Maybe you need to dig even deeper. Maybe there is some kind of connection between each victim and nothing that is supernatural."

"You may be right. But what could it be?"

"You will have to figure that out, but…"

"You want me to be careful."

A scratching nose caught my attention.

My eyes lowered to the table.

There scribbled into the wood were words.

Rosemary… needs… your… help…

Was this a ghost? I eyed the whole place, trying to find anyone. But like always no one was present. Not even a ghost was in sight.

"Weston?"

"Do you see that?" I asked, pointing to the counter.

"Am I supposed to be seeing something? Because all I see is the same countertop that I replaced a few months back.

Okay, so, now, ghost writing was a thing.

I gathered the folder up. "I have to go."

"But your break is almost over."

"I know, but this is important," I said. "I'll make it up later. I'm sorry, but I seriously have to go."

"Fine," said Melinda, folding her arms over her chest. "But don't expect to be paid your full amount."

"That's fair." I left the building and got in my jeep and drove to Caster Valley Apartments.

As soon as I arrived, I was shocked to see flashing police cars and an ambulance. I got out and walked over to a lone elderly woman.

"It's awful," she said, tears falling down her face. "It's truly awful. That poor girl... Only twenty-five and had her whole life ahead of her." The sad emotions from her were breaking my heart to pieces.

"What happened?" I asked softly.

The woman frowned. "They said it was an allergic reaction. They said she did it deliberately. I know my granddaughter. She wouldn't do this. Someone did it to her purpose. You have to find out why, Weston."

It was the elderly woman again. "You..."

The woman vanished.

Ghosts were the same as always.

I then saw Rosemary. She was in her receptionist uniform. She had that same blue hue around her. She was waving her hand in front of people. Before too long, her eyes met mine. Confusion and surprise filled the air around me.

"Weston, you can see me?" she asked as she ran over.

I nodded. "So, you know you are..."

"Among the dead?" she asked. "I didn't want to admit it. But no one else can see me, but you. How is that possible?"

"It's a long story. Can you tell me what happened?"

"I was on break. A gift was left on the desk just for me. I thought it was a secret admirer. I should have checked the ingredients. I would never eat blueberries intentionally."

"I believe you." I sighed and then kneaded at my forehead, exasperated. "Well, this blows my theory completely out the window."

"What theory?"

I shook my head. "It's not important. I was wrong anyway. Is there anything you remember?"

"Not really. It was pretty much a normal, same as always, day. Oh. Wait."

"What is it?"

"I did notice a woman staring at that picture on the wall."

"What picture?" I asked.

"The one that was taken in 1978," she stated.

"Is that the one with the businessman, his daughter, and the movie star?"

"The one and only," she said. "Sometimes people come in and glance at it from time to time. But this woman, I believe, was staring deeply at the photo as though they were remembering something or thinking about something. I watched her for about ten minutes before she finally left. It was strange."

"Could you tell me more about her?"

Rosemary shook her head. "No, all I know is she had beautiful, long blonde hair. She was slender, I know that. She didn't have anything special on. She had on jeans and a blouse with a cardigan. She didn't turn around. She just took off."

"I see. Do you know anything about the photo? It might be nothing, but you never know, it could be important."

"Not really," she said before she sighed. "I honestly can't believe I'm dead. I still had so much of my life I wanted to do."

I wanted to reach out and hug her, to give her some kind of comfort. But I didn't. I was too afraid of seeing her death. "Jess…"

"You wanted to know about the photo." She took a deep breath. "The man in the photo as I said was a businessman…"

"No, I mean. I know that already. I mean, is there anything more specific you could tell me?"

"No, if you want more you could talk to my nana. Though, I haven't seen her. I should though, right? She passed away two days ago. I mean, I know I'm a ghost and all, but I thought I'd at least see her. Do you think she crossed over already?"

"Rosemary…"

"I'm rambling, aren't I?"

"It's okay. I didn't know your grandma passed. I mean, we never hung out, so… I can't tell you if she crossed over or not."

"I see," she said, sadness rooted deep in her emotions.

"Is there anything else you can tell me?"

"I mean, I can tell you a little bit about the people in the photo. It's not much, but I do remember my nana mentioned some stuff."

"What kind of stuff?"

"Well, the businessman was very powerful. He was one of the investors in this apartment building. He was quite handsome; I heard my nana say that many times. He was kind and charming, but was very impatient when things didn't go his way which made him lash out."

"What about his little girl?"

"I don't know much about her. According to my nana, the businessman adopted the little girl. However, she never interacted with the little girl. No one knew much about her."

"What about the woman?" I asked. "She was a movie star, right?"

Rosemary nodded. "That's correct. She was here to film a scene. Nana was invited to see it, but then the accident happened."

"What can you tell me about the accident?"

"Well, several rumors have been around for decades," she said. "No one could find anything specific so officials just chalked it up to faulty wiring. But bear in mind. I wasn't there. I have no definite proof."

"Was there anything, I don't know, say, strange about it?"

"Come to think of it, yeah," she said. "Nana believed that it was sabotaged intentionally."

"Can I ask you one last question?"

"Sure."

"Was the photo taken before or after the incident?"

"Before," she said. "Why?"

"Just curious," I said.

Rosemary smiled. "Curiosity killed the cat you know."

"So the saying goes. What are you going to do now?"

"I have no idea. I wish though that I could give the police a piece of my mind for saying that I would do this on purpose."

"I know it's not much. But I will try and help. I'm still trying to understand myself and this ability. But I will find a way to help you and other ghosts."

Rosemary smiled. "Aren't you sweet," she teased. "But then again, I always knew you were. I'm going to stay here I suppose."

"Thank you for talking to me," I said.

Rosemary shook her. "No, thank you." She then grabbed my hand. I was overcome by her emotions of gratefulness before a vision flashed in my mind.

I found myself behind the receptionist counter, filling out paperwork, when I started feeling weird. I coughed and coughed and then dropped my pen and looked at my hands. They were red and breaking out in hives.

Swearing to myself, I looked at the muffin panicked before making wheezing noises. I needed my EpiPen. I tried to move to where I kept it in my desk, but I fell to the floor, breathless as I fought to breathe...

I let go quickly, coughing as I touched my throat.

"Weston, is something wrong?"

I blinked. "Uh, no, I just... I remembered something. I have to go."

Rosemary vanished.

24

As soon as I was inside my Jeep, I leaned back in my seat breathless. That vision was horrible. I pulled out my phone and dialed Norman's number. Unfortunately, it went to voicemail.

"Norman's voicemail here, if you are calling because you have information on conspiracy theories then do not leave a message and instead email me directly…

I rolled my eyes. Only Norman would make such an odd voicemail.

"…However, if this is about an important case and an emergency then by all means leave your name and your message at the beep."

Beep!

"Norman, it's Weston. Listen, I'll make this as brief as I can. Rosemary is dead and the police have once again ruled it as a suicide. I need you to find any information that can about her death as well as anything about her family history. I have this gut feeling that there's something important. Also, I need you to do one more thing as well. I need you to research a photo. I will send it in a text message directly after this voicemail.. Please get back to me when you can."

After hanging up, I went to my messages and sent him a picture of the photograph that I had taken and left him a text.

This is the photo I was talking about. It dates back to 1978 and taken at Caster Apartments. I do not know the names of the people represented, but I do know that it consists of a business, his four-year-old daughter, possibly adopted, and an actress. Supposedly, they died from an elevator faulty wiring.

I started up my Jeep. However, before I could drive off, the passenger door opened, and in moseyed in Angela. She seemed strangely different. She was in a short black dress and black heels and her eyes were an unusual bright green. Her emotions seemed off like there was darkness oozing out of her.

"Uh, Angela, what are you doing?"

Angela's eyes widened and I could have sworn they would pop out of her head. "Oh. Well, I'm hiding."

"Hiding from my cousin?" I asked.

"Yes!"

"Why are you hiding from my cousin?" I asked. "I mean, shouldn't you be with Hayden instead?"

She didn't answer. Instead, she smiled coyly and moved so she was leaning over, showing off her cleavage as her small golden hoop earrings dangled. I had the urge to gag but controlled it.

"What are you doing?"

Her confusion filtered around me. "Why is it not working on you?" she asked.

"Why is what not working on me?" I asked. There was some kind of weird energy coming off her. It felt like it was buzzing across my skin like she was trying to get me to do something. But judging by her surprised expression and emotions, whatever it was, wasn't working.

"That's impossible," she said. Realization filtered through her emotions. "Oh. You aren't attracted to me, are you?"

Without fear, I shook my head and gently tried to push her back. "I'm sorry. You are a beautiful woman, I admit, but I feel nothing for you."

She sighed and leaned back. "You're gay. Oh, that is such a shame because not only are you handsome, but you also have the most delicious energy I have ever felt and the strongest life force I have ever encountered."

"Angela, you aren't making any sense and to be frank, I am uncomfortable right now."

She huffed and then tied her hair back. Before I could ask her to leave, she then gripped my hand so tightly I felt her nails piercing my skin.

I flinched. Not at the pain, but at the fact her hand was cold to the touch and a dark cloud felt like it was clenching around my heart and chest.

Before I could snatch my hand away, she gripped it even tighter to the point it felt like it would either bruise or break. I couldn't help but gasp as waves of pain. But the pain didn't feel to be coming from her directly but from someone else.

I found the strength to jerk my hand away.

"Are you okay?" she asked, surprisingly polite and sweet. "You seem a bit shaken up and extremely pale."

"I'm fine." I wasn't. My strength was depleting and my head felt like it had a ton of pressure in it and was pounding, but I willed myself not to pass out. "Uh, I don't mean to be rude, but could you please get out of my vehicle?"

Angela's eyes narrowed. "Whatever." She then yanked the door open. "I can't believe I wasted my time."

I watched hazily in the side mirror until she was no longer visible before I leaned over and quickly opened the glove box. There was no chocolate. After slamming the door shut, I leaned back in my seat, holding my hand to my throbbing chest as I closed my eyes, hoping to relieve the dizziness.

Knock!

Startled, I whipped my head to the window where I heard the knock.

There stood my cousin.

Dizzily, I hurriedly rolled down my window and it was then I noticed a chocolate bar in his hand. "Carter?" I asked. "What...what are you doing here?"

"Giving you this," he said, handing me the chocolate bar. "I got another one of those weird texts that said I needed to bring this to you at this address."

As quick as my trembling hands could, I tore open the chocolate bar, and then bit into it. The second the crunchy, chocolatey taste hit my taste buds, I felt my energy start to come back slowly.

"Thanks."

"These mysterious texts sure seem to always be saving you. You must have a guardian angel."

I shook my head. "I doubt angels would save me considering…"

"Considering what?" he asked. "That you're gay?"

I shrugged. "I mean, you know what religions say. What if they are right?"

"I doubt they are. You know I don't believe in that sort of thing. Besides, who you are as a person matters more." He then smiled. "Now, do you mind if we get off this topic and get on the topic of why I was ordered to bring you a chocolate bar?"

"I…" I couldn't tell my cousin the truth. He didn't need to worry about me. And yet, those texts he was receiving did always manage to help me. Who was it? Was it my grandma? No, that didn't make sense. She couldn't work a smart phone.

"You what?" he asked.

"I kind of forgot to eat. I was on my way before I stopped when I saw police cars and an ambulance. Jennifer passed away."

Carter nodded. "I know. It was on the radio and already rumors have spread. It must have been a shock for you."

"It was. I guess seeing it and not eating caused me to feel a bit faint." I had to lie. I made sure not to bring up Angela. That experience was too awkward.

"I imagine your empathy also caused some of that."

"It did."

***

After making sure my cousin left, I headed for the museum. I didn't know why exactly I was going there. I supposed it was a feeling, a hunch.

Either way, I made my way inside. It was still afternoon. The museum tended to close at six. Fortunately, not many people were inside. By not many, I mean like one to three people, who were over by the planes.

Instead of finding Mr. Newman, to my surprise, I found Jasper. He was standing by the desk with his arms folded. I could feel immense anxiety coming from him.

I called out to him.

He jumped, startled. "Oh, Weston, hi," he said, nervousness jumping sporadically in his emotions.

"What, uh, what are you doing here?"

Jasper shifted on his feet as his eyes bounced around for a few minutes before he settled. "Well, I needed to... I mean, I'm here to speak to... It was one of Melinda's errands. I'm supposed to pick something up." He was lying or hiding something. I wanted to bring it up but thought better of it.

"I see."

Jasper nodded. "I was just waiting, but I mean, the item could be in the curator's office."

"Maybe we should check it out."

His eyes widened. "Uh, would that... I mean, wouldn't be get into trouble?"

I shrugged. "I don't think so. Come on."

We passed through the art section of the museum and went down a hallway that was labeled Curator's Office. Seeing the door ajar, Jasper opened it further.

"Should we go in?"

Jasper shrugged. "I, uh, I doubt he'd mind. I mean, this was...this was your idea, right?"

I wish he hadn't brought that up.

With a heavy sigh, I walked in. It was a small office. It was nothing spectacular. There was a small couch and a desk that was cluttered with photographs and other pieces of history. There was a book shelve and a filing system. In the corner, I could see a coffee maker with a mini fridge. Did Mr. Newman live in his office?

Just then, a sudden explosive pain erupted in my head like an erupting volcano. I think I might have cried out in agony at the intense level of pain, but I wasn't sure.

As quick as the pain came, it quickly lessened enough for me to open my eyes to a sliver just enough to see Jasper standing in front of me. His eyes were fixated on the air, but there was something wrong with him. His eyes, which were usually brown, were now silver.

"Danger," he said in a monotone and creepy voice. "Someone close is in danger."

"What are...?"

"You mustn't go," he said, sternly.

"Go where?"

"No, she'll... She'll hurt... You must..." His voice trailed off as his eyes widened. "No! Watch out!"

"Jasper, are you okay?"

Instead of responding with words, he walked towards me like he was in a trance of some kind as tears trailed down his flushed cheeks.

"He'll die."

"Who?" I asked.

He still didn't respond. Instead, he reached out and grabbed my hands. Pain, and not just in my head, but also in my heart. I nearly gripped my chest as I gasped at the intensified sense of urgency and panic shooting through my psyche.

With a yelp, I yanked my hand back and fell to the floor with a bang.

Sudden footsteps ran and a person knelt. With slightly blurred vision, I saw saw Mr. Newman. He pulled a chocolate bar out of his coat and handed it to me. "Here. Eat that. It will help."

With shaky hands, I peeled back the wrapper and took a bite. The second the milk chocolate hit my taste buds, my energy levels came back. With new rebound strength, I gazed over at Jasper. Mr. Newman grabbed him when he started to lash out.

"No! Stop!" shouted Jasper.

Mr. Newman held him by his shoulders firmly, lowering them both to the floor before he started shaking him gently. "Jasper, come on, kiddo, snap out of it."

The silver in Jasper's eyes faded back to brown as he fell against Mr. Newman. "D-Dad?" he asked as an air of confusion swirled around him.

I blinked. Mr. Newman was Jasper's dad?

Mr. Newman smiled, relief pouring out of him in waves. "I was afraid I lost you there for a minute." He then glared at me so intensely that made me want to vanish.

"I..." I tried to say.

Jasper grabbed Mr. Newman's arm. "He doesn't know," he said, through gritted teeth.

Mr. Newman's tension relaxed. "I see. Come on. Let's get you settled into the couch. It's better than the floor. You need it after that."

Embarrassment flooded his emotions as I watched Mr. Newman help him up and move him over to the couch.

"Dad, I'm fine," Jasper said. Even though, he was obviously in pain due to wincing and massaging his head.

"I don't believe you, kiddo," Mr. Newman said. "I also can't believe you're here. When on earth did you get back? And why wasn't I notified?"

Jasper rubbed at his forehead again. "About a week ago," he said. "I've been settling into a new apartment and trying to find a job. I told her not to contact you. I came here to surprise you when I…" He paused, swallowing as he averted his eyes.

Guilt swamped me even though I wasn't sure why. "I'm sorry."

Jasper eyed me. "Whatever could you be sorry for?"

I shook my head. "I'm not…sure," I replied as I rubbed the back of my head. "Are you okay?"

Jasper leaned forward. "Uh, migraines suck."

Mr. Newman said something under his breath that sounded like a swear word, but I couldn't make it out. He then pulled out a orange bottle from his jacket and handed it to Jasper.

Jasper looked at him. "You kept them?"

"Always do in case you ever came back, kiddo."

Jasper took the bottle. "Thanks. I hadn't gotten a reflill lately. So, these will help a ton."

Mr. Newman smiled softly before he picked up this clipboard. He must have been going over his inventory when he heard the commotion. Taking a breather, I watched as his gray eyes softened. "Weston, could I have a word with you? Jasper, I want you to stay there and rest."

Jasper's eyes widened. "Dad, I…"

Mr. Newman shook his head. "I don't want to hear it, son. Those headaches of yours are incredibly painful."

Jasper leaned back against the couch, fiddling with the bottle in his hand that he hadn't opened. "Yeah, I know."

Mr. Newman and I walked out of the office. "I must say it is a surprise to see you here, Weston."

"I know, sir. I wanted to talk to you. But I encountered Jasper. This isn't his fault. I talked him into coming into your office to see."

"And why is it you wanted to see me?"

"I was hoping you could catch me up on what I missed with you and Norman's discussion."

"I see. Well, you didn't miss much. We were discussing theories. Mr. Forrester sure has some rather interesting ideas. Though, none of which I agree with."

"I know the feeling well. When I first met him, he was going on about aliens." I chuckled nervously.

Mr. Newman, to my surprise, had a small grin. "He has the making of a conspiracy theorist."

I swallowed the sudden lump in my throat. "I also wanted to apologize for what happened." I reached into my wallet. "I know it's not enough, but if the water damaged anything…"

"Weston, you do not have to worry about that. I do not apologize for my behavior. I have to come off as strict in this place. Eyes are everywhere. And your name is around the town a bit more. People might not know completely about you being psychic, but I have kept an eye on you. Your powers attract attention. Also, as for what happened, that wasn't your fault."

I listened to him with wide eyes. "You... Wait. Wasn't my fault?"

Mr. Newman nodded. "I see," he said, rubbing at his chin. "Your powers alone were not the cause for the sprinkler system."

"But..."

"Trust me," he said.

I gave him a pointed look. "You're protecting someone."

Mr. Newman's silver blue eyes narrowed. "Stay out of my emotions."

I gulped.

"Forgive me," he said with a long sigh. "It's been a long day."

"Nothing to forgive," I said.

"It's just a long story," he said. "I can't show favoritism or any kind in public. I have a reputation to uphold. I hope you understand that."

"Not fully, sir, but I'll try."

"Good. Now, I get the distinct feeling you came here for another reason."

"I did. You see, Rosemary is dead. Melinda gave me this crazy idea. But now, with Rosemary, it seems like it was just a coincidence."

"Rosemary Curtis is dead? I had heard someone passed. News travels fast in this small town." He rubbed at his chin again. "Tell me about this theory?"

"Well, Melinda mentioned a succubus, and I was wondering if they were real or not."

"I'm no expert, but it is possible they exist," he said. "A succubus isn't uncommon, but they are rare and are usually associated with demons. Typically, they feed on sexual energy. I suspect we aren't dealing with that as none of the victims had been in any sexual intercourse."

"Yeah, that's what Melinda told me as well," I said. "Thank you, Mr. Newman." I then rubbed my hands nervously. "Uh, about Jasper…"

"What about him?"

"Are you really his dad?"

Mr. Newman shook his head. "I'm his adoptive dad. I found him when he was four. He was in a car accident that caused amnesia. His mother, before her passing, asked me to take him in, care for him, and keep him safe."

"Oh," I said.

"Weston, I appreciate you talking with me." His eyes then narrowed. "I wish you didn't have to be involved in all of this. But I knew it was only a matter of time before fate willed you in. I will do my best to keep your activities hidden. But do be careful on your own. Your abilities already make you a huge target."

"I'll be careful. Will Jasper be okay? He said he was on an errand for Melinda."

Mr. Newman's eyes widened. "He's working for Melinda?" He then sighed heavily. "Oh, why did he have to associate with her of all people?"

"It's not his fault. He nearly fainted and was brought into Melinda's shop. She offered him a part-time job."

"Nosey witch," he muttered. "Don't worry about Jasper. I'll take care of him. He just needs plenty of rest." I could feel his love and adoration from him. He deeply cared for his adoptive son.

"What was that?"

"Migraine," he said, but even though he was trying to keep a tight lid on his emotions, I could feel that he was lying. No, not lying exactly. But keeping something hidden. "He gets them from time to time. They can be scary. I know how to help him deal with him."

"He's lucky to have you."

"Thanks, Weston. Now, you better get going. I imagine you have lots to do. Also, I appreciate your donation for helping fix the damages, but don't think this will be enough."

"Understood, sir," I said, bowing my head. I knew he was putting on an act. I had to play along.

"Good. Off you go. And no more pranks."

I left the museum. As soon as I stepped outside, the cool evening air hit me. I sucked in a deep breath.

Feeling a hand brush against mine made me flinch and move back. When no vision invaded me, I relaxed. At least this person was real.

I turned around. A young woman with blonde hair was in front of me. She was dressed in casual clothing. She had on black lipstick and her blonde hair was tied back, showing off golden hoop earrings.

Wait. This was the woman from the night Norman passed out. She was giving off that strange dark feeling again.

The woman smiled. "Hello. We meet again. It must be fate. I heard what happened in there and came to check on you. You had quite the scolding."

"I deserved it."

"You don't seem at all like a troublemaker. But I guess appearances can deceive you."

"Yes, well, I'm sorry. I have to get home. My grandma is expecting me."

"You wouldn't happen to be the grandson to Ruth Hawthorn?"

"Why do you want to know?"

She looked taken back before she brought her hand to her mouth and giggled. "My, you are exactly like your grandmother. Both are so skeptical. Although, I guess I am being rude. I'm Ella. I wanted to bring a dessert for Ruth as a thank you gift. I sadly cannot visit her. Could you give it to her in my stead?"

"I suppose." The second she went to place the dessert in my hand, a flash of black zoomed in front of me, and a claw scratched me causing me to drop the dessert.

"Ah! Bad kitty!" shrieked Ella.

I saw Mel, who was by my feet. Her bright green eyes were narrowed in anger. I leaned down and scooped her up. "I'm sorry. This is my cat. She is usually friendly. But she can be quite protective."

Ella sighed in anger. "Well, maybe you should keep her on a leash. My dessert for your grandmother is now ruined thanks to your cat. I will have to make a new batch."

"I apologize."

"Damn right you do." Her fists clenched before she huffed off.

"Why on earth did you do that?"

Mel jumped from my arms. "Me? What about you? Picking me up like that? You are lucky I didn't claw your arms to death and bite you."

"You were making a scene."

Mel hissed. "I was making a scene? For a psychic, you sure are stupid. Didn't you feel the darkness that woman was putting off?"

I glared at her. "I did. But I was still trying to be polite."

"Hmm, if you say so," she said as she sat and wagged her tail back and forth.

I rolled my eyes and then knelt. The dessert that fell was a muffin. I reached out to touch it.

"Don't touch that, idiot!" Mel yelled.

Before my fingers could even touch the gooey substance, a bone-chilling presence alerted me. Nervously, I saw someone new. A man I had never seen before. His hair was dark and he was dressed in a suit and red tie and his eyes were almost black.

"Who…"

Mel jumped in front of me. "Leave," she hissed.

The man paid her no mind as he kept his gaze on me. "Stop her."

He then grabbed my hand.

I gasped at the coldness. A terrible darkness invaded me and I choked as vision engulfed me.

I found myself trapped somewhere dark. I didn't have any sort of light but I could hear what sounded like dirt hitting something wooden. Heat was blistering my skin as the air was thinning.

I shouted out for her to stop, but she never did.

I banged against the wood more and more until I welcomed the darkness…

The sudden vision ended and I wound up on the ground, coughing. The sense of terror swirled around me like a twister. Before too long darkness invaded my vision and I think I hit the ground.

25

My eyelids fluttered open briefly, a blurry humanoid person was looming over me with their nimble fingers cascading through my black locks. I didn't need perfect vision to know exactly who this was. The glob of orange and the scent of salt water was pretty much a giveaway not to mention the peaceful emotions.

"Hayden?" I asked, but my voice came out a bit hoarse and dry.

He shushed me gently. "Just rest," he said. "Save your strength, Weston."

Groaning, I turned over. My cheek bumped against something broad. The fabric felt like a pair of jeans. Before I could say anything, my eyes started sliding shut on their own accord and I instantly fell back into darkness.

The second time I woke, after finding my glasses on top of my head and putting them on, I was surprised to discover that I was in my bedroom.

At first, I was confused. I mean, how did I get here? The last thing I remembered was being with Mel outside of the museum, meeting Kayla, something about a muffin, and then a ghost, a vision, and then...

Putting a hand to my pulsating head, I slowly sat up. A glance at my watch told me it was 7:30 pm. How long was I out for?

Whispered voices from downstairs had me carefully getting out of bed and making my way down the stairs.

"Do you think he will be okay?" I heard someone ask. That voice sounded like my cousin.

"I believe he will be, Carter. I'm glad you brought him home," my grandma said.

"This is the second time I found him out cold. Do you know what happened to him?"

"I can't say for sure, but maybe we should ask him," she said as her eyes locked onto mine.

Carter turned in his seat. "Weston, hey, how are you doing?"

I made my way over and sat down. "Better, I suppose. I do have a bit of a lingering headache."

My grandma placed a hand on my forehead. "I have the perfect remedy for such dreadful things." She walked over to the counter and opened the cabinet and pulled out a jar with tea packets. She pulled one out and then started boiling some water.

While she was doing that, Carter turned his attention to me. "So, want to tell me why I found you passed out in your Jeep?"

"I was in my Jeep?" I asked, confused. "That isn't... How did I wind up there?"

"No idea," he said. "Your unknown savior texted me your location and I found you passed out in your Jeep."

"Here you go, sweetheart," said my grandma as she set the cup of tea in front of me. The scent of peppermint was strong.

"Thanks." I wrapped my hands around my cup, feeling the warmth against my palms.

"Weston, you can tell Carter the truth."

"Are you sure he should be involved?"

Grandma touched my hand. "If he's been receiving texts to help you, then, yes, I say he needs to be involved."

I sighed.

"What truth?" Carter asked. There was an air of curiosity and concern radiating from him.

I took another sip of my tea before I answered. "You know how I told you about my empathy?"

"Yeah," he said.

"Well, I didn't tell you everything."

"What do you mean, cousin?"

"I'm a psychic," I replied.

"Excuse me?"

"It means," Grandma interrupted, "that Weston here not only has the power to feel others' emotions, see ghosts and even get visions of their deaths through physical contact with them or by touching an item they worn as they died, even touching the death spot, and…"

"So, you're a ghost whisper or something?"

"If that is how you want to think of it, sure. I try not to draw attentions. I'm still not sure how it all works. And at times, I am left with more questions than answers. But it does give me some insight."

"Okay, let me see if I got this. You can see and talk to ghosts, feel emotions, and get visions of their death. Do I have that right?"

"Add telekinesis to that list, then, yes," I said.

"Hold up. You're a spoon bender as well?"

Grandma rolled her eyes. "Carter, his abilities come from my side of the family. We can only do small mediocre things. It honestly saved time. If we needed something from across the room, we could make it move toward us. Like this," she said, holding her hand out and making my cup slide to her from across the counter.

Carter's eyes widened more and I could feel his concern radiating off of him in intense waves. "And you can do that, too, Weston?"

"Yeah," I said. I expected him to be angry at me for not telling him everything. But instead, I was just met with worry.

"So, then, what happened to you was because of you being psychic?"

"Kind of," I said. "I met this woman named Ella outside of the museum. She wanted to bring a dessert to you, Grandma. A muffin, I believe. But it was knocked out of my hand and then... I saw... This spirit showed up and touched me. I saw his death. I don't just see it, though. Because of my empathy being so strong, I also partially experience it."

"And I'm guessing that's bad?"

Grandma nodded. "It can be for him, Carter. Delving too deeply into an emotional connection can drain your cousin of nearly all of his energy... Wait.

Did you say Ella? Hmm, I have only heard her name mention. I don't think I ever met her."

"That's strange," I said. "She seemed to know you as she wanted me to give you a dessert."

"Huh, my memory must be declining. I do remember someone mentioning her name and telling me that she was cruel and to avoid her at all cost."

"Cruel how?" asked Carter. Of course, he would be curious.

"Mind you, some of it is only rumors like of her calling a restaurant and cussing them out for not answering the phone on time. Others claimed she even hurts animals and some even claimed she killed her ex-husband when she found out he cheated on her. Though, I never experienced it myself. As I said, I don't think I ever met her."

"She does sound pretty cruel," I said.

Carter hummed. "So, it wasn't Ella that was the problem. It was the spirit?" he asked. "That's why you passed out, I mean? Will this kind of thing continue to happen?"

"Probably," I said, shrugging. "Maybe with some practice and training, I could get a handle on it."

"But what if you can't?" asked Carter with overwhelming concern in his voice.

"Then he will have to live with it, Carter. It shouldn't be hard. He'll just have to keep something sugary with him at all times."

I groaned. "Great," I said as I buried my head in my arm.

Carter's hand landed on my shoulder. "Don't worry about it, cuz. You'll be fine. I will keep a watchful eye out."

"By those weird texts you are receiving?"

Carter shrugged. "If that is what it takes. Whoever it is, they must be watching out for you."

Before I could respond, the door busted open startling all three of us. We all turned our head simultaneously to find Norman standing in the door and dripping wet.

"Sorry for barging in like this," he said. "I had to come and bring news." After he removed the matted hair out of his eyes, his gaze landed on us. "Oh, is this a bad time?"

Carter shook his head. "Not at all," he said. "I was just about you head out." He grabbed his coat.

"Oh, well, be careful out there. It's been pouring like crazy. The stupid cab driver wouldn't dare drive up here. So, the idiot dropped me off at the end of the drive."

Carter smiled. "People in this town are superstitious," he said as he put on his coat. "Remember what I said, cuz. If anything happens, I'll be there."

I nodded. "Thanks again, Carter."

The second Carter left, with us hearing his car start and backing out of the driveway, Norman came over. "So, that message I got from you, it turns out your hunch was spot on. It took a lot of digging, but I found something interesting."

"What did you find?"

"Something that is going to shock you," said Norman, smirking.

That had my attention. "Don't keep me in suspense."

He opened the files and took out a copy of the photo from the apartment complex. "Let's start with this," he said. "This is the photo you wanted me to look into, correct?"

"Yes."

"Well, it turns out something is interesting about the people."

"What about them?" I asked, trying to keep myself from fidgeting too much.

"Well, I first started digging to see if there were any other deaths around that time. Sure enough, two were listed. The first one was a middle aged man named Richard Silverstein. It was rumored he was murdered by his wife but there was no valid proof. It was reported in the autopsy that it was a suicide by, get this, sleeping pills."

"No way," I said.

"It gets even wilder than that," Norman said. "There was also Lucy Silverstein, the wife of Richard. She died exactly two days after her husband's death. It was rumored she offered herself because of either guilt or the gossip that she possibly killed her husband. Bet you can guess what was in her autopsy report?"

"She too died from an overdose of sleeping pills?"

"Ding! Hole in one!" exclaimed Norman with a grin. "Of course, this all took hours upon hours of research. There was nothing in my father's police reports. So, I had to contact an extremely informative person and you'll never believe what I learned."

"What?"

"There is a deep conspiracy," he said.

"What kind of conspiracy?"

"It starts with the actress, Danielle Parrett," he said. "Come to find out that she was doing some low-budget murder mystery or something like that. Anyway, I got a hold of Millie Marks. I doubt you know her, but she runs this huge paranormal podcast. She's actually loosely related to me somehow. Anyway, she provided me with a butt load of information. She is like me. She tries to piece together all things strange…"

"Norman!" I said, trying to bring him back to reality.

"Just listen," he said as I tried to make sense of his rambling. "Do you know Alan Marks?"

"Kind of," I said, scratching at the back of my head. "I think I saw an article on my phone a few weeks ago. I didn't read it, but I believe the article said he was some big time detective in Nebraska."

"That's that guy!" Norman said with enthusiasm. "He's Millie's father. He and his wife aren't just detectives. I'm not sure you heard about this, but they get involve in some rather…abnormal investigations. In fact, his wife is sort of like you. She can also talk to the dead. Not exactly like you, though. You might be slightly more powerful than she is."

"Wait. She can see ghosts?"

"Yeah," he said. "I mean, they are psychic like you. You didn't know?"

I shook my head. "I never knew there were others like me. I assumed I was the only one."

"Well, you aren't," he said. "Anyway, back to what I was saying. I contacted Millie directly because her father's father, aka, her grandfather, used to live here in our hometown. He was a hell of a P.I. back in those days. But one day, low and behold, he was fired and forced to move. Luckily, Millie told me that he kept all kinds of records before his death."

"Why was he fired and forced to move away?"

"Because he was onto something huge," he said. "When he did one of his interviews, he questioned why the twenty-three year old actress met up with someone in secret…"

"Okay, but…"

"Hold on. It gets even more interesting when you find out that the man was none other than Richard. According to Millie's grandfather, Richard was having an affair with her."

"Yikes," I said. "Did the report say why he did it? I mean, the guy had to a motive for cheating right? Were he and his wife having marriage problems?"

"No idea," Norman said. "There was nothing that indicated that. I do know that Millie's grandfather found out that Richard made a crap ton of calls to, none other than, Timothy Bloomington."

"That's Barry's father, right?" I asked.

"The very same," he said. "I doubt it's all that important, but he was the one who hired the director of the filming company. Can you guess who it was?"

I shrugged.

"Derek Jenkins," he said.

"He was Jerry's father."

"Indeed he was."

"I didn't know Jerry's father was a movie director."

"That's because you're a hermit," Norman joked. "But honestly, I didn't either. Jerry never spoke about his family."

"I'm guessing there's more to this story."

"So much," he said with a smirk. "The real kicker is that Millie's grandfather was forced to move because he was being blackmailed. He didn't say by whom, but he contacted Dustin Hunter, aka, Henry Hunter's father, because the man was not only the photographer who took the photo, but apparently had some important information. However, Dustin went missing before he could talk to Millie's grandfather…"

A cup-shattering broke us out of our conversation.

26

Norman and I both turned our attention to my grandma like we were in sync. While her emotions were closed off to me, I could see the pain crinkling around the edges of her eyes and also the sadness shining.

"Bless the heavens above," she whispered, signing the cross with her hands before clasping her hands like she was praying.

I was out of my chair in a blink of an eye and strolled over to her side being mindful of the broken pieces of porcelain all over the floor. "Grandma, what's wrong?" Without hesitation, I placed my hand on her shoulder gently to comfort her.

The second my hand landed on her shoulder, I became overwhelmed with intense emotions ranging from anxious to full blown terror.

Before it could go any further, something or someone shoved back. Instinct took over and I went to catch myself only I was so dizzy that my vision blurred and I slipped or tripped and landed heavily on the floor. I vaguely registered pain radiating from my hand, but I was too focused on getting my breathing under control to care about anything else.

"Weston!" a voice called. It sounded like my grandma.

Suddenly, hands were touching me.

"Don't touch me!" I screamed. Out of reflex, I used my telekinesis to push the intruder away from me.

I vaguely heard the thud. I would have helped had I been in the right state of mind, but I was too caught up in overwhelming turmoil.

"Weston!" shouted Grandma. "Get a hold of yourself!"

A flash of fear shot through me. That tone. It sounded too much like my mom's condescending one. With that knowledge, a surge of guilt and shame sparked inside me, outweighing the panic and the other turmoil of emotions still rattling inside me. Gradually, I started coming back to myself. I lowered my hands that I hadn't been aware were on my head. I shot my eyes up to see my grandma. She was staring back at me with concern.

"I'm sorry," I whispered.

Grandma knelt, pushing away the broken mug before grabbing a hold of my hands. I couldn't protest. Luckily, there were no spontaneous emotions this time. Just tranquility. "Sh. It's okay. Just breathe with me. In and out slowly," she commanded softly. "You are safe. I want you to listen to me and do exactly what I say."

"O...okay," I said, shakily.

"Good. First, list five things you can see aloud."

I obeyed. "You," I said, trying to focus. "I see you. I see the floor. I see the counter. I see the table. And I see the cabinets."

"Good. List four things you can touch."

I touched what was in reach. "Your hands, the floor, the counter behind me, and my glasses," I said, less shakily.

"Three things you hear."

I listened. "I can hear the fan, our voices, and...the rain."

She shushed me. "Keep going. List two things you can smell."

That was a little difficult. I closed my eyes and sniffed the air. A bright smile spread on my face. "I smell your flowery perfume and the apple pie you made two days ago."

She giggled at that. "Nice. Now, what do you taste?"

That was even more difficult. I licked my lips. "I taste something minty. Is it tea?"

She nodded. "How are you feeling now, sweetheart?"

Examining myself, I found that my breathing was better and my sight was no longer tunneling or starry. The ringing in my ears had also dimmed immensely. A strange calmness seeped into me and numbed my panic. I watched as she brought her hand up. A part of me wanted to flinch away, but I held still. She gently touched my head and ran her fingers through my hair. I couldn't help but turn my attention away. She shouldn't be doing this. I shouldn't be burdening her like this. She was an elder. Wasn't I supposed to be caring for her?

"I'm sorry," I managed to get out. I felt stupid and unbelievably weak.

"None of that," she said, sweetly. "Panic attacks happen to any of us."

"It was more than panic," I said. "I felt your emotions so strongly. It's the first that has ever happened."

My grandma sighed. "I figured. You both need to drop this investigation immediately."

"Grandma, you aren't…"

"There are things you don't understand," she said. "Dangerous things you can't even comprehend."

"We can't just drop it, though," said Norman. "I know we can't. We are on to something important."

Grandma sighed. "I guess it's time you know everything then since you're not going to quit investigating."

"What do you mean?" I asked.

She got up and walked over to a sink and opened one of the drawers. She picked up an item that looked like a photograph. She came back and showed it to me without saying a word.

I examined the photo. It was black and white and there was a group of people on the Caster Bridge. To the far left, in his usual business suit, was Timothy Bloomingdale. He had his hand on his daughter's shoulder as she stood in front of him with a lollipop in her mouth. Next to him was some guy I had never seen before. He was in a leather jacket and jeans and he was hugging a young woman in a white dress. Strangely, she looked similar to my grandma. Next to them was a man, who I assumed was Derek Jenkins, who was sitting on the bridge next to a young woman, who was also wearing a white dress, but her face was turned away from the camera. Another young woman, who had to be the actress, Danielle Parrett, was kneeling. There was a man beside her...

"I've seen him," I said.

"Seen who?" she asked. I pointed to the guy standing beside Danielle. "That's Richard Silverstein. Like Norman said, he died."

"I know," I said. "I saw his ghost."

"Weston..."

"Trust me. I remember. After I met Ella, his ghost showed up and touched me. I saw him being buried alive. I didn't get the sense he overdosed nor did I see where he was buried." I then gazed back at the photo. "Why are you showing me this?"

My grandma knelt beside me again. "Because I don't think these deaths are random," she said. "I, too, have felt that something was off. I never could figure out what. And with my age, I can't get around well enough to do much. But I suspect that the person who is killing has to be her," she said, pointing to a lonely woman off to the side with a scowl on her face wearing a dress. "That's Lucy Silverstein. I don't know for sure, but it makes the most sense." She pointed to the guy who was standing by Danielle. "That's Richard, her husband, and he supposedly had an affair with Danielle."

"So, what, she's doing this for revenge?" I asked.

Norman shook his head. "I don't think so. I mean, if this was revenge, it doesn't make any sense. Her husband is dead. And she apparently overdosed on sleeping pills. Her revenge would have been fulfilled when her husband died, right?"

"You make a good point, Norman," Grandma said. "To be honest, I wish I knew for certain. I'm not omnipotent. But I will say that we did know that Lucy killed her husband. However, without a body, no one could prove it. But we all knew the truth. Weston, sweetheart, you shouldn't get more involved. If anyone gets an inkling of your powers, they may try to go after you. I don't want to lose you. You are my only grandchild."

I grabbed her arms gently. "Grandma, you won't lose me. As much as I want to back out of this, I can't. Rosemary just died."

Her eyes widened. "Rosemary? Oh, that poor girl. But why? She wasn't involved."

"I don't know that either," said Norman. "But I do have some information on that. Her full name was Rosemary Curtis and she was forty-four."

"Forty-four?" I asked. "That's impossible. She looked like she was in her mid to late twenties."

"I know," he said. "Shocked me too when I read the details. She has some crazy good genes."

My grandmother glared. "Boys, you do know that some men and woman age differently, don't you? Some women don't look a day over thirty. But, some, me included, look our ages."

"Well, yes, that's true," Norman said. "Other than that, I found no information which is wild to me because this is a town where secrets don't stay buried. Rosemary literally had no known family other than her grandmother who did indeed die two days prior. But they were natural causes."

"I had no idea she passed," Grandma said, grabbing the photo and pointed to the woman sitting by Derek. "This was her. She and I were nurses together. Poor thing was always shy around people, but she could always cheer people up just by her presence. Of course, after Richard and Lucy's deaths, I never saw her again. I tried my hardest to find her. I figured she was grieving. She was always close to Richard and Lucy. Those three had been friends longer than I had known them."

"I think I know," Norman said.

Lifting my head, I saw Norman holding a manila folder in his arms. "I apologize to you, Ms. Ruth if I caused you any distress because of all of this."

I shook my head. "It wasn't you, Norman." I stood up and leaned a little against the counter and rubbed my forehead. "I didn't hurt you, did I?"

Norman smiled. "Nah, you just knocked me on my ass."

A pillow flew out of nowhere and whacked Norman in the face.

"Crude language is not tolerated in this house, Norman Forrester," growled my grandma. "You better be lucky I won't wash your mouth out with some of my herbal soups."

A small smirk formed in the corner of my mouth at Norman faltered and his eyes widened.

"Did you just hit me with a pillow, Ms. Ruth?"

"You bet I did. Next time it will something much harder if you so much as swear in my presence again. Do you understand?"

"Yes, ma'am," he said in a small voice. My grandma was a strong believer in God and she believed that swearing was the devil's road to Hell.

I then frowned as guilt gnawed at me. "I'm sorry."

Grandma cupped my face with her warm hands. "No need for that. It's hard for you to control your powers sometimes."

"Well, yes, but I should have better control over my emotions."

"Sweetheart, you're telekinesis is hard to manage when your entire existence is ruled by your empath abilities."

"I know that, but…never mind. Can we go back to what we were talking about a few moments ago?"

"Sure," she said, petting my head.

Norman came over and sat with us. "Mind you, this is only a hypothesis, but I think that someone wanted to shut Rosemary up. I think someone else is behind this. I doubt she was part of the plan, but maybe she knew something. Or maybe, and again, I'm just guessing, but maybe all these deaths are some weird test… or maybe there's something deeper."

"What makes you say that?"

Norman's forehead scrunched like he was thinking deeply. "I'm the son of a detective, finding patterns and clues should be in my blood. These deaths all seem completely random. Not to mention, the autopsy reports…" he trailed off.

Grandma gasped, paling.

"Grandma, are you okay?"

She shook her. "Huh? Oh, yes, honey, I'm okay. I'm just thinking."

"Ms. Ruth?" Norman asked, gulping like he was afraid to say whatever it was on the tip of his tongue. "I don't mean to distress you, but I... I think, and this is just a hunch, but I think Rosemary's grandmother had been covering something up."

Tears shone in my grandma's eyes. I held her hand as gently as I could to give her some comfort as I looked at Norman. "You also think your dad is covering up something, right?" I asked.

"Big time," Norman said. "Why else would he be so intent to label these deaths as suicide? I have been over all the medical reports on the case, and nothing comes up."

"So, Rosemary was deliberately killed because her grandma knew something and Rosemary got a hold of that information, is that what you are thinking?"

"Yeah," he said. "I was also kind of hoping you could help me. I can't do anything with it with my talent. So..."

I felt my grandma's anger through the contact of our connected hands. "Norman Forrester, are you crazy? Didn't you see what happened? He doesn't have control over his abilities. What if something like this happens again? He's already experienced a ton of passing out spells and now a panic attack..."

Norman's calm emotions had a spike of guilt in them. "I..."

"I do not want him involved in this any further!" she yelled as my cupped started rattling.

"Stop it," I said. It was like I wasn't right here.

"Weston!" shouted my grandma, who was staring at me like I've grown a second head.

I firmly placed my hand on the counter to keep myself from falling as I rose to my feet. My stupid legs felt like jelly. I hated panic attacks. "I don't have much of a choice," I said with as much conviction as I could muster. "We have to prove my innocence and we have to stop her from killing who knows who else."

"Weston, don't do this, sweetheart," my grandma pleaded. "You just experienced a severe empathic episode with me. You don't need to accidentally have another one."

"More people may turn up dead," I said. "Besides, we need to stop... Wait a second."

Grandma and Norman both stopped their argument to stare at me. "What is it?"

"We haven't asked one important question."

"What's that?" asked Norman.

"Why did this start up now? Norman is right. Something is missing. Lucy did enact her revenge years ago. She also died. That should have been her peaceful journey. I haven't seen her spirit at all. You know, I hate to say this, but I think we need to visit the site where this all began."

Norman looked at me. "You mean, start at the elevator incident?"

"Exactly," I said. "We should go now while we still have time."

Norman faltered. "Weston, I think Ms. Ruth is right. We can investigate this in the morning. I only meant to come here and tell you what I have found. I didn't come with the intention of us investigating."

"Norman," I said and then sighed "You're right. I'm in no condition to investigate tonight. I'm just worried. What if we don't have that much longer to figure this out? What if she attacks someone else soon? I don't have foresight, but..." I paused, thinking.

"But what?" he asked.

I ran a hand through my hair. "I just have this awful feeling something bad might happen."

Norman's calm emotions had a swirling hint of confusion as he smiled. "Then we'll figure it out. We'll start tomorrow morning at the Caster Valley Apartments." His smile widened. "Ooh! This should be fun."

I rolled my eyes. "Norman, this isn't a game, you know?"

"Come on, man, I know that. I'm just super excited to see how your powers at work. I get to see you in action."

"Great. Way to put pressure on my shoulders," I teased.

Norman grinned. "That's my job, after all. Besides, we can do this."

I hoped so.

Grandma sighed. "I won't stop you from doing this, sweetheart. But I want you both to sit down." Norman and I obeyed. She took a seat as well. "You both need to be extra careful." She went over to a box and then sat it in front of us. After popping off the lid, she handed us each three vials of salt. "These will come in handy."

"Mr. Newman already gave me a vial," I said.

"Good. The more the better," she said. "While I know you are the only one who can see them, sweetheart, these will come in handy for you as well, Norman. When you throw salt, make sure you have enough in your hand to throw it like a scythe."

"Wait a second," interrupted Norman. "Why do we need salt?"

"No interruptions," she said, glaring at him. "I'm getting to that if you let me."

"Sorry, ma'am," Norman said like he was a young boy who got his hand stuck in a cookie jar.

I nearly laughed at Norman's hurt puppy dog look. He wasn't used to my grandma's tones.

"Salt is pure and has for centuries been used against warding off evil. Vengeful spirits fall under that category. You can throw it at the spirit to temporarily stop them from doing harm. Salt can also be useful if, say, a person becomes possessed. The spirit will be burned."

"Wait. Possession?" asked Norman.

She gave him another glare.

"Being quiet," he said.

"As I was saying, some spirits can possess certain individuals usually only vulnerable people. I'm no expert, but I researched this with a very special friend. He told me that you can also make a circle around yourself or around someone else as protection."

I rubbed my hands. "So, does this mean my gift is useless if someone is possessed?"

Grandma nodded. "Yes."

Norman looked over at me. "Are you going to be okay?"

"Hopefully," I said.

He then smiled that dopey grin of his. "Well, I am here for you. You aren't alone."

I managed a small smile before turning back to my grandma, who also smiled as she said, "I leave him in your hands, Norman."

Norman slapped my shoulder. "I've got his back. You can trust me."

I rubbed the soreness. "Thanks."

27

The next morning, Norman and I sat at the kitchen table. He had stayed the night because the rain was terrible all night and because he had no money for a cab. I had offered to drive him home at one point, but he refused. I had to wonder if he and his dad argued again, but didn't have the heart to ask him about it.

"I can't believe I was off with the names. I was almost positive there was something there. But your hunch was spot on," Norman said as he ate a spoonful of cereal.

I looked at him as I sipped on some tea. After last night, I felt better, but still a little jittery. And with Norman's melancholy mood, I was beginning to feel a little worse. So, I decided to try and cheer him up.

"To be honest, my first thought was some creepy woman was trolling or dressed up as a clown going after names that rhymed," I joked.

That got a small smirk out of him before his frown came back.

"You know, sometimes coincidences just happen."

"I know that, Wes. I was just hoping for once I was right."

"Well, in a way you were. The names were important just not what we thought. We both assumed the killer was going after a person with the same first and last initials, but it wasn't like what we assumed. It was deeper."

"You got a point. I just hope we can figure out why and how to stop all this. Maybe it will bring justice to those we lost and help them find peace. Do you think we'll learn anything by going to where the incident happened? I mean, it was years ago. I doubt there will be anything now."

I shrugged. "Who knows," I said. "But we have to try. Maybe we'll find a clue that was missed that will help us figure this out."

After breakfast, I first called Melinda and let her know I'd be late before I drove us to Caster Valley Apartments.

"You ready?" he asked, grabbing several folders.

"As I'll ever be," I said. "There won't be any police here, right?"

Norman shook his head. "Nah, they already let everyone back in."

"I see." He and I walked inside. Not much had changed. I mean, I didn't expect it to anyway. It was just such a shame that Rosemary wasn't here. And instead there was an older man behind the counter.

"Can I help you?" he asked.

Norman flashed a smile. "We're good. We're just here to visit my grandmother."

"Oh, do you need help finding her room?"

Norman shook his head. "No, I know where it is. Thank you."

Norman and I then headed over to the elevator and he pressed the button to call the elevator. "I'm glad there are only five stories."

"Same," I said, crossing my arms.

As soon as the elevator door opened, I was greeted with the sight of the businessman, his father, and the actress.

"Are they here?" asked Norman as we stepped on the elevator.

"Like always," I said. "And before you ask, they can't talk to me. It's like they are stuck or something."

"Or maybe something is keeping them here," he said, searching for something.

"Like what?"

"Not sure," he said. "Do you notice anything about the ghosts? Is anything different?"

I gazed at the three ghosts. They were the same as always. "No, they…"

"Wait." Norman hit the stop button on the elevator.

"What are you doing?" I asked as the elevator made a sudden halt. With a jolt, I fell against the ghost of the little girl, her father, and the actress. As soon as my hand made contact with them, all sorts of emotions filter into my head before visions invaded my mind.

Flash.

I found myself coughing before coughing as my blurred vision watched the adorable little girl and her handsome father try and reach for each other...

Flash.

I found myself clutching my stomach as I fought to breathe, clinging onto my father who was bent over...

Flash.

I found myself hurling forward as the elevator jerked as I reached out for my daughter only to watch in horror as she too coughed and fell, her head colliding with the railing...

I pulled back and sagged to the floor as I tried to get myself under control as I felt warm tears streaking down my face.

"Weston!"

I blinked as something was shoved into my hand. It was a piece of chocolate.

"Eat," his voice demanded.

With shaky hands, I tore the paper and then ate the chocolate. "My head is killing me," I moaned, wincing and leaning back against the metal wall.

"What happened?"

"I touched them all," I said, shakily. "I never touched more than one ghost before. It was like my head couldn't focus. One second I'm the actress, then the little girl, and then the father. It was like the visions couldn't focus on just one. I feel like... I feel like I can't separate them."

Norman got on his knees in front of me and touched my hand. His calmness engulfed me like a soft wave. "You're Weston Brooks," he stated. "And you're my newest best friend. That is who you are.

Those ghosts that you saw, you aren't them. You are here and you are safe."

"Thanks, Norm," I said, smiling softly.

"Norm, I like that," he said, grinning as then removed his hand. "Sorry, I didn't know how else to help you."

I shook my head. "No, that helped immensely," I said. "I feel better. I just... my visions have a downside. I experience the death from their point of view. I don't see it like I'm an observer. It's more like I'm the victim themselves."

"Yikes," he said with a wince. "I would hate that. No wonder you have a hard time disassociating."

"Not to mention, I was the child." Tears unwillingly welled in my eyes and I rubbed them. "I don't get why she had to die. She was so innocent. And the emotions were horrible."

"What did you see?"

"I'm not entirely sure," I said. "From the dad's point of view, it looked like she had some form of head trauma, but…"

"You are legit!" he exclaimed. "That was the in the medical report."

"You had doubts about me?"

Norman shrugged. "What? Psychics are sometimes fakes, you know?" he said. "I didn't think you were a fake. But I didn't know how accurate your visions were."

I rubbed my forehead. "I understand that. Also, why did you stop the elevator?"

"Oh. I wanted to check out something from up high," he said. He climbed using the side rail and then pushed up on the ceiling. "I know it's here," he said as he continued to push until a hatch door opened. "Yes. Wes, give me a boost. I want to check if anything is up there."

I boosted him up by his shoes and legs.

"You aren't staring at my butt, are you?"

An embarrassing blush heated my cheeks. "No," I muttered.

After chuckling a bit, Norman crawled up through the hatch.

"See anything?"

"It's too dark. You got a light on you?"

"Yeah," I said, pulling out the flashlight from my pocket and tossed it up to him.

"Thanks." He caught it and then I could hear him move around above me.

"Norman?"

There was no response.

Something in the air changed and I turned. The businessman, his little girl, and the actress were all staring at me directly this time. They each smiled before vanishing as Norman's voice came from above.

"Weston, I found something!"

"What did you find?"

He dropped in from the hatch and held open his hand. In his palm was a gold hoop earring. It appeared to be super old judging from the discoloration. And strangely it also seemed oddly familiar. Where had I seen that before?

"How did you know that was up there?" I asked.

"Oh, just a feeling," he said. "I told you that my abilities can sometime lead me to things. Well, this is one of those things." He then turned over the earring.

"Do you think this was left by Lucy? Could this have been where she died?"

"Only one way to find out," I said. I nervously braced myself as I picked up the earring and closed my eyes. No vision invaded my mind.

"I got nothing," I said, opening my palm.

"What does that mean?"

"It simply means that this earring wasn't on her during her death. I only get glimpses of someone's death if they had the item on them at the time."

"Oh," he said. "I get it. Her earring could have simply fallen off when she sabotaged the elevator."

"Exactly," I said. A thought then crossed my mind. "Hold on."

"What?"

"Something doesn't add up," I said.

"What do mean?"

I touched the elevator. "If the elevator was the cause of their deaths, I would be seeing it. But I touched this elevator a zillion times. It never occurred to me. I just assumed based on what I heard."

"Weston, what are you going on about?"

"The vision... They were each coughing just before or right as the elevator started shaking..."

"Okay, but she could..."

I grabbed his arm. "Norman, listen to me. Barry, Henry, Jerry, they all had something in common in all my visions. They coughed and felt like they couldn't breathe. And these ghosts all felt exactly like that as well. Norman, they were so scared."

"What are you saying, Wes?"

I paused. "What if…all the victims were poisoned?"

28

We left the apartment building and stood by my Jeep. I examined the earring again. "This is bugging me big time."

Norman glanced at me with a wisp of confusion waving around him. He had apparently gotten out Manila folders and had the spread open on the hood of my Jeep. "What is?"

"This earring," I said. "I know I have seen this before. I just… I can't recall when or where." I sighed and laid my head on my arm.

"It'll come back to you," he said before he went silent.

I watched him as he was flipping through papers. "What are you looking for?"

"I'm trying to find their medical reports," he said. "I know I have the elevator incident report." He then pulled out a few pieces of paper. "Here they are." He sat them on the hood of my Jeep one beside each other. "Get this, the daughter, businessman, and actress were deceased by head trauma. The incident report states that the elevator dropped five floors from the brakes not working properly." His hazel eyes then glanced at me. "But you insist that they could have been poisoned. I don't disbelieve you. After all, I suspected that someone was deliberately hiding something."

"Didn't they list Barry, Henry, and Jerry's death as suicide? Did it say to what kind of suicide they committed?"

Norman flipped through a few more pages before examining them with an intense gaze. "It says here they all overdosed from sleeping pills."

I frowned. "Why would they take sleeping pills if they were all behind the wheel?"

"I've been thinking about that, too," he said with a hand under his chin.

I gazed back at the item in my hand. "Norman, have you ever tried to locate using an item?"

Norman's eyes shot up. "Excuse me?"

"Like have you tried to use something from the past to locate anyone who might wear the same thing?" I asked.

Norman blinked. "Do you mean you want me to use that earring to locate anyone in our town who might wear the same one?" he asked and I nodded. "Dude, that earring is so old. I bet it's from about forty or fifty years ago. It would never work. Besides, you forget, my ability requires a name to work."

"Guess we are back to square one."

A black cat jumped up on my Jeep and sat in front of me, wagging its tail.

"Mel?"

"Who else, genius?" she asked, her eyes seeming to narrow.

Norman's excited emotions had me looking over at him. He had a bright smile on his face as he gathered his papers and folders. "So, it is true. You really can talk."

Mel glared at him. "Of course, I can," she said before licking at her paw.

"I have questions. How can you talk? Were you cursed by a witch? Are you able to shapeshift? Are you Melinda in disguised? Her name is Melinda and yours is Mel. That can't be a coincidence, can it?"

Mel placed a paw over his lips. "Do shut up, Norman," she said.

I nearly giggled at the way Norman's eyes widened comically.

"What are you doing here, Mel?"

Mel's eyes found mine. "I heard you two knuckleheads needed some help. So, here I am at your service."

"How convenient," Norman said, a bit sarcastically.

"Do you want my help or not?"

"We would," I said. "In fact, we need to find out who wears an earring similar to this one." I showed it to her.

Mel peered at the earring before she sniffed it. She then made a disgusted face. "Hmm, I do faintly seem to recall a girl about your age who wears an earring like that."

"A girl my age," I said. "Well, I know Zelda. She and her dopey friends would never wear earrings like this. They have more expensive tastes."

"Dude, it's kind of freaky you know that."

"What?" I asked. "I'm simply observing. It has nothing to do with me being gay."

"I wasn't insinuating that."

"Sure," I said. "Anyway, I'm not the biggest know-how on jewelry, but this material feels lightweight and cheap."

Norman giggled. "Man, I hate to say it, but your gayness is showing."

I glared at him. Without meaning to, my telekinesis kicked in and sent him falling backward. He landed on his backside.

"Ow!" he said, pushing himself up. "I was only kidding. No need for that."

Guilt swirled in my stomach. "I…I didn't mean…"

Norman smiled. "No harm done. I shouldn't have teased you about that."

I shook my head. "No, you didn't do anything wrong. I'm afraid my powers are being weird. Usually, I'm more in control," I said, placing my head in my hands.

Mel tapped my cheek. "Did it ever occur to you that your abilities might just be simply growing?"

I blinked and shook my head. "That never occurred to me at all." I scratched Mel's head as she purred. "You really think that my powers are growing?"

Norman smiled. "If the kitty says it, it must be so."

Mel glared at him. "I'll gorge your eyes out, Norman Forrester."

Norman laughed. "You must be related to Melinda. You have her attitude."

Mel meowed. "I am not her. Now, I'll help you remember, Weston. Close your eyes."

I obeyed.

Norman giggled. "Is this a mediation thing?"

Mel and I must have been thinking the same thing because we both yelled at the same time. "Shut up, Norman!"

"Okay. Okay. Sheesh!" he said, and an image of him with his hands up in surrender showed up in my mind and I nearly smirked at it.

"What am I supposed to do now, Mel?" I asked.

"Use your empathy on the earring," she said.

My eyes opened at that. "What?"

Mel's green eyes narrowed to slits. "You must be able to feel emotions tied to items, right?"

"Only to items of the dead when they died," I stated, rubbing the back of my head. "Funny enough, I can't sense anything from items that are tied to the living."

"Useless empath," teased Mel.

I touched her nose. "That's not kind. I'm still trying to understand my powers."

Mel pushed my hand away with her head. "I know. You seriously need to train those mental walls inside that brain of yours. You don't realize it, but you shine like a beacon. You need to learn to protect yourself." She then sniffed the earring again. With a grimace, she turned her head away. "I don't know how you can't sense it when I can see and smell darkness on that so clearly."

"What did you say?"

"That you need better shielding?"

I shook my head. "No, you said darkness."

"That earring reeks of darkness. I can see it oozing out if it," she said.

"Darkness," I said as I thought back and then smacked my forehead. "Angela!"

Mel and Norman mouth gaped at me with confusion.

"Angela," I said again. "She had an earring similar to this one. That's where I remembered seeing it. She also had an aura of darkness around her."

29

Mel jumped off my Jeep and ran to who knows where while Norman insisted that he needed to do some more research. I decided to check out my cousin's house. More importantly, to check out Angela's room. Maybe she was somehow tied up in this matter somehow. Or at least that's what my instincts were telling me.

After dropping off Norman at the library, I headed for my cousin's house. Even though I had Carter's number in my phone, I decided to drop by unannounced. Maybe if I did this, I could get access without being suspicious. As soon as I pulled up to his house, I noticed that his car wasn't in the driveway nor did I see Angela. I didn't even know if she had a car. Honestly, I didn't care whether she did or didn't. I just didn't want her to be here.

I only had an hour before I had to go to work, but luckily I called Melinda ahead of time to let her know I would. Surprisingly, she wasn't angry and told me to come in when I could.

When I got out of the car and made my way to the front door, I knocked. No one answered. I tried the knob. It was locked.

This was perfect.

After a quick glance, I closed my eyes and concentrated on the lock. Hearing the click, I smiled and then unsuspiciously walked inside. Closing the door behind me, I locked it.

The first thing I noticed when I walked in and inspected my surroundings was that the living room was a shamble. It was like a fight or argument had broken out. There were balls of cotton littering the carpeted flooring from the torn up pillows. There was also broken glass from wine bottles and wine glasses. What on earth happened? Were Carter and Angela okay? Did Angela do something to my cousin?

Avoiding the mess, I walked around the couch and headed down the hallway, trying to find Angela's room which I think I found due to the hot pink door and the purple butterfly dreamcatcher hanging on hook.

I tried the knob but it was locked too. Tapping into my powers again, I tried to use my telekinesis to unlock the door, but I was met with a weird barrier that nearly made me fall back into the wall behind me. Now how was I supposed to get in?

"Weston," a voice said, "what are you doing here?"

Startled out of my skin, I jumped. Turning around panicked, I found my cousin in front of me. He was in a black overcoat and dressed in a nice-looking suit. It looked like he had just come from a funeral.

Shaking myself out of my thoughts, I looked at him startled. "I, uh…"

Carter crossed his arms. "Did you break in? No, that isn't like you. Dammit, Weston, you used the powers that your grandmother demonstrated to me, didn't you? Are you here to snoop around?"

I held my hands up. "I did use my powers, yes. But it's not what you think. I do have a good reason. I swear it."

"You better have a damn good reason."

"I do," I said. "At least, I hope I do. I mean..." I sighed and ran a nervous hand through my hair. "I should have told you this before, but the day you found me nearly passed out, I had a run in with Angela."

"Angela?"

I nodded. "Yes, she snuck inside my car. She said she was hiding from you and then she tried to hit on me."

"Wait. I thought she was with Hayden Lakewood? He is all she talks about. I didn't understand it considering she still occasionally makes remarks towards me. The whole thing is bizarre."

"Believe me, I know. It confused me to. And I needed to…"

"Is this about Hayden?" he asked. "Are you jealous?"

I was taken aback but then nodded. "In a way, yes, I am. But I also really want to protect Hayden. If she is hitting on you and trying with me, I don't want his heart broken."

Carter rubbed the back of his head. "Fine," he said. "I'll let you into her room on one condition.

You only, and I mean only, find out if she is hurting Hayden. I don't trust Angela at all, but she does have the right to her privacy."

"I promise," I said.

As Carter unlocked the door with a key he pulled out of his wallet, I asked, "So, cousin, uh, what happened in the living room?"

"Angela and I got into a fight."

"Oh, do you want to talk about it?"

"Maybe later," he said.

"Okay, so, then, were you at a party or a funeral perhaps?"

Carter shook his head. "No, why would you..." He then assessed himself. "Oh. I was on a date."

My eyes widened. "You had a date?"

Carter shook his head. "Not saying a word about it. I am not jinxing it. I may not be superstitious, but this might be something special and I don't want to ruin it. If there is a next date, I'll share. But it's not official right now."

"I want to hear about it."

Once Carter opened the door, he gasped. "What in the actual hell?" he bellowed. "What is all this?"

"What?" I asked, peering inside. Instead of a nice room with a bed, dresser, and all others essentials for a bedroom, it was instead painted all black and only had a futon in the corner. Glancing around, I saw a cloudy, shadowy, figure pointing to the closet. "Do you see that?"

"See what?"

"The dark shadow," I said.

"Dark shadow?" he asked. "I think you might be hallucinating there, cuz."

I rolled my eyes and walked over to the closet. Opening the folding doors, I saw a shrine. There were candles and pictures of all the victims all crossed out in black. There was even a picture of Lucy Silverstein. I knew because a nameplate was labeled under the photo and there was even an Ouija Board.

Carter came over. "What in the holy…"

"Don't say it!"

Carter shrugged. "I was going to say in the holy ghost of almighty."

"Sure you were," I teased. "Also, is this some kind of shrine?" I took out my phone.

"What are you doing?"

"Taking a picture," I said. "What does it look like I'm doing? The police need to see this."

"And they would probably arrest you. Think about it? You are their number one suspect after all. They'll question how you got the picture. I'll take the photo." He took out his phone and snapped a photo of the shrine and the rest of the room. "I can't believe she would do this."

Hurt and betrayal radiated from him. "Carter, man, I wish I had been wrong. I'm sorry."

Carter shook his head. "You have nothing to apologize for. I knew Angela was manipulative. But for her to straight up murder people?" he asked. "I mean that is a whole other level of messed up Why would she do this?"

I shook my head. "I'm not sure. But I doubt it's good."

Carter nodded. "You might be right." He then knelt. "What's this?"

"What's what?" I asked as I knelt beside him. I watched as he picked up something.

"It's a note." As his eyes read over it, I felt the confusion in his emotions spike. "Here you make sense of it."

The second I took it from him, I prepared myself for a vision. I got nothing. Honestly, I was glad about that. Instead, I glanced down at the note. "Wait. This...this is Hayden's handwriting."

"Are you sure?"

"Positive," I said before reading the note out loud. "This beautiful poem is for you, my dear one. Roses are red and violets are blue. Oranges are orange just like the sunrise. Under the moon, you blossom. Buds of lilacs, lavender, and even lilies smell as lovely as you. Enjoy your day with laughter and smiles."

"Not the greatest poem in the world," replied Carter. "It doesn't even rhyme."

I smirked. "That's why I know this note is for me."

"What?"

My smirk slipped. "Hayden and I made up this secret message game we found once on the internet. It was a way for us to tell each other what was going on through texts or notes. We would also tell each other special things only we would know." I took out my phone and went to the notepad app. "Take the first letter of each row." I typed T.R.O.U.B.L.E. and then turned it to my cousin. "Hayden's in trouble."

"Okay, but anyone could know that secret message. It's not unique."

"True, but trust me. I know Hayden. This is for me. He wants me to know he is in trouble. I can't explain it, Carter."

"If you say it is, then I trust you. Just think you both need better poems. Those sound terrible."

I laughed. "That's how I know it is Hayden. He and I can't rhyme worth a penny." I stuffed the note into my pocket. "We should go before Angela gets back. When she does, ask her about Hayden and then text me, okay? And text that picture to Norman instead of the police."

"Are you crazy? If she is killing people, the police need to know."

I sighed. "I know that. But if she has a hold of Hayden, I want him safe. And, I shouldn't be saying anything, but we think the police are involved in this. Norman and I think we discovered some big cover-up. I can't into all of this. But if Angela suspects anything, she may end up hurting or killing Hayden. Give me a few hours to try and find him and get some answers myself."

"Fine, but you owe me."

"Noted," I said.

30

I left my cousin's house and drove to work. Of course, as soon as I stepped inside the magic shop, I saw Jasper, who was sweeping the mahogany flooring. He stopped mid-sweep as his eyes landed on mine and stood as still as a statue.

"Hi," he said with an air of nervousness.

"Hello," I greeted before walking over to the counter.

"Melinda said you'd be late."

"Yeah, I had stuff that needed to be taken care of," I said.

Jasper continued sweeping. "Melinda said the same thing," he said.

Just then Norman barged in, causing the door to swing open violently.

"Norman Forrester!" Melinda yelled as she poked her head around from where she was hiding behind the bookshelves. "I swear to all of the magical curses, if you so much as break my door, you're going to get turned into a toad."

Norman grinned. "Would you make me the handsomest toad there ever was?"

Melinda glared. "Don't push your luck."

Norman chuckled. "Oh, come on, I bet I could be one of the best toads and even have a hot girl kiss me to change me back."

Melinda rolled her eyes. "You've watched too many fairytales."

Norman laughed at that. "I don't watch fairytales as much as I read the Grimm ones."

Melinda grinned at that. "Oh, so, you and I do share one thing in common, Norman Forrester. It's such a shocker."

"Maybe it just means we're a perfect match," he said with a mischievous grin.

Melinda rolled her eyes. "And you had to ruin a good moment."

Jasper and I shrugged before I turned my attention to Norman. "I'm going to guess the reason you are here is because of what my cousin sent you?"

Norman's eyes unwillingly turned away from Melinda to me. "Oh, yes," he said as he made his way over to me. "I honestly can't believe it. Angela is behind this. I hardly know her, but she has been in trouble with my dad so many times. It was nothing major just caused some public disturbances."

Discreetly, I took in everyone's emotions to see. Norman was feeling calm. Jasper, while not expressing it, had an air of anxiety swirling around him. And Melinda like always was a blank. But her expression was dark.

"Melinda?" I asked.

"Angela Silver," hissed Melinda.

Jasper rubbed the back of his neck. "I'm sorry, but did something happen? Who is Angela Silver?"

Melinda crossed her arms. "A no good—up in everyone's business—busybody. She tries to come in here, but never can."

"Why?" asked Norman.

"Bad apples like her are bad for business. She'll spoil all my good customers."

Jasper gripped the broom as more nervous energy spewed from him. "Aren't you worried you'll be sued for discrimination or something?"

Melinda jumped up on the counter and waved her hand like she was shooing the idea plum away. "People have tried to threaten me with that argument and never got anywhere. Besides, this is my business. I don't decide who is allowed in. My shop does that for me. You could say that this shop is magical. It decides who is and isn't right. It's not based on a person's skin, sexuality, or anything like that. It's based on how good-hearted a person is. Angela is not. She's filled with darkness."

I scratched the back of my head. "How does the shop decide that?"

Norman grinned. "Ooh! Is there a magic spell?"

"Nothing of the sort," she said, throwing a lollipop.

It hit Norman's forehead and he rubbed it. "Geez," he said. "I just asked. No need to sucker punch me with a lollipop."

"It's her specialty," whispered Jasper.

Melinda grinned. "Jasper, do you want to be hit as well?"

Jasper gulped. "No, ma'am," he said and I could feel the waves of fear.

Feeling sorry for the guy, I decided to intervene. "Let's get back to Angela," I said, trying to get us back on topic.

"Yes, back to Angela," Norman said. "Well, I can't go to this with my dad. I think we need to catch her in the act. If we do something now, she may catch wind of it and we could blow this whole thing up and she could take off or cover it up."

"I had the same thought process," I said. I reached into my pocket and touched the piece of paper from Angela's room. I couldn't tell them about Hayden being in trouble. If Angela knew, there was no telling what she'd do.

Norman sighed. "We just have to come up with a plan," he said. His phone then buzzed and he checked it. "Sorry, but I have to get going."

After Norman left, I felt piercing eyes on me. Turning my head, I found Melinda glaring at me suspiciously. "What are you hiding?"

"I'm not hiding anything."

"That's not what your aura is telling me."

I then gripped the counter as a flare of pain erupted in my head. "Not again," I whimpered. But this didn't feel the same as last time. For one, it wasn't nearly as intense. And the second was that, it was super quick and didn't mess with my vision as bad. And when I checked on Jasper, I only saw that strange silver flash in his irises before fading back to their usual brown. So, then, was this pain…not from him?

Was it Hayden? Was he in trouble? Before I could think anything else, more pain erupted along with a startling stream of powerful emotions. I sensed fear and anger the most rattled my system. I don't know if I gasped as blurriness entered my vision and voices invaded my hearing.

"Weston?"

"Is he okay?"

"Weston, can you hear me?"

"Should we call an ambulance?"

I covered my ears. Their voices were like screeching nails on a chalkboard in my brain. And the cars honking outside just made it that much worse.

"What do we do?"

Soon, everything stopped and I was able to open my eyes. I found myself on my knees with my arms wrapped around myself. I uncurled and leaned back against the counter. Melinda was beside me along with Jasper. I went to talk, but there was something hard in my mouth that tasted like cherry. In my hand, I saw a white twig sticking out. I pulled it out.

"Did you give me a lollipop?" I asked.

Jasper smiled, relief flooding from him. "Thank goodness. It was Melinda's idea. You just collapsed suddenly."

I turned my head to Melinda, who was staring at me weirdly. "What in the magical community happened to you, Weston? Your whole aura went wild. Did..."

I shook my head. "No, no. I'm okay. I think my blood sugar levels dropped again," I said, running a shaky hand through my damp hair. I'd apparently been sweating. I went to stand only to nearly fall back down.

Jasper grabbed my arm and I flinched a bit at the contact. His concern felt like a hot coal. He must have noticed my pained expression because his emotions spiked with guilt.

"Sorry," I said. "I'm...I don't do well with sudden contact."

Jasper wasn't offended. He just nodded and released his hands. "I understand. I can be like that when my migraines get bad. Will you be okay?"

"I will be. These things happen. Thank you for helping me."

"Oh, you two are precious," said Melinda playfully as she stood from her crouching position and ran hands over her dress.

My face heated up. "Melinda."

She just grinned. "I'm only teasing. Why don't you head home? You'll be no good if you fall over. Jasper, do you mind giving him a hand?"

"And you lower my pay even more?" I asked. "No thanks."

Melinda laughed. "I'm not docking your pay this time. Now go on. Jasper, make sure he makes it to his Jeep."

"Should he be driving in his condition?"

Melinda smirked. "Ooh. Good point. Maybe you should drive him home."

My face heated up more. "Melinda, stop it. I know exactly what you are doing."

Mclinda raised her hand, a smile never leaving her face. "I'm not doing anything other than making sure you are well."

"Yeah, right," I said, not believing her. She was trying to play matchmaker again.

Jasper's confused emotions were making my head pound even more. So, I slowly walked to the door. But before I could open the door, Jasper pulled me back just in time because a man a bicycle seemed to going way too fast.

"What the…"

"Are you okay?" asked Jasper.

"Uh, yeah, yeah, I'm okay." I couldn't help but notice Melinda in my peripheral vision, eying Norman weirdly as well as smirking creepily. She was too weird something.

I left the shop with Jasper following me. "Are you sure you're okay? I mean, that was a close call you just had."

"Yeah, I'm okay. I should thank you for saving me. I didn't even see it."

Jasper rubbed his neck nervously. "Y-yeah, I mean, I'm pretty good at spotting things and hearing things. At least, that's what my doctor's always were impressed with." I knew that was supposed to be a joke, but there was something strange in his emotions. It felt like he was hiding something.

"I wish I had that," I said.

"Will you be okay to drive?" he asked as we reached my Jeep.

I unlocked the door. "I should be. Thanks again," I said, climbing in.

Jasper grabbed the door before I could shut it. The confusion in his emotions changed to nervousness. "I know this is sudden, but would you be willing to get a coffee with me one day?"

I blinked at that. Was he asking me out on a date? That was ridiculous. "Uh…"

His disappointment pierced my heart. "I'm sorry. I don't mean it like that. I just… I… I wanted to show my appreciation to you and Melinda."

I gripped the steering wheel. "You don't need to go out of your way for us helping you out. It was the right thing to do." There was disappointment in his emotions that broke my head. "But if you insist, then, we can get together some time. I mean, obviously, not today."

Jasper nodded as the disappointment faded to relief and a small ray of hope. "No, I know. You need rest. That attack must have been awful. Trust me. My migraines are somewhat similar."

"Oh, I know," I said. "And thanks again, Jasper." I touched the door. "I need to get home and rest now."

"Right," he said, letting go of the door with a nervous laugh. "Sorry. Be safe heading home."

"I will." I shut the door and then started my Jeep before pulling away from the curb with Jasper in my rear view mirror.

31

The second I got home and stepped through the door, my grandma pulled me into a quick hug which startled me.

"Uh, Grandma, is everything okay?"

She pulled away and cupped my face as she gazed at me with narrowed eyes. Her emotions were a mystery to me, but I could feel some pain from her. Her eyes softened and she ran a hand through my dark hair that I was sure was sticking up and even greasy.

"I am fine, sweetheart. I was just worried about you. We haven't exactly talked much since what happened. I know you still have tons of questions about things. And I am willing to tell you. No more secrets."

I nodded. As I went to take a step, a wave of dizziness hit me so suddenly that I gasped and placed my hand on the door to keep myself steady as I blinked rapidly, hoping it would disperse the feeling away.

"Weston?"

I swallowed thickly. "Sorry. I feel woozy."

My grandma's eyes closed as she sighed. "When was the last time you ate?"

"Uh, this morning," I said. "I skipped lunch. But Melinda did give me a lollipop."

She grabbed my arm and pulled me towards the kitchen. For an elderly woman, she sure had a strong grip.

She fed me food for three people. There was chicken, green beans, salad, rolls, fries, and even cookies for dessert. I couldn't eat all of that. I settled for a few pieces of chicken, salad, a roll, and one cookie. I did feel famished as these attacks did a number on my energy levels. But at the same time, I didn't feel that hungry.

While I ate, my grandma watched me like a hawk as she also talked about her life. She talked about how she struggled with her powers for about a year and how her family barely helped her through it as they worked hard in factory jobs and retail to make ends meet. She even told me about how she met my grandfather. She had saved him one day from falling off a ladder. She told me how they fell in love but he passed away before my dad was born due to an illness. She then talked about my father and how he was a lot like me as a child.

I took this all in and tried to monitor her emotions which were hard to read. Though, I sensed the love she felt deeply for her family, my grandfather, and my father. She truly loved them dearly. I couldn't stop my thoughts from wandering to Hayden and how much he meant to me.

Once I finished all my food, I went to help her clean, but she stopped me. "No, sweetheart, I will handle cleaning up. You go on up to your room. I'm sure you had quite the day. And getting some rest early will help with that."

It didn't feel right to leave her to clean everything, but I also knew it was better not to argue. So, I kissed her cheek softly and headed up the stairs.

Once inside my room, a feeling of anxiety, panic, and heartbreak flooded through me. I leaned against my closed door and sank to the floor with my knees drawn to my chest as I fought to calm my emotions. Were these my emotions? Were they my grandma's? I couldn't tell.

Without warning tears had begun to fall straight down my cheeks unwillingly. I tried extremely hard to wipe them away, but I couldn't. My thoughts, no matter how hard I tried not to, went to Hayden. I scrambled for the note in my pocket with trembling hands. Eventually finding it, I took it out unfolded it, and began to anxiously go over and over the note, both out loud and internally.

I closed my eyes. Then both in anger and frustration, I crumpled up the paper and threw it as hard as I could on the opposite side of the room.

The rain had started to pour as I leaned my head back against the door and cried silently. Things in my room were rattling from my powers that I could feel swirling inside me like a hurricane. I clenched my knees and calmed myself, listening as the rain continued to pour, but the rattling stopped. I leaned my head against my hands. "I need you, Hayden," I whispered to myself. "I need to know you are okay."

I don't know how long I sat there before I slowly climbed to my feet and then fell on my stomach on my bed. I brought my left hand up to my face and stared at the bracelet I still had on. A part of me wanted to get rid of it, to get rid of the reminder of him. But I couldn't. His birthday present was special. It was a reminder of our bond. It was also a reminder of how I missed him so much. I then watched, surprised, as my bracelet glowed turquoise as a strange heat surged through my head.

"Weston," his voice called out to me in my mind.

Confused, I sat up. "Hayden?"

"Weston," the voice said again.

"Hayden? Where are you?" I turned my vision towards the mirror hanging on the wall; a rippled image of Hayden's face stared at me. I quickly got to my feet and moved over to the mirror. I touched the glass softly. "Hayden, what is this? What are you doing inside of the mirror?"

Hayden didn't respond. He was lying on the ground somewhere. Wherever he was, it was dark, which didn't help with locating him.

"Where are you, Hayden?"

"Weston, help me."

"Is it Angela? Is she hurting you?"

"No." He was lying. Even if he wasn't physically here, I could still read his emotions.

"You're lying. Why are you lying to me?"

"Please, Weston." The begging in his voice startled me. He's never begged like this before.

"Tell me where you are."

"Caster Bridge," he said before the image of him vanished.

With that in mind, I waited until it was dark and until I heard and felt my grandma sleeping before I opened my window.

Mel suddenly jumped in.

"You scared me," I said, startled, placing a hand to my racing heart. "What are you doing here, Mel?"

Mel's glowing green eyes constricted. "Stopping you from doing something stupid," she said. Her green eyes glared at me.

"You can't stop me from rescuing Hayden. He needs me."

"And he's also leading you into a trap."

"How do you even know that?"

Mel sighed. "I just do."

I rolled my eyes and moved Mel aside by swatting my hand and then climbed out the window. "I'm still going." I carefully made my way down the roof and used the vines like before to help me down the rest of the way.

Mel jumped down like it was nothing. For a cat, I supposed that was true.

"You do realize this is going to be seriously dangerous, right?"

"Yes, that thought has occurred to me," I said as I walked to my Jeep. "But I don't care. Hayden needs my help."

I opened the door and Mel jumped into my seat. "Well, since your heading into a trap, I might as well tag along."

"No way, Mel," I said. "If this is truly a trap…"

Mel glared at me. "Then you are going to need backup. So deal with me tagging along."

I sighed. "Move over."

Mel meowed happily and jumped over to the passenger side.

I rolled my eyes and got in. It was time that I saved Hayden.

32

Once I parked my Jeep, I turned to Mel. "Stay here, Mel," I ordered as I opened the glove box and pulled out the flashlight I had in there.

"No way," Mel said, turning her head towards me. "I'm here to not only protect you but make sure you also don't get into trouble."

"I know, but I don't want you hurt. Besides, you can keep an eye out. If anything happens, you can get help."

Mel glared. "Fine, but you better be safe and you owe me some fish."

I laughed and petted her head. "Duly noted," I said before I got out of my Jeep. When I pushed the button on my flashlight, it didn't turn on.

Stupid thing, I thought as I hit it a couple of times with my palm before it came on. Using the light, I cautiously made my way to the bridge. As soon as I got close enough, I saw him. He was leaning against the railing.

I tried to keep my heart from leaping out of my chest at the sight of him. He was just as beautiful as always. Minus the fact that his ginger hair was dirty and that his eyes had dark smudges under them. There was also a dark bruise on his forehead like he'd been hit with something.

"Hayden!" I yelled, dashing over to him.

Startled, Hayden's beautiful turquoise eyes landed on me. "Weston, what are you doing here?"

"Saving you," I said.

He rubbed his palm. "I wasn't sure you'd come."

I cupped his face. "Hayden, no matter what, I will always come."

Without a second thought, he grabbed my face tenderly and kissed me. This kiss felt different. Not like our first. This one felt desperate, but also like he was apologizing. But for what I didn't know. I didn't care. I just grasped his shoulders and kissed him back. I missed him so much. He constantly consumed my thoughts day in and day out no matter how hard I tried to push the thoughts away.

Light raindrops were starting to fall and thunder rumbled in the distance, but luckily, we pulled away before Hayden's emotions could invade me.

I asked, "What's happening, Hayden?"

His eyes filled with tears and deep saturated guilt poured from him in waves. "I'm so sorry, Weston. Please understand. I didn't have a choice."

I held his shoulders. "Hayden, I don't understand. What could you have done that was so terrible?"

Before he answered, horrible pain erupted in the back of my head and I collapsed. Even though my vision was blurred, I could see Angela smirking.

And then blackness overcame me.

***

When I was aroused to consciousness, I first found that my head was pounding crazily. The second was that my vision was blurred. Third, as I went to rub them, I found my hands were constricted behind my back. After blinking some of the blurriness, I turned my head. I was on the bridge.

"What...?" I tried to ask but a weird soreness in my throat prevented me from talking.

"About time you woke up," a woman's voice said.

Glancing up, I saw it was Angela. She was smiling sinisterly as she leaned down to my level. For a second, I thought she was going to kiss me which made my stomach churn with bile. What was she going to do to me?

I stammered from the soreness and coughing, "Hayden?"

"He's fine," said Angela.

"Why...?" I swallowed. What did they do to me?

Angela smiled. "Why are we doing this? Simple: vengeance."

"Huh?"

"Don't be afraid," she said, smirking as she touched my cheek. Dark emotions started swallowing me whole making me recoil from her touch.

"I'm...not," I managed to cough out.

Angela's sinister smirk never left her face as she leaned down. I tried to move back, but only ended up falling on my back.

"Don't," I said through the hoarseness.

Angela smiled and whistled.

And then Hayden walked over. "What do you need?"

"Hold him," Angela said, pointing to me.

Hayden nodded and moved as he grabbed my shoulders forcefully and sat me up not too gently.

"Hayden," I whispered.

Hayden didn't say anything.

"You can't save him. He's under my influence," said Angela. "It was too easy. He was attracted to me enough that my gift allowed me to manipulate him with a simple kiss."

"Are you a succubus?" I asked, sassily, after a small coughing fit.

"A succubus?" she asked, laughing. "That's funny. No, I simply have the gift to control men. Only works through attraction. It doesn't work on you sadly."

I closed my eyes as anger swelled. I concentrated hard to connect with powers so I could undo the ropes on my wrist, but I couldn't detect the usual warmth. It was as if my powers were weakened. Was that what she did?

"What have you done to me?" I finally managed to ask.

Angela smiled. "So, it does work like she said it would."

"Like who said?"

Angela didn't answer. Instead, she said, "What I gave you was some kind of potion. She said it would prevent you from using your powers against me. Of course, it will wear off soon. But by then, you will no longer be a thorn in our side."

"Why? I never did anything."

"Didn't do anything?" she scoffed. "You got too nosey. If you had just minded your business none of this would be happening."

"What are you saying that if I hadn't started investigating, then you wouldn't have involved Haydn in your twisted mess?"

"Unfortunately, no," she said, frowning. "I was going to kill him, but I noticed how close you two were and decided to use that to my advantage."

I glared at her. "You were going to kill him because of your jealousy?"

Angela paled. "How did you know that?" she asked before she leaped on me and pinned me, her nails gripping into my shoulder blades.

Sudden pain erupted in my head before spreading throughout my whole body. I could feel tears pricking at the edge of my eyes as I fought not to scream.

I squeezed my eyes shut.

"NO!" shouted Hayden.

The pain vanished and my eyes opened to see Angela on the ground.

Hayden stood in front of me protectively. "Do not hurt him!"

Angela stared at Hayden with surprise. "How did you break through my influence?"

"I may like you, Angela, but I'm not in love with you," he said sternly before he turned his attention towards me. His eyes were soft and he smiled.

I smiled back, but it slipped immediately as I watched in horror as Angela crept up on him. I saw something glisten in her hand. Before I could warn Hayden, she sprinted and stabbed Hayden in his shoulder.

I nearly screamed from the pain that was forcing its way into my brain and shoulder.

The second Hayden collapsed, I scrambled over to him. I wanted to place my hands on his shoulders, but they were still tied. "Hayden," I said as tears welled in my eyes.

Hayden's pain-filled eyes gazed at me as he held his bleeding side. "Weston, you're okay, right?"

"I'm okay," I said before raising my gaze. Anger pulsated through me as I glared at Angela with hatred. She had no right to hurt him.

With all the rage inside me, my telekinesis knocked her back. Even with my hands still tightly secured behind my back, I managed to clench them into fists with my nails digging into my palms as the ire inside me flooded my mind.

The wind started to whoosh like a freight train and tree limbs began to creak and crack. I didn't want to just scare her. I wanted her no longer to exist which was very unlike me.

Feeling Hayden grip my bicep, the ire inside me faded quickly.

"Don't do it," he begged.

"But…"

"She isn't worth it," he said. "Hurting her would haunt your soul forever. You are too kind to ever hurt another human in cold blood."

Tears slid down my cheeks as rain drizzled around us. I laid my head on his chest as my energy was drained. "I'm sorry."

Hayden's hand wound up in my hair as he petted my head. "It's okay."

My head shot up in time for me to see Angela getting to her feet. She grabbed the knife that had fallen to the ground and pointed it directly at me.

"Time to end this," she sneered.

Before I could do anything to stop her with my powers, salt sliced through the air and hit her. Angela screamed before she dropped to the ground as a ghost stood over her. She had long black hair, amber eyes, and was dressed in a short black dress.

"How did you do that?" she asked, glaring at me.

I shook my head. This wasn't my doing. I could tell because I wasn't feeling the warmth when I used my abilities.

"Did it work, Mel?" asked a familiar voice.

Shocked, I turned my head to see Norman. He was standing there with Mel, who was sitting on the ground.

"Salt worked," Mel said. "Good aim."

Norman smirked. "I'm glad it worked. I can't see anything other than Angela, so I'll have to take your word for most of it." He then regarded me. "Hell, Wes, I can't believe you allowed me to miss this party, Wes," he joked.

I rolled my eyes but felt relief. "Yeah, some party," I said. "How did you know?"

Norman smiled. "Mel told me you were in trouble."

"I had it under control."

"Liar," he said, smirking growing.

33

While Angela was knocked out, Norman ran over and untied my wrists. "You are so luckily that Mel came to me when she did. You might have been in serious trouble."

"Yeah, yeah," I said. "I know." Once my wrists were untied, I rubbed them. "Norman, can you tend to Hayden for me?"

"Sure, but why?" he asked.

"Because I have a ghost to chat with," I said.

"Ah, got it," he said, tending to Hayden.

"Are you Lucy?" I asked, standing up.

Lucy's eyes narrowed. The anger emitting from her had me faltering and gritting my teeth. I'd hope with some training that I could stop anger from hurting me.

"How do you know my name?" she asked, sneering as she advanced towards me.

"Long story," I said. "Did you possess Angela?"

"Why should I tell you anything?"

"I just want to help you," I said.

Lucy blinked, but didn't say anything.

"Can you tell me why you killed Barry, Jerry, and even Henry?"

Lucy's anger dissolved into shock. "Excuse me?"

"Jerry, Henry, and Barry," I said. "They are all dead, murdered."

"Murdered?" she asked.

"Yes," I said. "Barry Bloomingdale, Jerry Jenkins, and Henry Hunter, they are all dead. Just like their parents."

Lucy stepped back. "Their parents... My friends... Mr. Bloomingdale... He's dead? And so are Director Jenkins and Professor Hunter? You're lying. They were my friends. How can they be dead?"

I blinked. What?

"You killed your husband, right?"

Lucy's anger rose. "Of course I did. I never denied that. I hid it from the police. I didn't want to go to jail. But I wouldn't harm my friends."

"Wait. If you didn't then..." I paused as I thought through everything. My grandma had been convinced it was Lucy. But could she have been wrong? I trusted my grandma. Was she behind this? No! It couldn't be her.

A clap had me turn around.

There was an elderly woman, holding onto her cane. I had seen the woman before. She was from the apartment complex. The woman who claimed to be Rosemary's grandmother. But something was different about her. Instead of her being in a white flowing gown and sandals, her sky-blue eyes narrowed as an air of authority surrounded her.

Norman gasped. "You!" he said, shocked.

"Norman, you can see her?"

Norman nodded. "Sure can. That should be impossible. You passed away a couple of days ago."

The elderly woman smiled. "Oh, that," she said with a strange kind of giggle. "That was nothing more than a mere old fake death."

"You faked your death?" I asked, and my eyes widened. "It's you! You are behind everything. Not Lucy. Not Angela."

"I am indeed, dearie," she said, grinning.

"But how did you disappear so quickly?"

"Simple," she said. "I just walked away quietly without you noticing."

"But that means…you killed your granddaughter. Why?"

The elderly woman's expression darkened before a sinister smile made its way onto her wrinkled face. "Oh, you mean Rosemary. Yes, that girl was indeed my granddaughter. I used her as test."

"What kind of test?" I asked, surprised.

"A test for you, dearie," she said.

What the hell did that mean?

"Excuse me?" I asked. "What do you mean?

The elderly woman smiled. "I needed something to lure you to me. I thought I had my chance on the elevator, but you managed to evade it. You're either more powerful than I thought or just outsmarted me. So, I manipulated poor Angela." Her eyes traveled to the unconscious girl still lying on the ground. "I noticed her hatred towards you. So, I manipulated her."

"What about…"

"Oh, you mean Barry, Jerry, and Henry?" she asked. "They were just food."

"Who or what are you?"

"Why tell when actions can reveal," she said, waddling over to me using her cane before she grabbed my chin. Darkness was encasing her emotions. I gasped and watched as some kind of smoke or condensation came out of my mouth. She breathed it in as her eyes glowed orange before she let go.

I collapsed, feeling utterly weird, and drained.

The elderly woman's face began to morph into a younger-looking woman until it was Ella who stood in front of me. "I knew it," she said. "I missed that taste so much."

"You're Ella Graceland," answered Norman. "You used to be a pediatric psychologist. I saw you once after my mother died."

"Really now?" she asked. "Funnily enough, I do not remember you."

"Yeah, figures," he said. "You did tell me to accept that I was responsible for my mother's death."

"Norman," I whispered, sympathetically.

"Did I?" she asked, innocently. "Hmm, must have slipped my mind. You mustn't have been anything good."

Norman's eyes glowered and I felt his anger rise. "Go to hell," he growled.

"My, not very well-mannered," she said. "No wonder I gave you that advice. You have no manners whatsoever." She grinned.

"Norman," I warned.

His eyes narrowed and glared at me. There wasn't anger this time. I felt pity. "You saw her, too, Weston."

"What?"

"You don't remember?" he asked.

I shook my head.

"I found a file and your name was listed."

"But..."

"Remember those documents I showed you? I thought it was my dad covering it up, but it wasn't. She forged everything. I bet you anything that she even manipulated Lucy to unintentionally murder her friends and maybe even her husband in 1978, didn't you, Belladonna?"

"Like the poisonous plant?" I asked.

"Yes, all those autopsies about sleeping pills were a lie. She was using belladonna just like her name sake."

Lucy gasped. "It can't be. She was my friend. There was no way she would do this. She couldn't. Weston, tell her. Tell her it isn't true for me. I know I did wrong, but please."

"Weren't you friends with Lucy?" I asked, tuning out Lucy.

Belladonna dropped the cane. "She was a perfect candidate. She had a psychic energy that she didn't even know about. I fed from her energy to keep myself young. Neither she nor any of our true friends knew about my true nature or my true age. I'm older than you can imagine."

"What was the point?"

"I needed to stop Richard. Richard knew of my true nature. He found out accidentally. I wasn't' cautious enough. So, I used Lucy to murder him."

"You bitch!" yelled Lucy as she tried to punch Belladonna before she groaned. "Being a ghost sucks."

I coughed before touching my throat. "What... What are you?"

Belladonna smiled. "You tell me," she said, grinning at me. "You're smart, right?"

I glared.

"You're a psychic vampire, aren't you?" asked Norman. "I did some research. You feed on psychic energies. I bet Barry, Jerry, and even Henry all had some psychic energy in a way."

Belladonna smirked. "You are correct," she said. "I took all they had left. My, I didn't realize you were the smart one. I used to think you were only dumb for trying to be funny all the time."

"Shouldn't judge a book by its cover then," he said with a lopsided grin.

Belladonna groaned. "You know, Norman, I do remember your taste. You only have a slight psychic bone. It was never appetizing.

"Screw you!" he shouted.

"Weston and Angela are the two who could fill me the most and for much longer without having to drain them immediately. Barry, Henry, and Jerry could only do so much."

"So, you fed from Angela?" I asked.

"Of course," she said. "Plus, if things went south, I needed her to take the fall. What better person."

Belladonna laughed.

"Weston..." Hayden whispered.

My eyes went to Hayden, blearily. His eyes were closed, but I could see the pain lines in his face as well as feel the waves from him pushing its way into my chest. I clenched my hands, wishing that mine were clench around his, to keep myself grounded. The emotions from everyone were getting to me.

Rain then immediately started pouring.

Finally, I had enough!

I bellowed, "STOP!"

Everything came to an instant stop. The voices, the sound of heavy breathing, the painful emotions, all of it just...stopped. All except for the rain that suddenly started pouring heavily, but strangely kept me dry as though it was protecting me. I bathed in the calmness for a few minutes before I could take another deep breath. I then rose to my feet, ignoring the faintness in my head as my vision blurred slightly.

Suddenly, a presence had me turn to find the man from the museum.

"Richard Silverstein?" I asked.

Lucy's eyes pierced mine before her eyes turned to Richard and she gasped. "Where... I... Rich! How are you here?"

Richard smiled at Lucy before he turned his attention to Hayden. "He helped me. He found out about Angela and Belladonna, so he used the Ouija board to summon me. I tried to possess him but couldn't. He's protected. This boy," he said, looking at me, "is helping to protect him somehow. I managed to find him, but I couldn't talk like I can now. I had to save my energy. All I could give him was a warning."

"Richard?" Belladonna sniggered. "So, you can see ghosts. I never knew the full extent of your abilities. I should have known. The way your eyes always wandered around even when you were a child, talking to imaginary people who weren't there. I always knew there was something truly special about you from the first time I tasted your energy. I thought it was just the empathy thing Ruth mentioned. But you can see ghosts. This just makes it even more special."

"You talked to my grandma? But she said... Wait." My mind flashed back to the picture and realization hit me. "No, it's you. You were her best friend. You were the one who nearly gave me that muffin. You were going to kill her and me with a poison."

Belladonna grinned evilly. "Oh, come now, it wasn't too toxic. Yes, it was belladonna, but it would have only caused you to sleep. There would have been no harm if you had just eaten the one I had given you on the elevator. But when you didn't I knew I needed to find another way to get you, so, when I saw you at the museum, I handed it to you to give to Ruth. Though, that one was indeed deadly. I wanted Ruth dead. You see, dearie, her home is protected. I couldn't get near. And Ruth hardly leaves her home for me to corner her, so I had to find an alternative way. You see, when I saw you on that elevator, I knew your taste immediately. It would have been better if I had taken you when you were a child, but your father took you from me."

"My dad…"

"You didn't know?"

I shook my head again.

"Oh, you don't remember, do you?"

"Remember what?" I asked.

"Oh, this is wonderful," she said, laughing.

"Can you make sense?"

"You were four at the time when you came to me," she said. "I pinned you to the couch and fed from your energy. I was going to take you away and keep you locked up. Your energy would have kept me young for years, but your dad ran in. I'm guessing Ruth warned him or something. I tried to hurt her, but you protected him even though you were weak."

I blinked. "But if that happened then why wait until now? Why didn't you do it years ago?"

Belladonna sighed. "I didn't have a choice. I had to go into hiding… Your father knew my face. So, I killed him by stealing his energy. I'm not a regular vampire. For one, I didn't get bit by a bat. I also don't drink blood. That's gross. And vampires also have to feed often. I can go months and years if I steal enough. I don't always have to kill, though."

So, why start killing now then?"

"Damn," Norman said. "How did I not see it before? This is about your daughters, isn't she? You find out the truth. Natasha, the little girl on the elevator, was your daughter, and you accidentally got her killed. But you recently found out that your other daughter was alive and well."

"What?" I asked.

"All of this isn't just a test for you, Weston. This also has to do with Natasha. The girl who was adopted by Timothy Bloomsdale," Norman answered. "I get it now. Richard was Natasha's real father. You and Richard had a one nightstand. And then you gave birth to not one child, but two. It was then Richard found out about you being a psychic vampire and took them away to protect them. He gave Natasha to Timothy, but hid your other daughter from you. It was only recently that you got information that your daughter actually survived. She was never on the elevator. She was taken away while another girl who just looked like Natasha was on the elevator."

"Those no good bastards!" she yelled. "They wouldn't let me see my daughter!" Her anger flared causing me to wince in pain. Her expression darkened and regret took hold. "I wanted them out of the way. I knew Lucy was mad at Christina for the affair, but she never knew that I manipulated them to do it. Well, mostly, I manipulated Christina. She had a crush on Richard, but she respected Lucy significantly. However, I fueled her crush. Of course, I had her drug Richard to make it seem believable…"

"How could you do that to my husband!" yelled Lucy.

"It wasn't until very recently though that I learned the truth. Richard, Derek, Timothy, and Dustin all were in on it. They hid her from me. I just wanted to see my daughter. I don't know where she is. They wouldn't tell me. I feed from their offspring, hoping they would know. They didn't and I killed them instead. I used my medical knowledge and forged the autopsy reports. I figured I would manipulate Angela. Being a psychic vampire I can tap into others emotions and manipulate them. It worked. However, I..." A guilt-crushing sadness radiated through her.

"It was her fault!" she yelled. "Everything that happened was all because of her!"

Richard dashed over to Lucy. "Lu, I get you're upset. I do. I am, too. I never wanted to cheat on you. You were the only one for me. You were the sweetest, lovable woman I had ever met. I was so happy to marry you, but then..." His regret pierced my heart like a dagger. "I don't remember what happened. Christina gave me a drink and then the next thing I know I was waking up the next morning. It never should have happened."

"Rich, no, it wasn't. I should have listened to you. I should have talked to you! I was so upset that I went to Belladonna for advice."

"You both aren't at fault for this," I said.

Before I could hear their response, I found myself on my back, staring up at Belladonna's bright red face. Furiousness was strong around her. "No talking to the deceased. This is my moment."

"You...you have telekinesis?" I asked.

"Not exactly," she said, smirking. "When I take some of the psychic energy, I can gain a little bit of the powers they possess."

Suddenly, Mel ran in front of me. "Don't you dare hurt him!" she hissed.

Belladonna glared at Mel with utter hatred. I could feel it spewing off her. "You witchy bitch!"

she sneered with a wicked grin. "I thought I got rid of you years ago."

Mel's body went rigid. "You can't get rid of me that easily, Belladonna."

Before she could make a move, she was sent flying back with a painful meow.

"Mel!" I screamed before feeling something pressing hard against my chest. Belladonna had her cane pressed against my chest.

"Now, it's time for you to die."

I tried to use my powers to throw her back, but I couldn't feel it. Luckily, I didn't have to do anything.

"Step away from the boy!" shouted Detective Forrester, pointing his gun at her.

Belladonna didn't say anything. Instead, she continued to press her cane into my chest harder.

I winced.

"Belladonna Graceland!" said Detective Forrester sternly, pointing his pistol at her. "I won't warn you again! Step away from the boy and put your hands behind your head!"

Belladonna smirked. "You know I never do as I'm told, Daryl."

Richard knelt and whispered in my ear, "Tell her that Rosemary was her real daughter."

"What?"

"Rosemary was her daughter," he repeated.

"But how..."

"Tell her now," he demanded. "If you don't, she'll kill you and the detective."

I didn't care about my life, but my friends and Norman's dad were too important. So, I turned my vision to Belladonna. "Rosemary."

Belladonna looked down at me shocked. "What?"

"Rosemary was daughter."

Belladonna gasped, paling. "No, no, that's not true. You're lying!" she yelled. However, pain laced through her and me as she turned her head around.

Angela was behind her, holding a dagger in her hand that was dripping with blood. I could feel her weariness and fatigue.

"Angela, dear," Belladonna gasped as she held her shoulder. "Why did you..."

"I heard your words!" she growled. "You used me! You used me to bring Barry, Henry, and even Jerry those muffins, so you could kill and drain them. And you used my anger, made me lash out at my best friend, and used my jealousy to make me manipulate Hayden! You violated my emotions!"

Belladonna reached out with her good arm and went to touch Angela's cheek, but Angela backed away from her and pointed the dagger at her.

"Don't you dare touch me!" Angela yelled.

My head pounded at the emotions pouring in all around me. There were so many, too many to focus on. It honestly hurt my head to even try and process each one. I couldn't take on this many emotions at once. It felt like my insides were being squeezed. Just when I thought I would succumb, a bolt of what looked like lightning came bolting down between the two of us.

Belladonna cried out.

The pressure of her cane dissipated.

I watched her eyes widen as horror overtook her emotions. "What did you do?"

I opened my mouth to try and speak but I felt paralyzed.

While distracted, I noticed Detective Forrester ran over and cuffed her.

That was the last thing I saw before I welcomed the blackness.

34

I sat on the hood of my jeep and watched the scene of Angela and Belladonna being taken to the police car. Hayden was being taking care of by the paramedics. Luckily, he hadn't lost that much blood. They had called his mom and she was standing by him, glaring at me.

Paramedics had checked me over. I had passed out from the overload of intense emotions and lack of energy, but luckily Norman, after getting me to wake up, told them that I couldn't stand the sight of blood. I knew he was just trying to protect me from going to a hospital. Honestly, I couldn't thank him enough for that.

Just then, something in my peripheral vision caught my attention. It was a strange, black, oily shadow. It slithered and then swirled through the trees until it stopped directly at Belladonna, who was over by the car. I tried reaching out with my empathy to get a sense of what it was, but all could feel was a strange sense of static.

"No!" a voice cried out and I watched as Rosemary appeared. "Weston, help!" She touched the blackness only to flicker and jolt back.

I wanted to call out, but it was like I was paralyzed, staring at the black shadow as it coiled around her. Belladonna shivered, but the black shadow continued to engulf her. She then started coughing which made me empathize with her.

A horrible feeling ripped through my chest. A crippling pain like no other stole my breath and nearly made me fall off the hood and onto the ground. I honestly wanted to lie on the ground and curl in a ball because this pain was intense. I felt like I couldn't breathe. I could feel Hayden's calm emotions trying to comfort me, but everything felt surreal.

As soon as the pain stopped, I uncurled myself. Tears dampened my cheeks. And it wasn't from the rain because that had ended a while ago. I must have been crying. But I wasn't sure if it was from the pain or sadness or both or from something else.

Before my very eyes, Belladonna clutched at her heart before slumping to the ground.

"Paramedics!" shouted Detective Forrester, who had been trying to help her. "I need some help over here!"

The black oily shadow gathered. I could see red glowing eyes boring directly at me before the shadow vanished.

Rosemary appeared in front of me and gripped my shoulders tightly and forced me to stare into her furious brown eyes. "Why didn't you help her? She did bad, yes, but she didn't deserve to die like that, Weston!"

I was stunned. "I...I didn't... I'm sorry."

Rosemary let go of me and sighed. "Yes, she killed me. I should hate her for that, but... When I learned she was my mother, I wanted to know her. But I heard the news of her passing. I wanted to meet her, to tell her the truth. I wasn't a psychic vampire like her. I never possessed that kind of power. I wanted her to atone for what she did in a jail cell. I didn't want her to be killed, Weston!"

Before I could open my mouth, Mel jumped into my lap. "Rosemary, leave Weston alone, okay? None of this was his fault. Whatever that thing was, well, I don't think Weston could do have done anything about it."

Rosemary blinked, but a bright smile came across her face. "A talking cat," she said. It wasn't fear in her voice. It was excitement. "Now I have seen everything." She tried to touch her but her hand seeped through. "Dang, I wanted to pet you."

Mel swatted her paw. "Stop that. Just because you can't feel it doesn't mean that I can't."

"Sorry, kitty," she said, giggling.

I leaned against my Jeep with confusion swirling around my head. Before I could question it though, the little girl, who was Natasha, came up to me. I knelt at her level as she smiled.

"Papa said I should thank you," she said.

"Thank me?" I asked.

She nodded. "Papa said that Mama is gone now. You tried to stop her. She wasn't always a bad person. Daddy told me so. She just sadly did bad things. Papa says everyone does bad things sometimes, but it's how you try and solve them that truly matters."

"Your papa is a very smart man."

"The smartest," she said and then licked her lollipop before she smiled again. "Could you do me a favor?"

"Anything," I said.

"Could you tell the boy over there thank you as well?" she asked, pointing to Hayden, who was standing beside his mom with a sling on his arm. "Without him, I wouldn't have gotten to see my papa."

I stared at her surprised. "I will tell him."

Natasha grinned. "Thank you. You are so kind, mister." She let me go and looked at Rosemary. "You're my sister, right?"

Rosemary smiled. "Apparently, I am."

"Cool," she said and grabbed her hand. "You have to come meet Papa and everyone." She then waved before they ran off.

"That is one sweet little girl," Richard said, standing beside me. "I wish I had gotten to know her and Rosemary, too."

"What happened?"

"I had a one night stand with Belladonna. It was before I even met Lucy. A part of me thinks Belladonna just used me to get back at someone."

"It's possible," I said. "Natasha and even Rosemary are very sweet." I watched as she hugged her adoptive father.

Richard nodded. "Indeed."

Just then Christina materialized in front of me. There was irritation drooling off her, but also some kindness. "I was told to thank you. You saved us."

"I didn't do much," I said.

She gritted her teeth but even though she obviously didn't want to be here, she still managed to be polite. "Well, still, thank you." She then turned to Richard. "I..."

Richard shook his head. "No need to apologize, Christina. We know the truth now. We have the chance to move on and be with our loved ones now."

Christina smiled. "You're right." She then sashayed over to the others.

Just then a young man in overalls appeared. "I just wanted to thank you, Weston. As you probably already know, I am in fact Jerry Jerkins," he said. "I interacted with you briefly at the mechanic's shop. Though, I was unable to do much. I could barely talk then as I was confused. But now that Belladonna has been put to justice, I can finally talk and move on. It's thanks to you and your friends."

I shrugged. "I didn't do all that much."

Jerry chuckled. "You did more than you think." He then looked at Norman, who was in what looked like a heated discussion with his dad. "Tell Norman that Mickey will be fine. It isn't his time. It was just a horrible case of pneumonia. He'll be right as rain soon. That man is touch."

"I got that feeling," I said. "I promise to let him know."

Jerry nodded and then walked over to Thomas and the little girl.

"Weston," another male voice called me.

I nearly jumped, but the soft emotion of worry had me shaking my head.

"Sorry for startling you."

"You didn't." I then looked at him properly. "You're Henry, right? You're friends with Mr. Newman."

Henry smiled. "That is correct, Weston."

I sighed. "Do all ghosts know my name?"

Henry smiled. "You would be surprised. Truth be told, I needed to speak with you."

"Why did you need to speak to me?"

"It's about your destiny," he said, cryptically. "You must help any and all ghosts to crossover properly. It's imperative. However, you must also be careful. Some ghosts may try and kill."

"Like that shadow?"

"Exactly," he said. "You have to be careful. You are the only hope to help ghosts like me and others crossover."

"I'm sorry, but what do you mean coming?"

"You have your powers for a reason even if they happened on from the incident when you were a child."

"You know about that?"

Henry nodded. "Ghosts can talk to each other. There has been much talk about you. The more you help ghosts move on, the better. Just watch yourself, okay?"

"I'm not sure I fully understand," I said.

A wave of sadness washed over me as I leaned further against my vehicle. I was exhausted but was fighting it.

"I don't mean for this to sound rude, but could you try and not feel sad right now?"

"What do you mean?"

I crossed my arms. "I'm an empath. I can feel your emotions even if you are a ghost."

"I see. Can you feel emotions from animals?"

"None, but Mel's," I said. "I think it's because she's a talking a cat."

Henry had a thoughtful look. "Interesting," he said with a thoughtful look.

I shrugged. "I don't know about interesting. It's definitely odd."

"I'm sure you'll find out the reason."

"Maybe," I said, unconvinced.

"You will," he said. "Just keep doing what you are doing. Help as many ghosts with unfinished business that needs to be resolved before they fully can crossover. Just like all of us who were killed by Belladonna. We can all move on."

"Wait. What about Angela? In a way, she was just a victim."

"She will be fine," he said. "Now there is someone who needs your help. Barry. He still has one more purpose for you to fulfill. It will be a hard task, but you can do it."

"What do you mean?"

"You'll find out in due time." His head then turned to side. "Now, it's time for us to move on."

He walked over to the group of ghost, who were all gathered around. They all waved at me before vanishing, leaving behind starry sparkles.

I was glad they finally found peace.

35

It's been a week. A week since the murders stopped. A week since Belladonna was killed. Angela was doing community service, and actually being a lot nicer to me and my cousin, who I had to tell everything to. And that made him annoyed and a bit angry that he got to miss out on the excitement. Not to mention that my grandma had been mothering me. I felt incredibly guilty for over-worrying her. It's also been a week since Hayden got hurt. I hadn't seen him at all since that night. Luckily, we got back to texting each other and letting each other know how we were. That was something I was grateful for.

And, yet, I still had a job to do which was why I was here at this beautiful white mansion, walking up the white brick stairs to the brown decorative door.

I turned to Barry, who was standing before me. "Are you sure this will be okay? Brianna hates my guts."

Barry smiled softly. "Don't worry. Just hand them the envelope and then say exactly what I tell you. It all should work out."

Nervously, I wiped my sweaty hands on my jeans. "I hope so," I said before ringing the doorbell.

The door opened and a blonde woman stepped up, a baby girl on her hip that was gnawing on some kind of chew toy. The woman pushed open the screen door. She was wearing a sundress while the girl was in a purple dress with a bow in her blonde hair.

"Hello, can I help you?" she asked.

"Uh, I... This is going to sound bizarre, but I was told to give you and Brianna this," I said, pulling out a red envelope and handing it to her. "It was from Barry."

The woman's eyes narrowed. "Excuse me? If this was from my ex-husband, then why didn't the police bring it?"

"Uh..."

Barry nodded. "Tell her that Norman had you deliver it as he was busy."

"Well, Norman, wanted to do it, but he gave it to me as they both got busy."

The baby on her hip looked at Barry and held out of her chubby arms to him. "Uncy!" she exclaimed. I sensed a bright flow of happiness.

The woman glanced at the baby and shushed her. "Uncle Barry's not here, love."

The baby pouted as her hazel eyes watered and her emotions gloomed significantly.

Out of my peripheral vision, I saw Barry make a silly face and the baby giggled.

"I should go now," I said. "I apologize for disturbing you."

The woman's eyes narrowed. "No need for apologies. You know, you don't seem like the monster that my daughter insinuates. You seem kind of sweet. Thank you for the letter."

I smiled softly. "There was one more thing. Barry wanted me to tell you that he was sorry that things hadn't worked out. And that it was never your fault. He knew you were unhappy and couldn't provide the love you two used to share on that one fireworks date you two had."

The woman's eyes watered. "How do you know about that?"

I blinked. "It's complicated. But let's just say that I can see him."

The woman blinked. "That's…"

"Crazy, I know."

"I used to blame him for everything, but I long since forgave him. I know now that we both were unhappy," she said. "I hope he finds peace. I know I have. Thank you."

I nodded and watched her walk inside before walking back to my Jeep. "I'm sorry if that didn't go the way you wanted, Barry."

Barry shook his head. "Nonsense, Weston. It went pleasant. Thank you. Hearing her make peace, well, makes me finally feel at peace as well." A white light hit him. "Guess it's time for me to go. Thank you."

I nodded. "Goodbye, Barry," I said as tears well.

As soon as Barry crossed over, my phone vibrated. It was a text from Hayden.

Come visit.

I drove to his house and walked up to the porch. Before I could knock, the door opened to reveal a little boy, who had to be about nine.

"Who are you?" the boy said with anger in his eyes.

"I'm a friend of Hayden's."

The boy crossed his arms. "Oh, the guy Dad hates and Mom doesn't trust. I forget that Hayden gets into too much trouble. How do I know you won't take him away or hurt us?"

Before I could answer, Hayden's mom suddenly appeared. "All right, Kasper, that's enough," she said. "Let him through now."

The boy, Kasper, looked at his mother. "But, Mother…"

"No buts, Kasper. He's a guest. Let him in."

Kasper grumbled. "Still don't trust him," he said as stomped off.

Hayden's mom had an air of annoyance around her. "Come in," she said with fake politeness in her tone that set me on edge.

She then walked away.

I walked in and then headed down the hallway to Hayden's room. Just then I heard the voice of Hayden's father.

"I can't believe you allowed that boy inside our home."

Hayden's mom sighed. "We don't have a choice. If we want to keep an eye on him, we need him close. That boy has powers, Levi! That boy has powers. Telekinesis is one of them. He used it on me. I even overheard gossip that he might be able to communicate with spirits. You know how dangerous that could be. And then there is also the incident with Belladonna. She was a psychic vampire and even she said that she never came across someone with spiritual energy like him."

"This is why you shouldn't have invited him in," Hayden's dad said. "That boy is trouble…"

"Trust me, I know!" she yelled a bit quietly. "I don't want him here either, but Hayden has this crazy fascination with him. While I don't like it, I do think this gives us an advantage to keep our eyes on him. I'm worried about him knowing about Hayden's magic. What if he does something to hurt our son?"

"Even more reason not to invite him into our house. I don't and have never trusted him. Did your curse work?"

"I'm not entirely sure. That boy is being heavily protected. Our son gifted him a magical bracelet. I don't like that. Plus, you didn't see how that boy is with our son."

"Either way, he is trouble."

"I agree. And the sickening part is Hayden is protecting him from us."

"That isn't the worst part," Hayden's dad said. "It's the fact that he can make our son smile and be happy. If it wasn't so disturbing, I would almost find it touching. I just wish our son could forget about that boy and settle with a girl."

I bit my bottom lip and then quietly made my way to Hayden's room.

I knocked.

No answer.

I opened the door and came in.

Hayden was lying in bed with his eyes closed. He was no longer pale and he didn't feel in pain either.

I smiled and made my way over to him. I settled in beside him and slid my finger through his wavy, silky soft ginger hair. Watching him, I knew he wasn't sleeping. And the grin spreading out on his face wasn't the giveaway. It was the fact that I couldn't feel any exhaustion. If anything there was light playfulness.

"I know you aren't asleep," I commented.

His grin turned into a smirk on his handsome face. "I hate that I can never surprise you."

"It's not my fault I got empathy."

His eyebrows furrowed as he opened his eyes and his turquoise eyes of his bore directly into mine as he sat up. "I'm not complaining. I don't care that you can feel people's emotions. I mean, sure, it was a little nerve-wracking to learn about it. But, Weston, you've always been empathetic. It's a part of who you are. I would never take that from you whether it's from your powers or not. And I'm pretty sure without the psychic enhancement; you would still be the same. You might not be as powerful as you are now, though."

I smiled at that. "You think so?"

He shrugged. "I mean, it makes sense."

I lied beside him and ran a hand over his cheek. His eyes closed as he leaned into my touch. "Hayden?"

He hummed.

I smiled. "I was wondering about the kiss at the bridge."

His eyes opened just as I felt some sort of anxiety or anticipation simmering underneath his calm emotions.

"Is something wrong?" I asked.

Hayden's turquoise eyes found mine. "That wasn't Angela's or Ella's…"

"Belladonna," I corrected.

"Whatever," he said, his warm hands holding onto my cold ones. "It was me. They didn't force me against my will. The second I saw you I must have broken through the influence a bit. I wanted to kiss you, Weston."

I opened my mouth but before I could speak, my phone vibrated in my pocket. With an irritated groan, I pulled it out and answered, "This better be important, Norman."

"Moody much, aren't you?" asked Norman, teasingly. "Don't tell me I interrupted something important."

I looked at Hayden. "You kind of did."

"Oh, were you and Hayden getting it on, Wes?"

I face heated up. "No."

He laughed. "I totally did."

"Norman, what did you call about?"

He continued to laugh for a bit before he cleared his throat. "Well, I was wondering if you could meet me at the magic shop. I know it's your day off considering everything that has happened, but it's kind of important."

"Yeah, okay. I will be there in a bit."

"Great." He then hung up.

I placed my phone back in my pocket. "I have to get going." I then leaned down and kissed his forehead. "Thanks for telling me Hayden. I had been thinking about that for a while. I meant to ask, how are you doing? Your shoulder must still be sore."

"Well, I was better, but now with you leaving, I don't think I will be," he teased.

I laughed. "I'm sure you'll manage somehow."

Just as I got up, Hayden grabbed my wrist. I swiveled my head. "What is it?"

Hayden didn't respond with words. He pulled me down until we were face to face. My eyes widened. But before either of us said anything, he cupped my face and kissed me.

I could feel my cheeks heat up again as I placed my hands over his and kissed him back with the same gentleness.

Rain then started pouring. Not only outside, which I could hear pelting on the roof, but around us. I could hear water hitting the floor and even feel the moisture. However, he and I and the bed were all dry. Before Hayden's emotions could overwhelm me, I pulled back to put space between us.

And the rain ceased immediately.

"You're going to have to explain why that keeps happening."

"You mean the kissing, right?" he asked.

I gave him a look.

He sighed. "Right, you mean the rain thing. I..."

I placed a hand over his mouth. "Don't explain it now. Do it later when we can be alone. I want to know everything."

His eyes widened. "You... You overheard something my parents said, didn't you?"

I nodded.

"Tell me."

I shook my head. "Not today."

I could then feel his smile on hand as he nodded. "I understand. You'll get an explanation. I swear."

"Thanks." I moved off the bed forcefully. I didn't want to go, but I knew I had to. "I'll text you, okay?"

"Weston, I know. Go on," he said, but there wasn't any malice or anger.

I hesitated but waved. "Get some rest," I said, smiling before I turned and left his room.

When I got in my Jeep, I smiled. That was our third kiss. Did that mean we were a thing?

***

When I arrived at the magic shop, Mel and Norman were standing outside. They appeared to be discussing something about the building. As soon as I parked, they both turned their heads toward me. I waved and then got out.

Norman smiled. "About time," he said. "We have to show you something." He pulled out a small card. It was small enough to be a business card. He then handed it to me.

After taking it and examining it, it was indeed a business card.

"Mel's Paranormal Agency and Magical Emporium," I read aloud.

"I thought it was a much better name," she said.

"Better name for what?" I asked.

Norman smirked. "Keep reading."

I continued to read aloud, "Store owner: Melinda Black. Lost and Found expert: Norman Forrester.

Psychic and ghost expert: Weston Brooks. Hold up. You involved me in this?"

Norman's enthusiasm leaked through his naturally calm emotions. "Damn straight! Wes, you have a gift. And this town needs to drop their superstitions, so you can be accepted. Besides, this also lets people who are having paranormal problems know they aren't crazy. They can come to us. Our mobile numbers are there if they have any questions. Melinda was the one who had the idea surprisingly. She's not only hot but smart as well."

Melinda glared at him. "You want me to turn you into an ant instead, Norman Forrester?"

Norman paled and gulped. "Uh, no," he said. "I'm good. I don't want you to stomp on me and end my precious life."

Melinda grinned. "Great. Now, I have to go inside and tend to the store now." She sashayed back inside the building.

I turned to Norman. "Are you sure about this?"

"Most definitely," he said. "Melinda and I talked about this while she gave you the week off. It was all her. She will be handling everything for us financially. We also get to choose the cases that are brought to us. Oh, and the best part: our agency is inside the magic shop."

"It doesn't sound that difficult, I suppose, but what about my job here?" I asked.

"Melinda has that worked out, too. You can still do both. She can explain it better. But you get to keep your current job. As I also get to keep my mechanic job. Mickey will be out of the hospital in a couple of days. So, it all works out."

That didn't sound so bad. I did like working in the magic store for several reasons. Looking at the stop, maybe this paranormal detective business thing might not be a bad thing.

I hoped.

Printed in Great Britain
by Amazon